CARMEN LOUP

"If happiness always depends on something expected in the future, we are chasing a will-o'-the-wisp that ever eludes our grasp, until the future, and ourselves, vanish into the abyss of death." — Alan Watts

ONE

CREEPING MISGIVINGS

* * * * *

May should've been dead. She'd taken volt after volt of electricity while rewiring the *Audacity*'s main console, yet she continued stripping and twisting. Humans were more conductive than the thick-skinned Tuhntians who had built the rocket ship originally. May knew this, and she usually wore gloves, but for reasons which are about to become clear, she hadn't bothered.

Her legs ached to stretch out, but she was nearly done reassembling the console after having dismantled it for the eighth time in search of a remote control system. She snapped the orange siding back into place under the dashboard and rammed her forehead against it, hoping to transmit her desires directly from her brain to the machine.

Xan tapped her shoulder, and she slid out from under the console, her feet numb, head swimming as she dizzily searched the control loft for the Tuhntian. Nada. Strange; he was there a moment ago.

An invisible hand grabbed her shoulder, shook it gently.

"Damnit, Xan. I nearly had it that time," she said, her

fingers feeling for the velcro strap buried in the dense purple curls at the back of her head. She pulled the FabriLife visor off her face and resisted the urge to chuck it onto the low pile neon-patterned carpet in the FabriLife Life Fabrication Arcade. Instead, she curbed her frustration enough to gently hook the visor over the waiting arm of the viewscreen which, from the outside, looked rather like a clunky 90's arcade game. Inside, however, it was packed full of sophisticated A'Viltrian tech and cultures of alien dust.

An army of magenta kiosks glowed around them, their screens flickering the words 'Insert gem to begin.'

May sat on the metal platform of the machine and buried her face in the space between her arms and knees. Her hair, which Xan had styled into a loosely curling bob, umbrellaed out the fluorescent arcade light.

Behind her, having left the simulation long ago on account of a headache, Xan sat cross-legged on the platform and combed her hair with his fingers. The electric shocks had been simulated, but he was certain her hair was frizzier than normal.

"Look, starshine, if we drop another hundred thousand crystals at FabriLife, one of us is going to have to get an actual job and, judging on past experience, it's going to be you, and if you have an actual job, you won't have time to obsess over reacquiring the *Audacity*, and that will send you curlicuing into a depression even deeper than the one you're in now. So let's get back to Largish Bronda, watch a scantplot, cuddle with our Big Mouth Billy Bass, and try to forget about the *Audacity*, eh?"

In reply, tendrils of smoke seeped out from under May's arms and curled into the AC return above them.

"Hey." Xan pulled her shoulders back, snatched the not-cigarette from her mouth, and swallowed it whole, wincing as his tongue put out the lit end.

She had been smoking a lot of them lately. Words such as "addicted" and "craving" and "premature death on account of lung cancer" pestered her subconscious again. For half an orbit, she'd been too busy being the most successful (or rather, the only) Earthling rocket racer in the known universe to think about smoking. Now that her ship was gone, and she was stranded on a cold, miserable island for the foreseeable future, the itch had returned.

"Why do you keep eating them?" she asked.

"Smoking isn't good for your air sacs!"

"Well, lucky me, I don't have air sacs." May leaned back against the FabriLife machine's aluminum base, fingering the roll of things which were not exactly unlike cigarettes in her pocket and considering flicking on another one. "That can't be good for your stomach."

He leaned back beside her, unconcerned. "I've probably eaten more of those than Aimz has smoked."

"I hope I'm not the first to break this to you, but it's turned your skin blue."

"Blue?! Me?" He looked at his hand in mock horror, then in real horror when he noticed the state of his nails. He chewed them when he was nervous, which is why he typically wore shiny LayFlex™ gloves. But he hadn't had any reason to be nervous lately, right? No revenge-bent robots after him, no Chaos goddess trying to kill him, no prolonged bouts of loneliness so deep he couldn't remember if he was alive or not. He was finally enjoying life again. So why did his nails look like that?

"I'm sure I'll be ok," he said, tucking his hands under his thighs for safe keeping. "Find out anything you didn't already know about the *Audacity*? I popped out at around the twelfth beoop. Those things give me a plivering headache. Got a new mauve faux buffatalo coat, though! Feel it; it's soft!"

He held out his arms to display the shaggy mauve coat he wore over a holographic tube top that he had insisted was vintage-chic. While May had regressed back into her smoking habit, Xan had regressed back into the habit of dressing like he'd gotten lost in the clearance aisle of a drag-queen-owned thrift store.

"Everything gives you a headache since we got here. Is that normal?"

He shrugged off the question and wriggled his soft arms at her until she petted him. "Soft," she agreed, then shook her head. "I didn't discover anything new. I don't think the

Audacity's set up to be remote controllable. I give up."

"For the rotation, or forever?"

"Forever."

"Really forever, or Earthling forever? Because you've said forever a couple times now, and I'm not sure how forever works on Earth, but forever on Tuhnt means... well, it means forever. Indefinitely. From now until the end of time."

It was, of course, the same on Earth. Though May wondered if she could convince him that forever actually meant 'until I'm desperate enough to try again.'

The faintly glowing anchor button for the ship was still snapped onto the lapel of her trench coat, and she unhooked it now. Across the back, the words "The *Audacity*" were painted in a magnificently spacey text, zooming proudly across the small green disc. If she actually intended to stop trying to contact the ship, she would have no reason to keep the anchor button. When she glared down at the button, it glowed greenly back, familiar, comforting, entirely unaware of the pain it caused her.

"Let's try using the teledisc one more time," she said, more to the anchor button than to Xan.

He shuddered beside her, remembering the horrible feeling of their atoms getting lost in the ether. "Please, anything but that. The ship's too far away to teleport onto, even with a high efficiency teledisc. If we hadn't bought atom insurance for that last trip, we would still be meandering about the cosmos in a billion bits!"

"I miss racing." She clipped the button back on her coat. Safe for now.

"I know, mun. I miss it, too! I mean, not the threatening hate mail, the many brushes with death, scratched paint, constant low-level nausea, and outrageous entrance fees...I miss the photo shoots, mostly. And 'talking smack' about the other contestants. That was always fun. But we've got plenty of gem to last an Earthling lifetime if you stop wasting it on FabriLife tokens." Xan realized he had been talking too loudly and smiled, embarrassed, at a be-sparkled FabriLife associate android who smarmed past them, digitally side-eyeing him for suggesting that FabriLife was a waste of tokens, though the associate knew full well he was right.

"But what will I do? All I have to do right now is look for the *Audacity*, sleep, and eat." She noticed she had pulled another not-cigarette from the pack and was flicking the flinted end with her fingernail to ignite it. She stopped herself before it caught and put it back. "I guess I can add 'quit smoking' to that list."

"Well, skip down to sleeping, eating, and quitting the cigarettes. You've still got three things to do! That's plenty of things. Also, we could just have fun!"

"Pardon." They both jolted a bit, too invested in their conversation to notice the FabriLife android with a large, tight FabriSmile on its FabriFace. "Your time is out," it said. "Gem up or leave." Its eyes went a flavor of magenta which May knew must be Danger Diophalothene, a color which she couldn't technically see, but was starting to perceive via context clues.

"Right, we're leaving, just," Xan paused to stretch out his aching legs with a hiss, "give us a blip to relocate our extremities, eh?"

"Request denied. Gem up or *leave*." The electronic associate bent at its sparkly waist, and its eyes narrowed digitally.

"Alright, we'll get off your mark," Xan said as they pulled themselves upright on shaky, pins-and-needles legs and hobbled out, leaning on each other like a pair of geriatric criminals fleeing a crime scene.

Once outside FabriLife, the biting cold distracted May from the feeling of blood returning to her legs. She pulled her coat around herself, burying her fingers in the pockets to keep them warm.

It was, unsurprisingly, snowing Uptown. After the war of Reversed Polarization which had destroyed Tuhnt two hundred orbits ago, a board of sympathetic Rhean Queens had generously offered the remaining hundred-or-so-thousand displaced Tuhntians the island of Snoodark as reparation. The city that these Tuhntians built there had been creatively dubbed NotTuhnt and had been built both above and below ground, to take advantage of every inch of the tiny habitable section of the island.

They wandered Uptown now, where the nicer establishments had been opening, one on top of the other, for decades, many dating back to NotTuhnt orbit 000. Downtown, they typically avoided. Anything below ground brought back unpleasant memories of their time in the abandoned Pontoosa Adventure Hole.

"Right, let's get you something to eat! Eating usually makes you feel better. Unless it's poslouian-slug-worms. Those made you feel worse," Xan said, scanning the layers of neon signs for a restaurant they hadn't eaten at a zillion times yet.

"I had food poisoning; they weren't cooked properly. You got sick, too!" She was offended at the insinuation that she didn't have a strong enough stomach for alien foods. "You're the one who can't eat a slice of bread without dying about it. Let's just go back to Bronda. I'm not hungry."

"It's a beautiful rotation!" Xan said, gesturing to the sky which was not quite as dark as it usually was and the snow which fell with slightly less conviction than normal. "We might as well explore Uptown, right? Look!" He nodded toward a glowing blue marquee which was magnified by a clear intershoot that ran in front of it. "Have you ever been to a perception-changing bar?"

"All bars. That's the point of alcohol."

"Well, yes, but I mean...eugh, this is different. It's fun!"

"If philosophical epiphanies are fun for you." The voice belonged to Xan's sister who had spotted them a while back but only now decided to announce her presence behind them. "Blitheon, you two are really unaware of your surroundings. That's how you get mugged, you know."

"No one's going to mug us, Aimz," Xan said as if he were reassuring a child.

Aimz sighed, clicking a button on the end of a thin, pen-like stick from which two perfect recreations of their faces emanated as holograms. "Mugged. This will hold up to a face scan, too. I've got all your crystals."

"Huh," May mused quietly, studying the image of her own face. "Literally mugged."

The 'mugging pen' had been invented, as most things are, with good intentions and with a different name.

"Enjoy perfectly detailed three-dimensional holographic images of your friends and loved ones," the Visage-Stick advertisements had said.

"It's as if they were really there beside you," the advertisements had said.

"So detailed, even top security face-scan systems are fooled," the advertisements had said. And that final advertisement had been the one to start the quadrillion-crystal lawsuits against Visage-Stick and popularize the invention as the universe's first and only 'mugging pen.'

Xan snatched the pen from her and zilched out the records before handing it back. She held it up again, taking another snap-shot of their faces.

"Alright, you lost your face-stealing privileges." He grabbed it back from her, cleared it again, and this time, tucked it into a pocket in his coat.

"Whatever. You'll buy me anything I want anyway." She winked at him. It was true. May and Xan had enough gem left from their short stint as rocket racers to support both Aimz and Listay, her undead girlfriend. "Listay sent me out to bring you this. She thought you'd be hungry." Aimz tossed May a perfectly round, maroon apple.

She almost refused, but her stomach growled pitifully at the sight of the apple, so she gave in and ate it. She had to eat five times as frequently as the Tuhntians, and it was beginning to feel like an imposition. "Thanks. Listay's growing apples on the Merimip?"

"Uh-uh, apples are trending on mainland Rhea right now, apparently. Some farmer from Earth brought them here, and Listay figured you'd want some." Aimz pulled another apple from her pack and ate it stem-first, tying the stem into a knot with her tongue just to see if she could still do that sort of thing. "Hey, want to start a bar fight?" she said, slurring around the apple stem which would not knot.

May did not *not* want to do that, but Xan gave her an urgently worried glance before taking Aimz by the shoulders to speak to her seriously. "Aimz, mun, your eyes look—"

"Fine. They look fine. Just myosis; it's bright out." It was not, by any means, bright out. It was never bright out.

Xan hogtied and gagged his creeping misgivings and shoved them into one of his many overstuffed mental closets, forcing a smile back onto his face. "Come on, let's go to the perception bar," he said to Aimz. "It's fun!" he repeated to May, enthusiastically.

"If you say so, blue." She tossed the apple core into the nearest refuse incinerator and the three of them crowded into the intershoot which sucked them up to the perception bar.

TWO

UNCONTROLLABLE MOIST EPIPHANIES

* * * * *

"Warning: Perception snacks may cause rampant existentialism, catastrophic identity failure, uncontrollable moist epiphanies, and, in some cases, fatal levels of empathy.

"Talk to your loved ones, a medical professional, and any relevant gods before partaking.

"We cannot guarantee a safe return to your original perception without the purchase of personality insurance. Message repeats—" The intercom voice was soothing but the words disquieting.

Dim lights and cool colors gave the perception bar the feel of an underwater cave. The soft light orbs floating near the ceiling could nearly pass for bioluminescent deep-sea creatures as they bobbed, occasionally bumping into each other with an apologetic boing.

Though the bar was thronged with waiting people, Xan (who was short for a Tuhntian) and May (who was shorter still) slipped through the crowd unnoticed and snagged a booth just as the last group was leaving. Aimz followed slowly, unenthused but willing to show up for free snacks.

Xan and May scrunched into one side of the booth, Xan impatiently scrolling through the introductory waiver pages on the holographic menu in the center of the table which, had May been given a moment to read them, would've likely convinced her not to stay.

"Ah! Look, new flavors!" Xan said as the hologram stilled on a web of category options. His finger dipped into a bubble which read "Recent Additions" and a hundred lines stretched from it, all with a short description.

"Alright." Xan rubbed his hands together with excitement as he surveyed the options. "What have they got? Newly hatched Rhean larvae receiving their first nutrient download? Wouldn't recommend that one, sounds boring. Who hasn't been a larva, right? Oh! What about struggling Udonian business owner who loves their wife but is unsure of how to show it? Better. Tuhntian historian with a penchant for collecting interestingly rusted bolts—oh, that! I'm getting that one."

He swiped on the digital bubble, flinging it into the corner where a small teledisc was set into the table. Moments later, a floating black orb which looked to May uncannily like a Magic 8 Ball floated above the teledisc.

Xan patted the floating sphere toward himself across the table. "See, you just pick what you want, send it on over to the teledisc, and zam! Perception snacks. They last about twenty blips, but they feel like they last for decades. An entire perception, mashed up, sieved, and jammed into a crisp. That's fascinating, right?"

May nodded. "How do they, uh...harvest the perceptions?"

"Orbits of highly invasive stalking. But it pays well. And the perception reapers are some of the nicest people, very professional!" He held out a hand under the sphere, and it deposited a sea-foam green crisp, but May stopped him before he could pop it in his open mouth.

"One of these perceptions is yours?"

"Well, there are millions of perceptions but...yeah. Ages ago, mind you. It was after I moved out of Aunt

Kalumbits's place but before...well, you know. I didn't have a job on account of the translation chip debacle, so I signed up. Why? Don't go looking for it."

"Why not?"

He shuddered. "Eh, it was so long ago. It's not relevant anymore. But you know what is relevant?" He tapped the screen. "An eight thousand orbit-old A'Viltrian coosmonger with serpentine palbeatus. Ooo...relevant!"

May thought that sounded like the least relevant option she had heard yet.

"Is the boredom leaking out your ears yet?" Aimz said, finally sliding into the booth opposite them.

"Mystery ball?" Xan asked her.

"Am I that predictable?"

Xan smiled, glad that he could, after all these orbits, still predict her, and dragged the digital bubble stamped with a question mark into the teledisc where another Magic 8 Ball appeared.

She tapped the sphere toward herself, grabbed it, and positioned it over her head, turning up her face and letting the thing drop a crisp into her mouth.

One moment she was chewing, the next she looked as if she could see the underlying structure of the universe and what, exactly, she should do about it. Then she was back to normal, eyes half lidded, unimpressed. She shrugged. "Not bad. A bit dry, and they really heaped on the inspirational background music in that one. But not bad. I want to watch May try one." She smiled, almost cruelly, as she coaxed another mystery crisp from her sphere and held it out to May.

This made Xan nervous. This made May nervous, as well. Aimz was altogether too excited about this experiment. Still, unable to muscle past her curiosity, May took one, popping it into her mouth, chewing, and realizing that, despite three centuries of effort, she would never have the resources to preserve the dying traditions of the Pringnette culture and that the few Pringnette elders who remained had already given up hope, meaning that her life's work had been in vain and—

"Whoa, starshine," Xan said. His hand was on her back,

and he watched her carefully. Why was he blurry? She rubbed her face and found that she'd been crying.

"Ugh, that was horrible."

Aimz held out another crisp to her; this one had a small chunk taken out of it. "Here, Earthmun. It's a wealthy heiress. Looks like you got a rough one."

Gingerly, May took the second crisp and crunched it. She lounged on a luxury starship for the thousandth time, feeling the weight of a million days wasted, without purpose, staring out at the expanse as her every need was attended to and—

"Ugh." May shook her head to clear it faster. "Also bad." She turned to Xan, horrified. "How do you cope?"

"With what?"

"Centuries!"

"Oh." Xan leaned back in the booth, or rather pushed back into it, as if he could be eaten up by the cushion.

"Hey, that's right!" Aimz said, snapping her fingers. "You've only got a handful of orbits left to live, don't you? That's got to be weird. You've got only this very tiny window to get everything absolutely perfect and then-zilch! You're gone. Done. That's got to be depressing," Aimz said, popping another crisp in her mouth and nodding off.

If she hadn't taken a perception-nap at that exact moment, Xan would've laid into her. Instead, he turned to May, who was staring wide-eyed at the table. "I'm sorry. Aimz never learned decorum."

"She's right. I'm wasting my life."

"That's not true," Xan said firmly. "You don't have to be doing something all the time to be worthwhile. Right now, all you need to do is have fun with me and Aimz and enjoy yourself, alright? Obviously FabriLife isn't the ticket and neither is perception snacking. We'll find something else! Teach me English curse words?"

Aimz jolted awake with a wild gleam in her eye. "I know what will help you get over your tiny lifespan."

"What?" May asked, miserably.

"Aimz, no, we aren't doing violence tonight."

"Violence!" Aimz shouted, jumping on top of the table in

one majestic leap. She reached a hand down to May. "Ever started a bar fight?"

"I haven't," May said, grabbing her hand and letting Aimz heft her up onto the table. Xan covered his face and slumped into the seat.

"Xan! I'm about to teach! Kalumbits always said I'd be an inspiring teacher and look, she was right!"

He motioned for May to bend down so he could whisper to her, and she did. "She's off her rocket. Don't listen to her."

"I just want to watch," May lied to reassure him. "You can go back to Largish Bronda if you want." Years of customer service work had built up a lot of repressed rage, and now that she was a few thousand lightyears away from Earth, she was ready to let that rage out.

"Right, okay, so," Xan said anxiously. "I feel I must remind you that you're not exactly…"

"What?"

"Well you're…"

"An Earthling?"

"Yeah and you—"

"Don't stand a chance against a bar full of Tuhntians?"

"Right so—"

"Rule number zero!" Aimz interrupted them, dropping down to one knee on the table. "Find a bar, any bar, that isn't a perception bar. There's a surplus of empathy in perception bars, and you're not going to get into a fight that doesn't soon devolve into hugging and crying. We've got to go Downtown."

"Eugh, Aimz, no. That's where—"

"Where all the Carmnians are? Tightly spotted." Aimz winked.

"Can I finish a sentence?" Xan asked.

Aimz and May watched, politely letting him continue.

"I…uh…well, yes, that's what I was going to say. That was a complete sentence."

"You're a Carmnian," May pointed out correctly.

Xan cringed, wobbled his head, but had to agree. "I am. Also, I would like to note, I'm a criminal! See how that works? No one trusts Carmnians. Not even other

Carmnians. Let's bowl."

"Bowl?" May asked. "With balls and pins? You have bowling?"

"Balls and pins? No, you bowl with a slamahar and tribilites. Just punt the slamahar at the tribilites and try to knock as many over as you can. It's fun! It's safe. The tribilites get a kick out of it. May," he dropped a hand onto each of her shoulders, "come punt a slamahar at some tribilites with me?" he begged.

"Bar fight," Aimz goaded over her shoulder.

"I don't know," she told Xan. "I just think punching someone would help me feel better."

"Eugh. Then punch me, not a stranger!" Xan said.

And Aimz obliged.

THREE

HUBRIS DAMPENER

✳ ✳ ✳ ✳ ✳

"Bar fight lesson one, my wee protege." Aimz snatched May's hand and pulled her at a flat-out run through the perception bar, the occupants watching them perplexedly. "When someone says you can punch them, always do it! Free punches!"

"Wait, Aimz, is Xan okay?" May stumbled, attempting to keep up or risk having her arm ripped off. They were outside now, but the adrenaline kept May warm as Aimz scooped her up and carried her bridal-style into the intershoot which plummeted them down to street level again.

"Eh, Carmnians have thick skulls. Don't stress it. You wanted to get in a fight, right?"

"Not with Xan!"

Aimz set May down but kept hold of her hand, yanking her three steps at a time down an icy staircase which was lit with string lights as it descended into Downtown NotTuhnt.

"Aw, stop worrying about him. He's tougher than you, you know."

15

"I don't believe that," May shouted down at Aimz as she attempted to keep her footing on the slick stone steps.

Aimz laughed. "Yeah, me neither. Zipzam?" She held out a plastic party popper to May who took it and pulled the string, a plume of green smoke clouding her head. Slowly, the smoke cleared. May smiled.

"Eh, you're right; he'll be fine. Let's punch strangers!"

"That's the ticket, Earthmun!"

The zipzam coursed through May's system, pulling all her thoughts and feelings to the surface like an emotional detox as they descended the staircase. "Xan says 'that's the ticket,'" she said, on the verge of tears.

"By O'Zeno, that zipzam's got your taxi maxed." Aimz giggled, jumping the last two steps and landing in the damp but cheerily lit underground city.

"You know that! You know that they do this to me, and you give them to me anyway," May shouted, then trundled into Aimz who stood at the bottom of the steps, laughing. "Sorry," she said, the zipzam beginning to wear off. Tuhntian drugs and alcohol couldn't stand up to her Earthling metabolism.

Downtown was dingy, dark, and humid, but in a festive way. Like a landfill the week after Christmas. The staircase ended in a city square, lush with fleshy underground plants strung with small lights. The square was bordered on one side by City Hall where those who called Downtown NotTuhnt home rotated through pretending to be in charge regularly.

In front of City Hall, a conglomeration of cheap souvenir vendor stalls flanked an enormous statue of Queen Carmnia made of chicken wire and concrete. The blue painted concrete on the statue's shins had flaked away in some places, revealing hexagons of rusted metal which held up the statue whose massive headdress not only touched the roughhewn rock ceiling but seemed to be growing out of it.

"Hey, Mom," Aimz threw casually up at the statue and patted its leg, more concrete flaking away under her hand.

"Oy!" shouted a round-faced Carmnian from behind a display of tapered sticks. "Smoke out the scourge with

Zilpappy's Smoke Sticks! Guaranteed to have an odor. Rumored to destroy the scourge at its source!"

"Zuxing scam artist!" Aimz shouted over her shoulder at them, then sighed at the three young Carmnians that were eagerly shoveling crystals at the vendor in exchange for a tube of sticks.

"Carmnia curio! I've got genuine Queen Carmnia curio for sale! Nail clippings, bottle of tears, and for the right price, a lock of verified Carmnia curls!" another vendor added to the cacophony, her stall hung with points of red and yellow lights which danced to a three-note tune emanating from the kiosk.

"Wish balls, get your wish balls. Good for two class-five wishes or five class-two wishes. Wash wishly," the next vendor monotoned from behind a folding table laden with an army of muddy balls.

Across the way, an identical stall with an identical vendor gave their own speech. "Anti-wish balls. Negate the side effects of poorly thought-out wishes. Free hubris-dampener included."

Aimz trundled onward, her hand tightly wrapped around May's wrist. She'd spotted her target: the Sunny Underside Cafe, a sagging shack decorated mainly with glowing signs which advertised the mind-altering substances sold there.

"Wait!" May dug her heels into a thick crack in the concrete and pulled Aimz to a halt.

"What?"

"Xan's not coming after us," May said, looking back up the dark and empty staircase.

"So?"

"So, what if you actually hurt him?"

"That was my intention, Earthmun. Now unpin it. Lesson two is important if you're at a physical disadvantage which, if I might be blunt, you are. Fight dirty! Anything's a weapon if you can sling it at someone hard enough."

"Why are you like this?" May asked a smiling Aimz, still playing tug of war with her hand.

"Orbits of loneliness?" She pretended to think. "No. No,

I've always been like this. Benefit of being a Carmnian, I guess. No one can blame me! Now do you want to release pent up aggression on a complete stranger who probably deserves it, or do you not?"

"I don't *not* want that."

"Oof, Earthmun, you're starting to sound like Xan. What does that mean?"

"I do want that, yes."

"Right, then! Rule five—"

"You mean lesson three?"

"Ah, zux three and four; they're boring. And this is a rule. Rule five is if someone's packing plasma, they're mine, alright?"

"You like getting shot at?"

"*Love* getting shot at. Also, have you ever seen Xan get angry before?"

May shook her head. She wasn't sure it was possible.

"Me neither! And as long as you don't die today, I might never have to. Now, the last lesson. Lesson six: don't walk in like you're about to start anything. Best bar fight is a surprise bar fight. Ready?"

May nodded, and Aimz finally dropped her hand. She shook it out to get rid of the pins-and-needles as she and Aimz sauntered through the open doorway.

The Sunny Underside was well stocked with Tuhntians.

Mostly Carmnians, judging by their unusual pallor and prominent, pointed noses.

All at least twice May's weight.

All dressed in clothing that provided great range of motion and plenty of sharp metal bits.

All dealing with personal issues which made them terrible grumps and drove them to mind-altering substances.

For a blip, Aimz surveyed the line of hunched backs at the dimly lit bar in the center of the shack. She bit her lip, focused. Starting a bar fight was a matter of craftsmanship in which she took great pride. She glanced at an empty hover stool which bobbed innocently in the corner, awaiting a bum to support.

"Actually, May, I changed my mind. Bowling does sound

like fun," she said before seizing the hover stool and flinging it into the line of bodies at the bar. "Bar fight!" she announced to those sober enough to hear, then she dived onto the counter, taking a few hundred crystals worth of alcoholic beverage along with her.

Arms as thick as baby blue whales grabbed Aimz by the collar and flung her into a startled trio of Carmnians who had been playing something like darts with miniature crossbows off to the side. The three darts-players switched targets and sunk several sharp darts into the arms which had flung Aimz across the room. The person attached to those arms roared in pain, and then the room erupted.

Through the tumult, May saw a flash of Aimz's pink hair and she dashed in toward it, biting, elbowing, and scratching at any appendage which got in her way.

"Fun, yes?" Aimz asked May as soon as she was in earshot. May was too busy dodging punches. She'd been noticed; people were punching down now.

She kicked hard at the back of an exposed knee (she'd spent enough time with Xan to know that even the sturdiest aliens had shit joints just like the rest of us) and felled a barrel of a Tuhntian who hollered as he rolled to the ground, clutching his leg.

"Look at that! You've definitely been in a bar fight befo —" A laser blast, the first one of the evening, zinged across Aimz's thigh, ripping a hole in her leather pants.

She yelped, jumped up, ran face-first into a fist, laughed as green blood faucetted from her lip and over her teeth, then cracked someone's nose over her knee.

May was of the opinion that it was time to go.

She grabbed Aimz by her jacket and pulled her toward the door, dodging laser blasts, the heat and light dangerously close.

"Aimz, come on," May shouted but didn't dare turn around as she used her forearm to block elbows which tried again and again to collide with her face.

At last, Aimz came to someone's senses (likely not her own, since her senses were rather more preoccupied with stirring up trouble at the moment) and plunged ahead of

May, steamrolling the bodies which had been blocking them from the entrance. Finally, the path back to the festive streetlights of Downtown was cleared from the bramble of appendages.

Before May could reach it, however, a fist to the temple hurtled her into a cool, black pool of nothingness. The floor smelled like rancid milk and whiskey.

✳ ✳ ✳ ✳ ✳

Xan now had two very pressing objectives. Objective 1: Pay the bill. Objective 2: Collect Aimz and May without getting stuck in the middle of a bar fight.

The first should have been the easiest, but technology can sense distress in its user, and when it feels it's under pressure to perform, it tends to bungle.

Xan tapped the bill-pay bubble. Tapped it several times. More than tapped, he drove his finger straight through to the other side of the hologram.

The overly sensitive digital menu, so shocked by Aimz's act of violence and picking up on Xan's nervous energy, had frozen, catatonic with fear. It couldn't even muster the total.

Rather than wait for the machine to calm down and get its servers together, Xan harpooned a sack of crystals from his pocket—at least double the bill—slipped out of the booth, thrust it at the attendant with a hurried, "No change," and bolted outside.

They were long gone.

He rubbed his aching head to coerce it into thinking faster. Aimz wasn't dumb enough to let harm come to May, was she? But she had been acting peculiar lately. Alarmingly peculiar. He would need reinforcements. Listay, Aimz's lover, was the ex-dead ex-general for the job. He had her on speed dial in his BEAPER for exactly this reason.

"What did Aimz do?" Listay asked the blip the BEAPER connected.

When Xan first met her, she had been half-way out of the grave, and he had been half-way in it. Her eyes were still cloudy, her deep purple skin still ashy with death, but her ruined dreads were gone, Xan having helped her re-style them into low maintenance box braids which she kept in a tidy roll at the back of her neck. Changing your hairstyle, Xan had explained to her, could also change your outlook on life. Or after-life, in Listay's case. Typically, he'd greet her with a tongue in cheek complement of her hairstyle. Not today. Today, he—

"Your hair looks great," he said, predictably. Then, before Listay had a chance to roll her eyes, he got to the point. "Aimz ran off with May! Wanted to start a bar fight. I lost them. Think they went Downtown?"

"She definitely took May Downtown." Listay knew this not because she was interested in bar fights, but because Aimz had frequently tried to drag her into them. Typically, she allowed it. Aimz had a surplus of energy, and if she could get some of it out by beating up unwholesome strangers, Listay wasn't keen to stop her. "I'm a beoop away by monorail. Don't wait for me. Get May out of there; Aimz is compromised."

"I'll pay for a teledisc," Xan said. "I'd pay for a hundred teledisc trips before engaging Aimz in an anti-bar-fight-fight."

He scanned the area for the round green signs which illuminated public telediscs. There were two nearby, but he was too far to read the coordinates on either of them, so he jogged to the nearest one and held Listay's image up to it, depositing a crystal into the charge-slot.

"Coordinates logged," she announced, then her image zipped out, and she reappeared in tangible form beside him, immediately sprinting off toward the below-ground staircase.

"When you say 'Aimz is compromised'...what...what does that mean?" Xan shouted after her, hesitantly picking up speed so he wouldn't be left behind.

Listay paused at the entrance to the underground to let him catch up. "It means she's compromised, so we need to hurry."

Steep stairs had never bothered Xan, but steep stairs combined with worry and adrenaline made him feel queasy as they descended. He hadn't been Downtown yet. If there was an area of town where Carmnians typically gathered, he wanted nothing to do with it. He glared up at the concrete face of Carmnia and said exactly the same Tuhntian words Aimz had said to it, but due to his tone, instead of translating as "Hey, Mom," it translated as 'Hello, Mother."

Aimz and May weren't difficult to find. They were recouping in a quiet area on a rusted bench which had been chained to the fence around City Hall, making fun of the oafish bar-goers while Aimz tipped a bottle of Fraguntassle first into her mouth, then over a scrap of cloth with which she dabbed a welt on May's forehead.

"Zuut, Earthmun, I gotta get you cleaned up before Xan finds us," Aimz said, then took another swig from the bottle.

"I'm fine," May insisted, the Fraguntassle stinging the cut on her forehead. She patted her rolled bangs down far enough to cover it and moved her jaw from side to side, making sure it still worked correctly. The adrenaline in her body suddenly realized there was nothing left for it to do and made a hasty retreat. She knew exactly where bruises would soon form. Exactly everywhere.

"May!" Xan launched at her, wrapping her in a quick hug, then holding her at arm's length to observe her. "You're not dead?"

"Of course not. It was just a bar fight."

"With Carmnians," he added.

"You're a Carmnian! What's so bad about Carmnians?"

Rather than explain, he looked to Aimz for help, but she was also waiting on his answer. His face curled into a grimace when he saw her, and he pulled a pocket mirror from his coat and held it up to her.

"What? I know I've got blood on my—" She stopped talking and grabbed the mirror, studying herself for a quiet moment. "Huh," she grunted, then snapped the mirror shut and handed it back to him, a haunted look on her bloodied face.

"What is it?" May asked, watching the pair as if this were some alien ritual she'd just witnessed. It wasn't.

Xan started to say it was nothing. Then stopped. He had promised not to lie to her anymore. He had promised her honesty, and she would get it. Just not right now. "Eugh, I'll tell you once we're back at Largish Bronda, alright? Please say that's alright. This isn't the kind of thing you talk about in public."

May nodded, but regretted the motion as it made her head throb even worse.

Listay grabbed Aimz's hands and pulled her up off the bench. "I'll take her back to the Merimip and watch her."

"I don't need to be watched. I need more Fraguntassle." She wiggled the empty bottle at Listay.

"Really?"

Aimz nodded solemnly. "Really."

"I'll get you a bottle to go."

"Two!" Aimz shouted after Listay as she entered the bar, parting the ongoing sea of bar fight with her elbows in order to reach the counter.

"May, I'm worried about you," Xan said, helping her up.

"Why, because I have a concussion?"

"You have a whom?" he asked.

May snorted, amused. "That's exactly what Aimz asked. It's an Earthling thing. Don't worry about it."

Listay pulled herself from the brawl, an opaque white bottle held aloft in each fist. "Fraguntassle acquired," she announced proudly. "Let's move out."

They walked back toward the statue of Carmnia and the towering flight of stairs, but May noticed something on Carmnia's left toe that she hadn't seen from the other direction.

A pamphlet which looked like it had been hand painted on roughly textured homemade paper danced stiffly in the watery breeze.

'Have you seen this rocket?' it asked.

May had seen the rocket.

In fact, May was extremely familiar with the rocket in question. Below the query, a beautifully illustrated image of the *Audacity*. Undoubtedly the *Audacity*. And this was how she knew: the hull of the rocket in the poster read 'Audacity.'

She snatched it down, staring at the image as if it might rip from the page and turn into the ship itself. Had she made this poster and forgotten? Impossible. Had Xan made it? She looked at him, but he was standing over her now, also puzzled.

"What is this?" May asked.

"It's a flyer."

"Yeah." Below the ship ran a line of coordinates. Xan typed them into his BEAPER and showed May the resulting map. "Should we go?" she asked.

"In my experience, people only seek me out because they want to kill, imprison, or have sex with me, and I'm not especially keen on any of those options right now. So probably not."

"They aren't looking for you; they want the *Audacity*," May clarified.

"Presumably because I accidentally stole it," he reminded her. "Please, let's just get back to Largish Bronda and forget about this ill-fated outing?"

May folded the flyer and tucked it into her bra. "Already forgotten," she said, then sighed because much of her evening *was* already forgotten. She knew Aimz had dragged her down there for a bar fight, she knew Listay and Xan had found them outside City Hall cleaning up, but she couldn't remember much else detail-wise. "Definitely a concussion."

FOUR
THE OFFENSIVE CHAPTER

* * * * *

Public teledisc teleportation was extremely convenient because there was never any wait. There was never any wait because no one could actually afford to use the things. At a hundred crystals per mile, the majority of society, even the majority of the Tuhntian upper class, was firmly priced out of regular public teledisc travel.

When Xan and May arrived on New Tuhnt, they had more gem than the richest of the upper class. After a failed attempt to teleport to the *Audacity* which had been thrust zillions of miles into open space and hundreds of FabriLife hours logged trying to work out a remote control for the ship, their coffers were dwindling.

And so, they used the monorail to get back home. Though awfully loud, the monorail was the most common form of mass public transit in the Flotluex system. Monorail stations were peppered throughout Uptown, and it wasn't long before they found one headed toward Snoodark Quarry which wasn't so much a neighborhood as it was a populated pit.

"Step off It, ya' zoup-nog Carmnians!" shouted someone

a few bodies away from them as they joined the crowd at the edge of the monorail platform. This was a popular vaguely threatening insult on Not Tuhnt, "It" being the name of the highest cliff on the island of Snoodark which overlooked an expanse of pointy rocks.

"Will do!" Xan waved good-naturedly at the someone.

"Zux off, trok-licker!" Aimz said even more good-naturedly and flashed an offensive Tuhntian hand gesture which looked like a complex shadow puppet. Listay shook her head, subtly moving between Aimz and the trok-licker.

May leaned forward a bit, her anger drawn like a magnet toward the large, bearded Tuhntian who had insulted them. Working at Sonic, she had smiled through snide remarks and wished her transgressors a nice day because that's what she had been paid to do. It had taken time to shed the habitual politeness Sonic had required, but rocket racers were expected to be nasty to each other, and she had eventually grown out of her customer service voice. Had Xan not put a hand on her shoulder to steady her, she might have given the bar fight a sequel.

"Hey, un-pin it, mun. They're not worth the trouble. Some people just aren't fond of Carmnians, that's all."

"Why don't you tell them to fuck off?" she whispered, keeping a rageful eye on them as the monorail steamed into the station and flung open its doors.

"Because you laugh at me when I say fuck," Xan explained, looping an arm around one of the monorail poles to swing around it.

It was true, May laughed when he said fuck, but she kept herself from laughing now as she sat in the seat opposite him. Translation chips didn't like switching languages mid-sentence, which was a shame, because Xan loved doing it. The frustrated chip tingled in her skull whenever Xan threw in a word she knew like "fuck" or "bongo" which he had learned from May and 'I Love Lucy,' respectively.

Also, his accent was strange because, just as May literally couldn't pronounce any Tuhntian word that required one to flex one's gloxalatal, Xan literally couldn't pronounce the hard "k" sound. He always put far too much gloxalatal into it.

Normally the chip accounted for this, but when he stopped relying on it and tried to speak English to her, the chip would shrug. "You know what that means," it would say. "I'm taking a break."

"Try another curse word," May suggested.

Aimz had been half listening from Listay's lap, but the mention of cursing had piqued her interest and she sat up, straddling Listay's thigh in a way which might have been edited out in a less racy book.

"Learning alien obscenities?" she asked.

"Yeah, you want in?" said May.

"I do very much want in, yes. Tell me how to make people cry in another language."

"You were never this interested in language studies at university," Xan said.

"They don't teach you obscenities at university."

"They do in the higher-level courses! But English isn't one of the ninety-two primary universal languages. Here." Xan dug in the pocket of his coat and pulled out a small rectangular magnet he frequently used to scramble his translation chip. "I've just got the one, so we get to share!" He leaned out from the pole, holding the magnet between his and Aimz's heads. "Alright, starshine, curse at us."

"'Shit,'" she divulged.

Aimz and Xan both repeated the word, but the "sh" came out as a clink which May physically could not have duplicated.

She shook her head, and Aimz rolled her eyes, leaning away from the magnet.

"I'll stick to the classics. That magnet's making my skull ache," she said.

Xan kept the magnet held to his head and pulled himself up onto the pole again, hooking a leg around it just for fun. "Try something else?"

"Alright, you can't get 'ck' or 'sh' out, so how about 'hell.'"

"Hell?" he repeated satisfactorily.

"Yeah. As in "Oh hell", "give them hell", or "what the hell."

"Easy! What does it mean?" He let the magnet drop away and rubbed his temple which throbbed from the pull of the magnetic field.

"It's where you go when you die to be punished for eternity."

"Punished? For what?"

"Not believing in it."

"Oh. Well, zuut, that's dark, isn't it? I suppose that's what makes it an expletive! In most of Tuhnt's major religions, when you die, your spirit gets recycled back into the Everythingness."

"How environmentally friendly of you."

"Right? I mean, there is a kind of 'hell,' I guess. If you really zux up, you could get stuck in between recycling and be doomed to wander the universe for eternities. They say that's how entities like Chaos came about. You get stuck outside of the recycling system and have to watch the universe expand and contract endlessly around you until you eventually evolve into something ultra-sentient and formless like her."

May laughed at the thought of Chaos having been such a horrible person that reincarnation rejected her. "Hopefully she's back in the recycling system now."

"Can you imagine? Little larval Chaos, nothing to do but wriggle indignantly at her attendants. Blitheon, I feel sorry for the people who take her in when she's a kid."

"So is anyone in charge of this recycling system?" May asked.

"Of course someone's in charge," Listay said now, pushing Aimz aside to talk to May. The concept of an all-powerful organizational entity had always fascinated Listay, and she had casually studied universal religions with an eye toward finding this organizer. "They have infinite names, but several organizations call them The Seam."

Aimz laughed herself off Listay's knee, hitting the sticky monorail floor with a thump. "You mean The Crack? Listy, darling, you don't actually believe in The Crack, right? We've already got hundreds of entities who show up to entity conventions and fill out their inter-galactic census.

Why invent new ones that don't pay their space-taxes?"

"Hold on. Space-taxes *are* a thing?" May interjected.

Listay gave May a look which said she was likely in some deep space-trouble but carried on. "The Seam doesn't exist until the universe contracts into nothingness again. They say The Seam was the first being to get booted out of the recycling program, and when they got bored of the nothingness after the universe ended, they convinced it to start expanding again. Thus, earning the title of The Seam in between the end and the beginning."

Aimz's face scrunched. "The universe just does that. It's like squeezing a sponge underwater. It gets smaller, then it gets bigger."

"Who's squeezing the universe sponge, though?" Xan said, concerned about how utterly enormous their hand must be.

"The Seam," Listay answered.

Aimz's hands circled emphatically in an attempt to catch a better explanation. "Physics! It's just physics!"

Listay patted Aimz's fluffy pink hair. "Of course it is, mun."

"There are a helling lot of entities already," Xan tried to agree with Aimz.

May laughed. "Good try, but that one doesn't conjugate."

"No? Why not?" Xan loved conjugating things and had picked up English conjugations eons ago, again, thanks to 'I Love Lucy.'

May shrugged. "Because it's a place."

"Right. Fuck's a lot better isn't it? I mean, it conjugates better."

"It does, but I don't think you can physically say it."

"I just did!"

"Not correctly, though."

"Fuck," he said earnestly. "Fuck."

"Alright," May motioned for him to bend down so he was at eye level with her. "Watch my mouth. Fff-uuuuu-CK."

His face twisted into an impression of hers.

"Ck," he said in a way which was slightly less like crashing into a drum kit than it had been last time.

May nodded. "Ck," she repeated.

"Ck?"

"That's it! Now say fuck."

"Fuck. Fucking. Fucker. Fuckly. Fuckest."

May laughed and waved him away. "Yeah. You've got it, blue."

FIVE

YUZKA FELTING

* * * * *

Snoodark Quarry was the last habitable section of the island to be incorporated into the city of NotTuhnt because it was the *least* habitable.

The quarry was bordered on one side by a densely overgrown forest full of miserable creatures intent on making others more miserable than they were. On the other side, it gave way to craggy fjords on the Rhean sea which was also inhabited by miserable creatures. And now that a housing development had sprouted in the heretofore empty quarry, the quarry *itself* was inhabited by miserable creatures.

May and Xan, upon arriving on the island, had purchased a Largish Bronda's FlexiDimensional HoverBus to live in and parked it exactly halfway between the forest and the quarry in hopes that their miserable neighbors on either side would keep each other at bay.

Largish Bronda's line of vehicles were well known in the Flotluex system for their reliability. They were reliably sluggish with a reliably clunky design and reliably mundane features. They were also reliably cheap, and since their only source of income had been blasted into the ether, May and Xan were trying to budget.

The HoverBus they chose was orange, naturally, but not Obtrusive Orange, like the *Audacity* had been. Obtrusive Orange had been long outlawed by the time this HoverBus was painted. May might have called this orange "Pumpkin Spice" had she been at all interested in giving creative names to colors.

They entered through an opaque yellow plasma door at the back of the bus to a space which might have featured on the cover of a 1970s issue of "House Beautiful," full of massive, slumping sack chairs, needless curves, and a recessed waterbed which doubled as a conversation pit.

"Hey, Billy!" Xan said when they entered.

"Hey, Billy," May echoed habitually. They were addressing their only decor piece, a Big Mouth Billy Bass which hung on the far wall. It did not acknowledge their return.

May flopped dizzily into a sack chair and tried to remember what you were supposed to do about a concussion. The only thing she could remember was not to think too hard, and that was rather counterintuitive at the moment.

She did not remember that Xan had promised to explain what was going on with Aimz and, as such, she didn't bring it up. This suited Xan rather well, and he curled next to her in the sack chair and wiped the splatters of blood—equal parts her dried red blood and crusty green Tuhntian blood—from her face.

"Thanks," she said, resting her head back against the chair and closing her eyes, which set her brain spinning like a gyroscope. She sat back up to still it. "Sorry Aimz punched you. I tried to get her to go back, but she's been acting strange lately."

Xan sighed and tossed the bloodied rag onto the yellow laminate counter which delineated the living room from the kitchen. "Yeah," was all he said. He flopped on her shoulder with about as much energy as the wet rag on the counter.

"Hey, Blueberry, what's bothering you?" she asked.

"Bothering me?" He shook his head and smiled. "Nothing! What makes you think I'm bothered by something? Chaos is off our marks, Sonan is gone, I'm not in prison, I'm with you, and Aimz is...alive. Everything's zing up to caliber! What could I possibly be bothered by?"

May dug a not-cigarette out of the pocket in the side of the sack chair. "Aimz punching you in the face, maybe." There was a trick to lighting them that she hadn't quite become proficient in. It involved holding down a button at one end and flicking the other end with a fingernail. She flicked it a couple of times unsuccessfully.

He shook his head. "She does that sometimes. But, I mean, I suppose if you're asking, if you're curious, it's a bit unlike you to—"

He paused to watch her as her face lit up blue with the light of the not-cigarette. She smiled and inhaled.

"I mean, you're smoking cigarettes again, and if you're not working on the fake *Audacity* at FabriLife, you're doing things like zipzam poppers and getting into bar fights."

"I'm not smoking *cigarettes*," May said. Xan plucked it from her hand and swallowed it whole. She got another out and flicked.

"Right. You're smoking not-cigarettes. May, are you depressed?" he asked.

She smiled crookedly at the smoldering cherry. "Doesn't translate," she said and puffed. "Mmm!" she said, remembering something. She fished the flyer from her bra and unfurled it on her knee. "This might be the concussion talking but..." she mumbled around the not-cigarette. Xan helped her by plucking it from her mouth and eating it. "If someone else is looking for the *Audacity*, they might be able to help me recover it. It's our only lead."

Xan groaned, sat back heavily in the sack chair, and rubbed his chest. "Please stop smoking those so I can stop eating them," he whined.

"Stop eating them so I can smoke them."

"Eugh," he stuck out his long green tongue and let his

limbs drop heavily over the chair. He made a wonderful impression of a corpse, because he rarely had to breathe.

May continued to scan the flyer, her free hand absently tickling his side. He convulsed with laughter and sat up; quieting when he saw that she was still staring at the flyer.

"You're really set on getting the *Audacity* back."

She looked at him seriously. "Your perception of time is different," she said. "If it takes you fifty orbits to save enough for another racing rocket, you'll barely notice. I could be dead in fifty orbits."

"Will be if you keep instigating bar fights," he grumbled.

"I've got to do something. Everything in town is staffed by robots. There are no jobs, there's no *Audacity*. What am I supposed to do with myself?"

"Retire?"

May laughed at that. "I never planned on being able to retire."

"Well, now you can! Spend your rotations lounging by vortex springs and felting yuzkas for the local larvae troupe chapter."

"Is that what retired Tuhntians do?"

"Only the fun ones," he said.

May doubted she would be a fun retiree. Without a clear and defined life purpose, she figured she'd die of boredom within the orbit. That was troubling. Thinking about it hurt, though. Not emotionally—it physically hurt her bruised brain.

Perhaps Xan could think about it for her.

"I think," she said, "I'd die if I didn't have a purpose. And I don't know if I have one right now. Is that bad?"

That was not something Xan heard often and, as such, he wasn't really sure how to reply. He pulled the sides of his faux buffatalo coat around her and scooped her close while he thought.

"It's not *not* bad," he said, finally.

"My brain's too fried for double negatives, Blue."

"But not too fried to ponder the purpose of life? Maybe put a tab on that thought process and come back to it later. For now, you can just exist. Nothing bad will happen if you just exist for a blip."

That was true, but she *did* think she had a concussion, and she had heard somewhere back on Earth that something bad, she wasn't sure what exactly, might happen if you slept on a concussion. She didn't remember how long she had to wait, but for safety's sake, she decided she wasn't tired yet.

Xan, however, was. His grip on her relaxed, and he wriggled deeper into the chair. While he slept less often than May, he stayed asleep for much longer than she did, and she didn't trust herself to stay awake if he was sleeping.

With safe-cracking stealth, she unhooked the BEAPER from his wrist and transferred it to her own. It made a sprightly booting-up noise when it sensed its wearer had changed, and the welcome screen danced out of it. The BEAPER asked her to confirm that she hadn't stolen it by promising that she hadn't.

"I didn't steal you," she whispered harshly at her wrist. This BEAPER knew her. She had worn it plenty of times before. It just didn't like her much.

She input the full coordinates from the flyer, realizing too late that the BEAPER's map had saved the coordinates to its history from earlier.

The map pinpointed the flyer's destination and offered several routes which would take her there, all with a small symbol which, when opened, explained that it would be much more pleasant to simply take a public teledisc there instead, and it would happily take you to within ten meters of your location for the low price of two hundred crystals with a convenience fee of twenty-two crystals. Just swipe—

May shut off the BEAPER, tired of scrolling down the ad's steadily smaller print.

Xan still slept cadaverously, and he hadn't been keen on the flyer anyway, so May headed back to the monorail alone.

SIX

MAY MEETS THE QUEEN

* * * * *

The flyer led her straight to Queen Carmnia.

It was early yet, and the Downtown square which held the statue of Carmnia was now empty apart from lumps on benches, some of which were people sleeping under piles of coats and some of which were simply discarded piles of coats. It was fashionable, at the time, to bring unwanted coats to this particular square.

Since she wasn't being schlepped along by a war-eager Aimz or a worried Xan, May took a moment to study the statue of the queen. Carmnia's skin was a pale blue shared by Aimz and Xan, and her nose was long and pointed like theirs, but the scowl she made beneath the massive golden headdress was unfamiliar. It looked as if she'd either told the statue artist an incredibly nasty joke or threatened to kill them.

In actuality, while posing for the statue, Carmnia had done both. The joke had been in reference to the artist working over her massive concrete crotch and the death threat had come because the artist hadn't unequivocally agreed that sculpting her crotch was a delightful privilege.

The BEAPER gave an impatient ding to remind May it was attempting to take her somewhere, and she walked past Carmnia, hoping she'd never have the displeasure of meeting her in real life.

The residential district extended along the chiseled stone walls of the underground Downtown. Rather than integrated apartments, leftover shipping containers which had carried the raw materials Rhea included in their reparations to the Tuhntians had been stacked into a Lego-brick complex, woven with intershoots and thin guardrails.

On the face of the containers, their owners had painted house numbers, but the last box in the first row, the one which the BEAPER's map insisted she enter, was painted with more than just its designated coordinates.

It played canvas to a detailed mural starring two Carmnians reclining in starburst clouds. These two Carmnians were strikingly familiar. May neared the mural, more certain with every step that leaving Xan back at Largish Bronda was the right decision, because he was already here. In mural form, anyway. Perfect likenesses of Xan and Aimz had been painted onto the side of the shipping container, reclining naked in starry clouds, like a celestial Botticelli.

Clearly, then, someone was looking for Xan, not just the *Audacity*. This was almost certainly a dead-end. But an interesting dead-end, at least. And if there was another rancorous robot ready to wreak revenge on Xan, May would rather know about it. She knocked.

Knocking, like ice cream or thumbs, is a cultural universal. Every civilized person in the entire universe knocks before entering.

The appropriate number of knocks, however, is greatly contested.

One knock is clearly not enough. No one knocks only once. A single knock is too easily explained away as a pipe sputtering, a tree branch falling, or a hungry ruffloo ricocheting off your door in hopes of catching its next meal.

Two knocks is the standard on Earth. Two healthy raps.

It's clear, definitive, and two taps echoes the two syllables of the word "Hello" rather nicely.

Three knocks is a touch excessive. Not unheard of and decidedly not inappropriate. Perhaps a bit rude, though. More of a "Hey, I'm here," syllabically.

Now, an Earthling who hears four knocks is grabbing a baseball bat on the way to the door because it is likely either a solicitor or the IRS. It's a kind of "Answer the door" or even "Get out here now."

Four knocks means business.

May knocked four times.

On Tuhnt, four knocks is used exclusively for food delivery.

As such, the person who came to the door was delighted to open it but not as delighted to see that the person on the other side wasn't holding the bowl of zipnite stew (lukewarm, extra salt) and a side of crawfish sticks (rare, hold the sticks) that she had ordered.

"Oh, you're not food." The coat-rack-thin Carmnian bent down to May's eye level, and the enormous plume of vermillion curls which obfuscated her eyebrows gave an urgent bounce. "You're not Tuhntian, either, larvling. Have you noticed?"

May pulled out the flyer and presented it to her. "Did you post this?"

The Carmnian took off the thin frames she had been wearing and squinted at the flyer, as if perhaps she was seeing it too clearly before and needed it to be a bit blurred before she could read it.

"Yes! Oh yes, mun, that's my flyer! Thank you for returning it to me, such a kind...I'm sorry...your name?"

"May."

"Such a kind May you are!" She took the flyer and began to shut the door.

"Wait! I have information about the *Audacity*."

She stopped closing the door but didn't exactly open it.

"You do?"

"Yes."

"About *Audacity*?"

"...yes." May was not fond of repeating herself.

"Oh my sweet larvling!" She patted May inside and shut the door.

The inside of the apartment was felted in fibers and draped with crochet. It looked more like the guts of a beast made entirely of yarn than the inside of a shipping container. Soft crocheted forms ballooned from the floor and lower walls, growing like mushrooms into things which might be mistaken for couches or tables. The Carmnian brought May to one of the soft bulbous forms and motioned for her to sit, then sat beside her, trapping May's hands in her own cold, jail-like fingers.

"Tell me! Please, I mean." The Carmnian wiggled like an over-excited terrier. "Please tell me everything you know about the *Audacity*."

"First, I want to know who you are and why you're looking for it."

The Carmnian pouted as if she had really hoped she could just get the information without having to give anything away.

May waited. She would not stand for pouting.

"Alright, well, my name is Kalumbits, but please call me *Aunt* Kalumbits, everyone does! Everyone did. Some people did. You know...just please call me that, alright? I would love you to call me that."

"You're Aunt Kalumbits?"

"Oh yes!" She bounced, the flash of consternation scared away from her expressive face. "Indeed. Oh, how nice." She fluffed out and straightened her hair with her fingers, pulling it a bit higher above her eyes. Just enough to make May suspicious that it was a wig.

"Is Kalumbits a popular name?"

"Oh, I should think not at all. No. Well, I once ran into a Rhean named Kalumbits. Nasty piece of work. All angles, her face was. And her hair! Oh, larvling, you wouldn't believe. And she had the nerve to disparage *my* hair. Hair is exceedingly important, don't you think? It can change your whole outlook on life! Do you like my hair?"

May relaxed now. Even if Kalumbits had been a common Tuhntian name, there was absolutely no doubt: This was Xan's Aunt Kalumbits. This made everything right.

"It's nice," she lied quickly. "You were looking for Xan, weren't you?"

Aunt Kalumbits swallowed hard. Her eyes became big and watery, and she put her glasses back on as if to cover them, but that only magnified her bright red irises.

"You know my Xan?"

May nodded.

Four knocks at the door.

"Oh, it's food!"

On the other side of the door, a delivery robot whirred pleasantly, proffering a box cocooned in a warm red glow. Kalumbits snatched the box and closed the door on it.

"Are you hungry, dear little larvling? You look hungry; have something anyway." She set the box down on what passed for a table and extracted a single, raw crawfish-on-a-stick which wasn't on a stick. May politely choked it down as Kalumbits popped open the soup and began to drink it.

"You weren't looking for the *Audacity*, were you? You were looking for Xan."

Kalumbits nodded. "Well, of course! But if I'm being honest, I've never seen a flyer with the image of Carmnian on it before that wasn't a wanted ad." She laughed lightly as if that had been a joke rather than a disparaging remark about Carmnians.

May hadn't found it funny and pointedly frowned at her. "How did you know he was on the *Audacity*?"

"Well, mun, I know Xan. An orange ship—he always loved orange things—gets stolen from a silo in Trilly by a Carmnian the same day Xan disappears? There wasn't any doubt, was there? I mean, the media kept it all south of the beak, didn't want to start a panic, but I knew. Now, circling back around here, where *is* my Xan? I need to see him. I'm sure he misses me!"

"I might be able to bring him to you," May said, wary of telling a stranger where she lived, even if the stranger was Xan's favorite aunt.

"When? Now?" She nearly flung the soup from her lap, stiffening with excitement.

"Well, I..." May had nothing better to do. There was no excuse worth giving. "Yeah, I'll be back in a minute." She said, knowing full well that "minute" wouldn't translate to anything meaningful, so Kalumbits would have no idea when to expect her back.

"Superb, larvling!" Kalumbits set aside her food and squeezed May like a drowning person squeezing a buoy.

May waited to be released. She did not squeeze back, because her arms were pinned to her sides. Also, she didn't want to.

✳ ✳ ✳ ✳ ✳

When May stepped through Largish Bronda's plasma door, no one greeted her, which meant that Xan was still asleep.

She found him curled on the sack chair and, May assumed on account of his unusually serious expression, deep in some kind of nightmare. She wondered what Tuhntian dreams were like, resolved to ask him later, then promptly forgot about it. Tuhntian dreams, she figured, were pretty much like Earthling's.

She was very wrong. Members of the A'Viltrial species, like Tuhntians, don't dream of isolated events. They dream of retro-reflected illimitable reality. Everything that is, was, and is to come in the entire cosmos compacted into a perfectly round orb of matter and anti-matter encased in an impermeable film of spacetime. Of course, since such a thing is utterly impossible, none of them have ever been able to make sense of it.

That's what Xan dreamed about.

Also, the fish was there. Everything was there, so naturally the fish was.

Big Mouth Billy Bass hadn't let Xan get a blip of decent sleep since they bought him three seasons ago, and now Billy was in Xan's dreams, producing a tuneless high-pitched whine at him. Xan was so disturbed by this dream that he didn't notice May slip the BEAPER back on him. He didn't notice her tapping his shoulder to wake him. Didn't notice when she ruffled his hair, flicked his nose, shouted "Wake up," in his ear, or pushed him onto the floor.

"'I Love Lucy' is on. I think it's 'Paris at Last'," she said.

Xan rocketed awake. "*Parlez-vous français?!*" He loved that episode.

"Good morning, starshine," May said to him, ironically. It was not morning and he was not her starshine.

"Eugh." He rubbed his eyes, pressing in against the ache behind them. "Do you hear that?" he asked, three times louder than necessary.

"No... Hearing through your eyes, are you?"

"Yes?" he said, his eyes still covered against the squealing. It was almost definitely coming from the direction of the Big Mouth Billy Bass hanging on their wall, but the moment he looked at it, the sound stopped.

May followed his gaze to the bass. "What's wrong?" she asked.

"It stopped." Xan shrugged. "I guess I have better hearing than you. 'I Love Lucy' isn't really on, is it?" he asked.

"No, I just needed to wake you up. I think I found Kalumbits."

"What about Kalumbits?"

"I think I found her," May repeated. She wasn't fond of repeating herself, but she was fond of Xan, so he got a pass.

"You?"

"Yes."

"Think you?"

"Found her, yes!"

"Here?!"

"Downtown. She posted the flyers."

"You went without me?"

"I promised to stop dragging you into things you didn't want to do. I never said *I* wouldn't do things you didn't want to do," May said.

"Fair point, that. Are you sure it's her? What did she look like?"

"Like you, but thinner and older."

"Like...like me?" He crashed performatively into the waterbed in the middle of the room, covering his face with his hands. "Blitheon's razor burn," he said from between his palms. "Did she have red hair?"

"Yeah, but I think it was a wig."

He groaned and rolled onto his side, grabbing a brocade pillow to hold onto. "Aunt Kalumbits isn't Carmnian. She's one of Vorcia's brood."

May plopped onto the waterbed beside him and propped her head up using her elbow as a kickstand. She was disappointed and tired but not surprised. Raw crawfish was not the kind of thing honest people ate.

"Who is she? She knows you and Aimz."

"Yeah, she better."

"Why?"

"She's also our aunt."

"Another one?"

Sighing, he stuffed the pillow he had been holding onto behind her head and grabbed another for himself, settling into the mire of despondence. "Chrismillion. We never really got on well."

"Can't imagine you not getting on well with anyone," May said.

"Yeah, well, imagine how she and Aimz got on. I've no idea why Kalumbits married her; she was flightier than a zipnite migration. She'd be gone for ten orbits at a time, come back with some 'priceless gifts' from her 'travels' which, unsurprisingly, were nearly always riddled with arcane curses. Have you ever tried to get a stubborn curse out of fine silk?"

"Did you try putting it in a bowl of dry rice?"

"I...no. What's rice?"

May laughed and shook her head; it didn't matter. "I told her I'd bring you to her."

He smooshed his face into the pillow and groaned. "Doo-e-aff-ta-go-now?" he asked, his voice muffled by the brocade.

"Not now. I told her I'd bring you back in a minute."

"How long's a minute?" he asked, flipping over.

"Exactly. She didn't know, either."

"And she was too proud to ask, wasn't she?" Xan smiled. The only thing he liked about Milly was that he always, without fail, could predict her. Like the Largish Bronda's Flexidimensal vehicles, she was reliably awful.

"Yep." May yawned.

"How long have you been awake?" Xan asked, concerned. By his count, it had been at least two rotations.

"Awhile," she said. "You're not supposed to sleep after a concussion."

"Ever?" Xan whispered, horrified.

"Everrrrr," May confirmed in a spooky warble. "No, seriously, I don't know how long. I guess I better try to sleep."

He stretched and turned over. "I'm going back to sleep, too. I've got a Tuhntian idiom for you: 'Never wake a Carmnian in the middle of a sleep cycle.'"

"Why, what happens?"

"They'll still be tired."

May snorted quietly and closed her eyes. Despite her body being tired, her mind was having a fiesta. She crawled to the pile of holobooks at the end of the waterbed. Snoodark Island was too isolated to pick up anything on the TV except corny scantplots, so they had purchased old holobook cylinders by the kilo at an estate sale.

The books had clearly belonged to an eclectic soul. They ran the gamut from absurdly methodical erotica to implausibly outlandish science fiction. May had been struggling through "Floaters," a speculative horror novel about a clan of fish-warriors who swam through the air, descending upon burgeoning civilizations and hoovering up their crops. The book itself wasn't terrible, but May had lost interest half-way through a chapter-long explanation of the plot of an unimportant novel which the main character (an enormous floating carp with a swim bladder malady) was reading.

She picked the holobook up now, considering it before stuffing it into the crack between the waterbed and the floor, where they stored the holobooks they knew they were never going to read. She found a book on the impact of trending vegetal microcosm exploration on impoverished mollusks and attempted to understand it.

SEVEN

SLAPDASHERY

* * * * *

Simulated sunlight peaked through the faux windows of Largish Bronda's FlexiDimensional HoverBus, waking May. She escaped the waterbed and turned off the faux window so she could see what actually lay outside the bus rather than the Largish Bronda Corporation's idea of a perfect morning.

Outside, predictably, was gray, cold, and dead. She flipped the simulated sunrise back on.

"Good morning, starshine!" Xan startled her from the kitchen. He had already made coffee and was cooking a potato-like vegetable that seeped purple starch and tasted uncannily of pineapple. A gift from Listay, straight from her vegetable garden.

"Purpatapple again for breakfast?" May leaned on the kitchen counter to watch Xan pop the last of the lumps into the Chrispopalactic Crisper which chopped and fried the vegetable instantly.

The fine art of *portmanteau* was absolutely lost on Xan. Tuhntian *portmanteau* exists, of course, but translation chips just aren't sophisticated enough to process them

47

into another language. "Grenanera," he corrected her. 'Grenanera' means 'purple potato-like vegetable which tastes uncannily of pineapple' in Tuhntian. He added, "Coffee?" which meant 'coffee.'

"Of course," May said as she floated the hover stool toward her and sat at the tiny counter. "We'll need it to keep up with your aunt."

Xan winced. "I was hoping you'd forgotten about that."

"You really don't want to go? But you're usually so..."

"Desperate for attention? Yeah, I know. But Milly's different. Her attention comes at a steep cost. If she says she wants to see me...it means she wants something," he stared out at the cheery faux sunrise, trying to guess what it was she could want.

"Well...yeah. To see you."

"When did you get so optimistic?" He finished drinking the pot of coffee without bothering to pour it into a mug, then combed his hair with his fingers to tame the proto-mullet he had been obstinately growing out for a season. He tried a mullet every couple hundred orbits, just to be absolutely sure they still looked terrible on him.

"Should we bring Aimz?"

"Blitheon, no. On their best behavior, Aimz and Milly are nuclear. With Aimz in this state—" He didn't like where that sentence was going, so he stopped saying it.

"What state?" May said, scooping up the last bite of crisped purpatapple.

"Well, I mean, Aimz isn't up for it right now. Come on." He tossed her empty plate into the disintegrator. "Let's get this off our marks."

✳ ✳ ✳ ✳ ✳

Xan had avoided going Downtown ever since they arrived a season ago, and now he'd been there twice in as many rotations. He hooked arms with May, hunching close to her as if they were about to walk into a haunted house as they descended the stairs.

"May, this place is really spooky. I mean, first off, it's underground. Nothing good happens underground. I've never once been in an underground location and had a good time."

"I thought you had fun in the Pontoosa Adventure Hole," May teased. "That's what your flag said." She was referring to the triangular novelty flag he had used as a censor-bar after his swimsuit had dissolved away in the gift shop of the Pontoosa Adventure Hole, an underground theme park turned abandoned pit of horrors.

"The flag was mistaken. I did not have fun in the Pontoosa Adventure Hole. In fact, the Pontoosa Adventure Hole is 90% of the reason I'd rather not have anything to do with underground locations."

"What's the other 10%?" May asked.

"Well, Trilly, where I grew up, used to be a thriving sirospletax mining town. Then one day, someone pulled on the wrong tree root and collapsed 600 miles of mine shaft and–poof–no more miners."

"Huh," said May. "There goes my plan to pull out some tree roots while we're down here."

"Oh, well, I mean you can probably pull out some smaller ones."

"No, no, you ruined it for me," she grinned at him cheekily and he relaxed a little. Her strange sense of humor, something that only he ever seemed to be in on, always put him at ease.

"There it is," May said, nodding toward the giant mural. She hadn't warned him about it. She probably should've.

"Blitheon's inconvenient pimple, that's scary," said Xan. "That's Milly, though. Huge, public, bordering on obsessive displays of affection. She must've forgotten what I look like, though…"

"That's exactly what you look like," May said.

Xan shook his head. "My nose isn't that long."

It was, but May didn't refute him.

"Last chance to turn back," she said.

"It's okay. It's alright. I'm ready to see her." And he stepped confidently in the direction of his own likeness. One step. He stopped. "But first, we need to agree on an exit strategy."

"Okay," May said. "If you decide you don't want to be around her, we'll leave."

"Where's your sense of decorum? We have to come up with a lie in case she tries to rope us into anything."

"A lie. The height of decorum."

"I mean, I don't like lying to anyone—"

"Don't you?"

"—but I don't want to hurt her feelings, either," he finished, ignoring her interruption out of decorum. "The wink-word is slapdashery. If either of us says 'slapdashery,' the other will make up a fake emergency and get us out of there. Alright?"

"What if the word slapdashery comes up in normal conversation?"

"Right, yeah, that's the sort of thing I'm likely to say, isn't it? What about anterior? That's a good word. No need to use that in conversation. And if I have to refer to something as anterior, I'll substitute with something else like 'frontmost' or 'before.'"

"Think you can manage that?"

"Probably," he said.

"Alright, anterior is the safe word," May agreed and knocked on the metal door, just twice.

Silence.

Two more knocks were met by a deeper silence from inside.

From outside, however, came a thump.

Followed by another thump.

Followed by a whispered curse.

The commotion came from behind the mass of shipping containers-turned-apartments. May decided to go figure out what it was, and Xan decided, a blip later, that she shouldn't do that alone.

Behind the stacks, in the alley, they found a pile of luggage trunks and a large minicraft (which was roughly the size of a mini largecraft), its shell dusty blue with neon green ovipositors spray painted at random sizes and intervals around it. The phallic shapes had been tipped with pink flowers, though, in an attempt at disguise.

Xan took an unnecessarily deep breath in and let it out with unnecessary force.

"That's Milly's old minicraft alright. Aimz vandalized it after Milly accidentally destroyed some science experiment by vaporizing a cream puff too early in the morning."

May tried to imagine what type of experiment, exactly, might suffer such a fate, but a third massive trunk launched from the minicraft and landed in the alley with a resolute thud.

"Aunt Milly?" Xan called out, jogging toward the trunks. From the door of the minicraft, Milly appeared in a heavy cotton patchwork coat, setting a feathered hat atop the trio of trunks. A gaudy visor across which scrolled the phrase 'Nasty Piece of Trok' in pink digital letters covered her eyes entirely, and she tilted her head up to see out from underneath it.

"Is that my Quaxlagon?"

"Quaxlagon?" asked May. "That's your full name?"

"Eugh, yes. Please don't make fun of it."

May laughed. "I wasn't going to! It's nice. Now I have something to call you when you're being a pest. Quaxlagon."

"Whatever you say, May June July."

Milly twirled over to Xan, throwing off the visor, and flung her arms around his neck, nipping his nose fondly. "It's so good to see you, larvling! So good. How long has it been? Why, manage me, the last time I saw you, you were half a crawfish shorter." She pushed him back, holding him at arm's length to inspect him. "Oh, and look at those kingly shoulders filing out. You always were a slight little thing. Gone a bit heavy on the snacks, though, mun?" She patted his stomach, and he self-consciously sucked it in.

"May eats a lot; it would be rude to not eat with her," he defended.

Milly tapped his face dismissively, then turned to May and gave her several pecks on the forehead. "Blitheon bless you, larvling."

May reflexively wiped her face with her sleeve, and Xan wriggled his nose to check that it was still on. Carmnian elders were fond of the nose nip. Xan wasn't.

"It's nice to see you, too, Aunt Chrismillion." Xan looked over her shoulder at the minicraft. "Is..." He paused, wondering if he really wanted to finish that sentence. He did not. But he finished it anyway. "Is Aunt Kalumbits... around?"

Chrismillion raised her chin just enough to be able to look down at Xan. "One aunt not enough for you?"

Xan swallowed, refusing to meet her gaze. "You know that's not why I asked."

Chrismillion's suddenly tight expression relaxed. "She was on Tuhnt when it was destroyed. If that's what you mean."

"Anterior," Xan whispered to May.

"Hmm?" Milly asked.

"Nothing."

"Well," May began, quickly deciding on an excuse to leave. "It was great seeing you, but we've got a thing back at the place."

Chrismillion squinted at her, then patted May's shoulders. "Nonsense, larvling! Come inside. I have a kettle of tea on, and all those trunks belong to Xan!"

May watched him for some kind of physical cue as to how much he didn't want to go inside. While the translation chip didn't do much to translate the strange faces he made, she'd known him long enough that she usually got the idea. She wasn't even getting the gist now. Nor a hint. Nor a modicum of an atom of a clue.

"Do we need to do the thing back at the place right now?" she asked.

He shook his head. The trunks had him on a reel, and Aunt Chrismillion knew this. That's why she had kept them.

"We'll stay for tea, but we do have to get going soon," May confirmed. Xan's mouth was a tight line, and his eyes looked like they'd been popped out, polished to a high shine, and set back in his face.

"Why don't you go ahead and start the tea?" May said, hoping to get away from Milly for a while to check in with Xan. "We'll be right in."

Aunt Chrismillion looked suspiciously from May to Xan. "You won't run off and take the trunks, right?"

"Promise. I don't think we could run with those trunks if we tried," May said and, satisfied, Milly went back into the apartment.

After the reverberation of the slamming metal door had settled, May nudged Xan. "Are you okay?"

"Not at all! Why do you ask?" he said as if she had asked him if he would mind scratching an annoying itch on her back.

"Didn't you...I mean, hadn't you already assumed Kalumbits was gone?" May felt like she was prodding a dead jellyfish on the beach with a sharpened stick.

"Heh," he choked. "I guess..."

"Come here." She opened her arms and he crumbled into them. "I'm sorry, Blueberry."

He shrugged; there was nothing she could do. Or rather, she was already doing what she could do. With a sigh, Xan straightened back up and ran a hand down his face.

"I've still got an aunt, I should probably try to reconcile with her. It was anterior to the war the last time we were anterior to anterior."

May wondered how the Tuhntian word for anterior as in 'before,' also meant anterior as in 'the front of someone.' I could go into cultural universals once again, but I wouldn't want to pummel a perished puntl.

"She freaks me out," May said.

Xan nodded encouragingly. "Yeah, that's something she does. I would like to say she's entirely harmless, but, well...I suppose she's mostly harmless. Let's have some tea," he said resolutely.

"You really want tea after what Sonan did?"

"Even Aunt Milly isn't cruel enough to poison me." He searched the cobblestones in deep thought. "I mean, I don't think she is. Zuut, now you've got me worried."

"Well, if it is poisoned we won't have to worry about spending any more time with her." May chuckled, and to her relief, Xan smiled back.

They entered the shipping container. The coffee table was set with a traditional pre-boloyten Tuhntian tea machine made entirely of cut glass. Half tea pot, half hookah, and half chandelier; it was one-hundred-and-fifty percent worth of thing. Six candles flickered around it, warming the tea. May had the eerie sense that they were about to summon Rube Goldberg's ghost and cautiously sat on the couch with Xan.

"Sit, larvlings! Oh so much to catch up on, isn't there? I did *so* miss you, Quaxlagon. I can't..." She paused to swallow, her voice had become hoarse. "I can't tell you how dreadfully sorry I am."

"Hmm," Xan agreed and accepted a cup of tea from her. He wondered briefly if she was trying to apologize in advance for poisoning him. But May drank her cup and gave him a nod. Nothing remotely like barley. More like peppermint, really. With a hint of fabric softener and a pinch of concrete. May, though she would never know it and had no formal training, would've made a top-notch sommelier.

"Can you ever forgive me, larvling? I do, I feel just *despondent.*"

Xan sipped the tea, politely swallowed, and vowed to never drink tea again. Even if it didn't kill him, it hadn't been worth the effort to lift the cup to his mouth. "Forgive you for what, exactly?"

"Oh, dear, will you truly make me say it?"

Again, he drank the tea. This time to keep himself from answering her in a way he might regret.

"I apologize for taking your costumes."

Xan silently waited for her to go on. May watched him, fascinated. He never silently waited for anyone to go on. Being around Milly had seemed to totally wipe his personality.

She huffed, slammed her teacup on the saucer, and went on. "I'm sorry I'm a horrible caregiver and that you wish I had died instead of Kalumbits. Is that what you wanted to hear? Will you forgive me for that now?"

Xan smiled tightly at Chrismillion. He set down the tea and turned to May. "May, what were you saying anterior to us coming in here?" He looked at Chrismillion without moving his head. "We have a thing to do at a place, I'm afraid, but it's been just delightful catching up with you. Keep the costumes, please, and thank you for the disgusting herb water. I detest it."

He stood and began to leave, but as he did, Chrismillion threw herself across the table to reach for his arm, knocking over all six candles in a way which was not only entirely and completely accidental, but also very intentionally choreographed and executed.

She yelped as the flames singed her coat, then rolled dramatically on the floor, the flames seizing the opportunity to start exploring the room. The fire turned its sights on the couch and began licking it up like a cat licking up spilled milk, but slightly more dangerous.

May and Xan leapt off the quickly succumbing couch.

"Help me pick her up!" May said, grabbing Milly's ankles firmly as Milly howled melodramatically. Xan scooped under her arms and hefted her up, totally unfazed, as if he'd done this before. He had, in fact, twice carried Milly out of a fire that she caused. This was nothing new.

Once outside, May dropped her end of Milly on the dusty rock and latched the apartment door to keep the fire contained.

Xan crouched in front of Milly, resettling her askew wig. "Are you alright?" he asked.

She coughed, waved her hand swimmingly in front of her face. "Quaxlagon, darling..." she coughed again, though she didn't need to, and Xan suspected as much. "Fetch your sister won't you? I do believe I am to die of smoke inhalation," she warbled.

"Milly," he whined at her. "If I bring Aimz you're going to die of murder."

"I want to see her! Why are you keeping her from me?" Milly sat up, miraculously recovered, her voice strong and demanding again.

"Goodbye, Milly." Xan put an arm around May's shoulders and tried to walk away, but unfortunately Chrismillion was not the kind of demon that disappears if you ignore it.

"Can I stay with you?" Milly grabbed the back of Xan's

furry coat.

"You've got the minicraft," Xan protested, turning around mid-stride.

"Yes, but I can't live in there. It's full of your trunks!" Milly said.

"Then I'll take the trunks back."

"Please." Aunt Milly grabbed his arm now and suddenly looked shorter than him, though moments before she had been taller. "I really do want to make amends. I..." She paused, her eyes glistening. "I loved you and Aimz and Kalumbits very much, and now that Kalumbits is gone, I want to fix things between us. Honestly, I do."

Xan had heard this before. Several times, actually. But he hadn't heard it in a few centuries, since he hadn't seen her in a few centuries, so he was tempted to give her an eighty-third chance.

"Aimz won't believe you." What he meant was that *he* didn't believe her.

"Just let me see her! You know what's in the trunks, I'd wager. Why not put on a show for me?" said Milly, a devilish smile twisting her face.

"I...yeah. You're suggesting we revive the Tinsel Merkin Fiasco, aren't you?"

Milly nodded so hard, her curls couldn't keep up. "And I've got connections at the *perfect* venue, the Grand Theater of Doing Things in Front of People in the Name of Entertainment in Snoodark's Folly! How does that sound?"

"That sounds..." Xan's head did a circular sort of maybe gesture. "Like a venue. What's Snoodark's Folly?"

"Queen Carmnia's sprawling manor, of course! How can you call yourself a Carmnian, not knowing Snoodark's Folly. Just shameful!"

Xan put his hands up submissively. "Alright, okay, Snoodark's Folly. Who do you know that works for Carmnia?"

"Oh, you know, some people." She waved a dismissive hand. "Just knock! Tell them Milly sent you."

"Sure," Xan said, hefting the three enormous trunks with a strength born of a desire to end this interaction as quickly as possible. "We'll definitely do that! Thanks for the tip." Then aside to May, he whispered, "We are definitely not doing that."

"Let me know when it is! And the dress code!" Milly called after them.

"Of course! Bye Milly," he said, already huffing under the weight of the trunks as they headed back toward the staircase.

"Don't wait long!" she said at their diminishing forms.

"Yep," he shouted through his teeth.

"Give my love to Aimz!"

They were out of earshot. Or, at least, Xan was confident they were far enough away that they could pretend to be out of earshot. Xan finally released the frustrated growl he had been politely restraining.

EIGHT

STUDYING BOTANY

* * * * *

Listay, having been reported as dead by the handful of her staff who had returned to Rhea after the *Peacemaker* crashed, was dealing with a legal conundrum that even she, a seasoned military general with a penchant for bureaucracy, couldn't get around.

Rather a lot of ordinary things become impossible when you're legally dead. Firstly, opening a bank account in the name of someone now deceased looks a great deal like some kind of fraud. Secondly, the dead don't typically go on paying taxes, and as such, the dead cannot apply for a job.

Frustrated, penniless, and dead, Listay had been forced to accept help. Help, as it so often does, came in the form of a buy-one-get-one free deal. The Largish Bronda Corporation had built a surplus of Merimip Ocean Ships and were so desperate to get them off the lot, they were giving them away with the purchase of anything larger than a keychain. So when May and Xan purchased the hover bus, Listay got a Merimip, a sleek little houseboat with a bulky, cumbersome glass dome on top.

This is how Listay came to after-live on a boat in the fjord with Aimz who, though never claiming to live there herself, could usually be found lounging around the boat somewhere like a feral cat full of kittens.

Usually, Aimz stayed at the Merimip under the guise of "studying botany" in Listay's "garden". The pair were engaged in a vigorous study session when the squeak of footfalls on the aluminum boat ramp alerted them to May and Xan's approach.

On Rhea, many hundreds of religions have been created for the express purpose of instilling sexual shame in the hearts and loins of all Rheans. Conversely, Carmnian culture dictated that modesty-be-damned; clothes were worn for style alone. This is why Listay answered the door shielded in the broad yellow leaves of a distant relative of the ficus, and Aimz joined her in proud full frontal.

"I hope you're prepared to out-do what you just interrupted." Aimz sported a wide grin and nothing else, leaning against the doorframe rakishly.

May had never purposefully imagined what Aimz might look like naked, but *had* she imagined it, she wouldn't have imagined this. She very pointedly averted her gaze.

"Oh, don't embarrass May," Listay interjected before Xan could say that he did intend to out-do what he'd just interrupted and make a fool of himself. "We'll get dressed and be with you in a—"

"Waaaait!" Aimz shouted as the stack of trunks behind Xan finally registered with her. She held her arms out to the trunks as if she were expecting them to hug her.

"Right?" Xan smiled.

"Listy, larvling, you're right. Let's get dressed." Aimz snatched the handle on the bottom trunk and pulled, dragging the stack backward into the boat. She paused and looked up under her arm at Xan. "Zuut, how did you carry them here without an electro-lift?"

Xan made a face as if a few hours of his life had just been purposefully skipped over by some all-knowing, omniscient hand. "No idea, honestly. May?"

May shrugged. "I know I didn't help."

Grunting, Aimz pulled the trunks into the boat and

shut the door, leaving May and Xan outside.

The Merimip bobbed genially at them, floating just a hand's width above the water.

"She's going to be a blip in there," Xan said and sat on the ramp, his back against the Merimip's door.

"Why, what's in the trunks?" May asked.

"Didn't you ask that on the way over?" he asked.

"What way over?"

"Oh yeah, right. Right..." Xan said, again perplexed by how they had arrived at the Merimip. "Well, they're the costumes and props from my old burlesque group, The Tinsel Merkin Fiasco."

"The Tinsel?"

"Yes."

"Merkin?"

"Uh-huh."

"Fiasco?"

"That's the one."

May thought about that. "What does merkin mean?"

"Oh, you don't have them on Earth? They're uh..." Xan bared his teeth, trying to puzzle together the most appropriate words. "Crotch wigs," he decided was tasteful enough.

"Huh. So those trunks are full of crotch wigs?"

"Oh zuut, no! No. That's the point, you see; it was a fiasco. We don't do merkins anymore."

"Ah," said May.

"Ah!!" said Xan, falling backward into the Merimip through the suddenly dematerialized door. He landed on his back, nose-to-nose with a beaming Aimz, the shiny red tinsel of her outfit tickling his forehead.

"Iiiit's Zecktrix!" She announced cheerfully, shimmying the tinsel in his eyes.

Against the monochromatic grey backdrop of the Merimip's interior, Aimz's pale blue skin, magenta hair, and sparkly red leotard made her look like a bad photoshop. May climbed into the bobbing ship, helping Xan regain his footing.

"Zecktrix?" May asked.

"Aimz's stage persona," Xan told her.

"No, no," Aimz said. "Persona implies a character. This is how I always am!" She did something strange with her tongue, like she was trying to lick the last bite of peanut butter from a jar, but sexily.

Xan nodded. "You're right, my mistake."

"Listay! Come look at me! Look at your zuxine Carmnian plaything!" Aimz shouted and Listay, now fully dressed and looking a bit sheepish, entered the living room.

"You look lovely," Listay told her, then glanced at May, trying to decide whether she should apologize for being almost naked in front of her, or if it was wise to not bring it up again. Aimz made the decision for her by launching at the second trunk and flinging it open, pulling out scarves and holsters and wigs and other things which would need a lot more time to explain.

"Where did you get all this? It's our stuff! Last I knew Milly–" Aimz froze. An impossibly thin peach scarf she had just thrown into the air made its decent, draping itself over half of Aimz's face. She spun, fixing Xan with one pink, blazing eye.

"Milly! I swear on every volt in Quanzar's laser-scythe, if you don't tell me where that tchaag is, I'll—"

"Aimz, look!" Xan said, pulling something from the trunk. "It's your plasma-plipper!" He began to juggle two glass balls connected by a string and a weak blue lightning arced between them.

"No–" Aimz batted them away. "Ow." She shook her hand which had caught the tail end of the plasma arc and been lightly electrocuted. "Where is she?"

"Alright, so, long story. As you know, May's been looking for the *Audacity*—"

"Shorten it."

"May found these flyers—"

"Shorter."

Xan cringed, mentally running through the plot thus far. "Chrismillion lives Downtown, and she wants to see you–"

"Good," Aimz said. May was grateful that one of her eyes was covered, because she'd never seen such a murderous gleam in them and she didn't care for it.

"Not good. Not a good idea at all," Xan said, snatching the scarf away from her. "So we compromised. And this is the good bit! We're getting the Tinsel Merkin Fiasco back together! One night only! If Milly happens to hear about it and come see us, fine! She gets what she wants, you never have to see her as long as the spotlight's bright enough. Good plan, eh?"

"Xan," Aimz crossed her arms. "Half of the Tinsel Merkin Fiasco is dead."

"Ahh-uhh, eugh..." he grimaced at the reminder. "We've got plenty of acts between the two of us, and May can work the lights. Besides, Old PinFlicker is in one of these trunks. It'll be like we never disintegrated-destructed-demolished-no-*disbanded*! Like we never disbanded."

"I'll organize the event," Listay said, delighted to be organizing something, for once, that didn't have life-or-death consequences. She was wrong, of course, but let's not get ahead of ourselves. "If you're putting on a show, you're going to need spreadsheets."

"Uh-huh, right, yes. Listay will do the spreadsheets," Xan said, unconvinced that any organizing had to be done at all because he had never been the one in charge of doing it.

"Chrismillion's never going to change. You know that," Aimz said, shoving Xan off the trunks so she could dig through hers again.

"Do I know that?"

Aimz snarled half-heartedly at him. "You're just like Kalumbits. She always gave Chrismillion more chances than she deserved." She tilted her head back, her gaze rolling back to the exploded trunk. "But I really want to do Zecktrix again," she said.

"So we're on?" Xan said, excited.

"We're zuxing on."

NINE

PHASERS SET TO STUNNING

* * * * *

Xan conveniently forgot to mention Milly's suggested venue at Snoodark's Folly, and so Listay had come up with the cheapest venue she could find. The tiny theater was snuggled beneath Uptown NotTuhnt's historic Sneepum Hotel, the first hotel built on NotTuhnt. It was the *only* hotel built on NotTuhnt. And for good reason. No one ever visited NotTuhnt if they could help it. Realizing this, the hotel manager had changed the welcome sign in the lobby to one which read 'Our sincerest apologies.'

It was opening night, which was also dress rehearsal and closing night, since they only planned on doing this once. May sat cross legged on the blue velvet floor of a backstage dressing room while Xan lugged a trunk into the room, dropping it with a plume of dust. "Ready?" Xan asked her excitedly, leaning over the trunk as if it might pop open and dazzle her too soon.

"As I'll ever be."

Xan propped open the lid to reveal his bounty, a mess of gold and silver spaghetti.

"What is it?" May squinted into the glittering maw,

feeling like she was trying to look into the sun.

"That's Fuxoona Glizell. Aren't they stunning?"

"Stun's a good word for it. I'm going to take a look at the tech booth," she said, standing to leave. "Try to figure out the lighting…"

"Make it bright. I want Aimz to think she's performing on the sunny side of Sarfooreimp! If she doesn't see Milly, she can't get upset about her, right?"

"On it," May said.

The tech booth had left much to be desired. A single switch labeled "House" at one end and "Stage" at the other was installed right in the center of a rather large console. After a great deal of searching, May found another switch underneath the console labeled "Off" and "On". She really would've liked to show her technological prowess just once, but alien technology thus far had been mostly ridiculously user friendly.

Gold-silked fingers appeared above the tech booth wall and were soon followed by Xan who pulled himself up, jingling, over the back of the booth, and perched on the dividing wall. Even in the dim light, the sparkles on his dress were mesmerizing.

He puffed his chest out, showing off a pair of fake boobs which shone like two small disco balls, and he shook his head to demonstrate the bounce of his thickly curled, silver-gold wig.

"What do you think?"

May wasn't exactly sure what type of reaction he was searching for here. "It's very shiny," she said.

He lay himself dramatically over the back of the booth, his legs kicking elegantly out in white, thigh-high, skyscraper stilettos.

"It's alright, mun," his voice shifted and, though the translation chip didn't pick it up well, he affected a masterful Queenly accent. "You can tell Fuxoona they're the most gorgeous Tuhntian you've ever seen." He winked cheekily, wobbled dangerously on the divider, then steadied himself.

May covered a laugh. "What if Xan gets jealous?"

"I swear on my ovipositor, I won't tell a soul of it!"

"Oh, alright," May cleared her throat and put on a delicate southern drawl for him. "Having basked in your singular beauty, I feel my life is complete and I can die a happy woman." Then, in her normal voice. "Good?"

"Good!" said Xan. "You should be on stage with me!"

"No," May said.

"No, right, yeah." Xan agreed. Then, again in a Queenly timber, he said, "Now help Mx. Glizell down, munny. Fuxoona's not the spritely young acrobat they once were!"

May left the booth the easy way, via the stairs, and got back to floor level below the lounging Xan. He reached his arms out to her dramatically and wriggled his fingers.

"Xan, you're—"

"Ah-hem!"

"Mx. Glizell," she corrected, "you're too heavy for me to lift, you know that?"

"Why! I might in all my life!" he said with faux offense and docked his fists on his hips before jumping down, May's hands around his sequined waist to steady him on his massive heels.

"Ah, there we are, larvling." He straightened his dress then, in his own voice, cursed. "Zuut."

"What?"

"Chrismillion's here. Did you invite her?"

"No," May said.

"Neither did I. Aimz and I used to tease each other that she had spies watching us all the time. We stopped teasing each other when we started believing it," he shivered. "Alright, okay, I'll keep an eye on Aimz, and you can keep Milly occupied, right? Yeah." He looked round nervously as if Aimz might plummet from the catwalk and attack. "Second thought: I'll watch Milly, and you watch Aimz. No. Third thought: Where's Listay? She can overpower Aimz."

May frowned at Chrismillion, studying her willowy stature. "I could overpower Milly."

"You're sure? She can be extremely persuasive. You've got to assume that anything she says is a lie straight out of the silo."

"I meant physically," May said, though she could

probably overpower her psychologically too, should she need to.

Xan shook his head. "If it comes to that…watch out for her nails," he said.

"Okay."

"And her teeth," he added.

"Got it."

"And her nose."

"Her…nose?"

"It's sharper than it looks and she will weaponize it," Xan confirmed.

"Oh…don't worry about it. You go break a leg," May said, gently shooing him away before Milly spotted him. She was still looking around the growing crowd like a meerkat with a periscope.

Xan tilted his head at her. "Do you expect that will help?"

The house lights flickered, warning the audience that the show was about to start so they should either sit down or scram. "Earth saying, means have a good show!"

"But why?!"

"I don't know, and I don't have time to make something up," she physically turned him around and started walking him in the direction of the backstage entrance.

"Alright, I'm going, mun! Aunt Kalumbits is late; I hope she arrives before my act…" he muttered as he went.

Convinced he was going in the right direction, May headed back to the tech booth, pondering why he had said that. He knew Kalumbits wasn't coming on account of her being dead. Perhaps, she thought, it was a strange alien custom to invite the deceased. No stranger than breaking a leg, at least.

May sat in front of the light controls next to Listay. There was nothing to do, but she enjoyed the illusion that being behind a control panel might give her more control over her life in general. Listay set a notepin which displayed a green holographic spreadsheet on the console.

"Twenty-seven people, all perfectly seated according to an algorithm which factors height, light tolerance, and the distance each of them is able to accurately throw tips from," Listay said with a practiced humility.

May studied the spreadsheet emanating from the notepin. "How did you factor that?"

"Square root of arm length, multiplied by muscle elasticity, minus one third muscle mass, divided by willingness to punt a crystal at someone," Listay said.

"Really?"

"No." Listay chuckled. "I asked them. Here." She handed May a llerke. "You haven't eaten in eight beoops; you must be starving."

May found it spooky how Listay always knew when she was hungry, but May was usually hungry, so there was nothing supernatural about it.

"Thanks," she whispered to Listay, flicking the lights from "house" to "stage". A single, red-heeled foot peeked out from the side of the stage and kicked at an old wooden box, the infamous PinFlicker. It was the size of an accordion, its many panels barely concealing tarnished brass innards and hosting an array of metal pipes which began to puff out a fuzzy melody as the internal music cylinder rolled under the many pins and pumped the small but powerful bellows.

Aimz strutted out in less than she usually wore plus a silver beaded headdress, hips gyrating, shoulders shimmying, arms dangerously akimbo. The crowd pelted crystals at her as a holy offering. She received the praise like a gracious god.

May kept watch over Chrismillion who sat in the back row, absently clutching a fistful of crystals to her décolletage. She wasn't watching Aimz. She was hunched over a little hand-held mirror, touching up her dark purple lipstick.

The music wound down to a distorted warble, and Aimz paused to fiddle with the box until it played again, quieter.

"Welcome to the show you pitiful ovi-suckers!" That got a hearty cheer from the crowd. "Most of you perverts have done this before, I can tell, but let's re-certify you. When I shimmy you—"

"Shout!" went the crowd.

"Blitheon, you're a snack-y bunch of submissives, aren't

you? Right, when I titillate you—"

"Tip!" they cried.

"And finally, what are you not going to do this evening?"

"Usurp your right to bodily autonomy by touching you or anyone else who excites us!" recited the crowd in practiced unison.

She smiled. "It's nice to see getting your planet exploded hasn't changed the scene. Now..." Aimz kicked off her heels and leapt from the stage onto the back of an empty velvet chair, then the next, using the unfilled seats as stepping stones to get back to the tech booth. The crowd twisted to watch her.

"Hey, you heard that? No touching," Aimz whispered into Listay's mouth. Listay looked as if she very much wanted to touch, but showed mighty discipline. Aimz cackled and leaned into the soundboard microphone. "And now," her voice reverberated. "Prepare your retinas for the brightest Queen-show since Blazita Fyresnatch's pyrotechnics accident: Mx Fuxoona Glizell!"

May was certain there wasn't a teledisc in the stage. Nonetheless, Fuxoona appeared in a puff of glitter right in the middle of it. Low-tech magic had created this effect. And, since a magician never reveals their secrets, even I have no idea how it happened. Damn magicians.

"You." Fuxoona pointed to someone leaning dangerously forward in their seat in the front row. "Be a larvling and crank my good friend PinFlicker."

A shadowed figure flung themselves half onto the stage to reach the box and wound it up, a new song wafting from it, a simmering tune with regular pops, like bacon seductively being fried. Fuxoona pulled a stick-on gem from a hidden pocket in their gown and slapped it on their bare chest.

"Do me a favor, larvlings. When you tip, aim right here." Fuxoona pointed to the faux cleavage with a wink. "I've got a lot of padding there. Any of you lonely zuxxers want to see why they called me The Legs of Trilly?"

The audience went wild for that, showering Fuxoona with crystals, adding to the mess on stage already. Typically, someone was there to clean up between acts, but that someone had perished on Tuhnt. Fuxoona kicked at a pile of crystals and tutted. "Zilla's off her mark this evening, isn't she? Zecktrix!" they shouted back to Aimz. "Where's Zilla?"

"Dead!" Aimz shouted back.

"Oh, heh." The persona of Mx Fuxoona slipped for just a moment and Xan's entire posture shifted, slightly, just enough to break the illusion that he was something other than Xan in a dress. The audience fell silent, and Fuxoona snapped back into place. "The Legs of Trilly!" said Fuxoona, to a slightly less enthused audience who had now been reminded twice of the destruction of their home planet in one stage show.

Fuxoona began to move like a slow-motion inflatable tube-man, then they were upside-down, doing things with their body May had no idea Xan could do. Arousal wasn't a sensation May had ever experienced, at least not toward another being. She'd gotten close a few times working on her old Honda, though. She did not experience it now, but she was entertained. And, clearly, the audience was up to their eyebrows in excruciating lust for Fuxoona. The theater bubbled with whoops, shouts, and moans of delight as the stage disappeared under a layer of crystalline tips.

"Aimz?" May asked, leaning over to Aimz who had parked in Listay's lap. "Xan's acting strange."

"Sure is, but zuut, the audience is responding to it!"

"No, I mean...earlier Xan said he was expecting Kalumbits, like he had forgotten. And just now—"

"Oh yeah, he's a little unstuck in time," Aimz said. "Common symptom for people like him."

"Symptom of what?!"

"Did he not zuxing tell you? Agh, of course he didn't. Listen, Earthmun, Xan and I—" The music ground to a halt, and Aimz paused to see why. On stage, Fuxoona followed suit with the grinding, but not the halting. "Showing off without me, Fuxoona?" Aimz asked from the back microphone, then launched out of the tech booth and walked wibblingly over the seats again to rejoin the spotlight.

"Aimz!" May hissed after her, but she was well out of earshot.

May looked to Listay for a hint at what Aimz had been trying to say, but Listay was entranced, leaning forward on her elbows, her eyes swimming around Aimz's hips, the corner of her mouth tilting up in a goofy half-smile. Listay, though in actuality there was nothing she could've done to prevent this, would later berate herself terribly for once again letting her guard down on account of a pair of beautiful hips.

Had she not been otherwise occupied, Listay might have noticed Chrismillion moving from her designated seat in the back of the crowd. May noticed. May sat up straighter, trying to figure out if she needed to hop over the tech booth wall and do something about it or not.

Milly slipped down the side aisle, headed for the silent PinFlicker. Just being helpful, May thought. Aimz looked at Milly with all the fervor of a starved lion spotting a sickly gazelle at the watering hole. Now, Listay noticed what Milly had done. But it was too late. Milly, though certainly she had approached the stage with the benign intent of winding PinFlicker for the performers, instead shoveled a handful of crystals from the stage into her purse.

"Blitheon's natal charts," Listay grumbled as she left the booth.

"Zux off, thief!" Aimz shouted, grabbing Milly by the front of her dress.

"Eugh." Xan discarded Fuxoona like a wet plastic bag and put a hand on Aimz's shoulder. "Let Zilla take care of it, mun—"

"Zilla." Aimz pushed Milly away from the stage, spinning around to intimidate Xan now instead. "Is." She stood up and he fell back, scrambling away. "Dead!" She flung herself at Xan, grabbing the string of gaudy gold beads around his neck and pinning him to the creaking stage. Someone in the audience began a clap, but another audience member coughed and silenced them.

"Stop saying that!" Xan wheezed around the choking beads. He wriggled until he had the sharp heel of his boot under Aimz's sternum and flung her off him, sending her flailing into an empty row of velvet seats.

The audience was beginning to get uncomfortable. Some half-stood, watching to see if this was a new experimental form of burlesque that hadn't quite settled into itself yet. Others slipped out the back. Still others raised their BEAPERs, preparing to call the police.

At the edge of the stage, Milly had recovered enough to get revenge. One word would send the theater into a complete panic. One word would set the police on Aimz's tail. One word would absolutely destroy the chance of another performance of The Tinsel Merkin Fiasco.

"Scourge!" she shouted like a 1930s horror actress. "Scourge!!!" she repeated, pushing her way through the crowd.

"Aimz," Xan said, climbing down from the stage. "BEAP Kalumbits about this, alright? I'm going after Milly. And, uh…" He looked lost for a second, as if he wasn't quite sure what he was saying or why he was saying it. "Ask Salesha to do her bit early, alright? I'll be back by the finale, I'd wager, then we'll all go to Martoly's Bar and have a drink." He tried to give her shoulder a comforting pat, but the mention of Martoly's Bar had re-ignited Aimz, and she ripped off her heavy silver wig and flailed it in his face, knocking him backward over a seat and pinning him to the sticky floor.

"You *blew up* Martoly's and *every other bar* on the zuxing *planet*, you *tchagg*!"

"I thought Aimz had gotten over that," May said to Listay as they watched the wrestling performers in the empty theater.

"You're the reason Milly left!" Xan flung the silken glove off his hand, pelting Aimz in the face with weaponized gold glitter, his signature attack.

"And you're the reason everyone except her is dead!" Aimz said, her eyes shut tight against the threatening glitter as she yanked out curly blond chunks of his wig. They weren't actually doing any damage to each other, and May and Listay both realized this, so they hung back, neither keen on getting covered in glitter.

"Here." Listay handed May an open bottle of Fraguntassle. "When they calm down, make Xan drink it. It seems to mitigate the scourge."

"What's the scourge?" May asked, accepting the bottle of opaque white brew.

Sirens interrupted her answer. Three triangular-bodied chrome police robots rolled into the venue. May yanked Xan (who had been gnawing gently on one of Aimz's hands while her other hand viscously ripped the stuffing from his fake boobs) behind a seat to hide him. She flicked his nose to get his attention.

"Ow." He cupped his nose, blinked at her as if she were a complete stranger, then re-adjusted his wig. "What was that for, mun?"

"The police are here," May whispered at him harshly, "Because you and Aimz started wrestling in the middle of the show. What's gotten into you?"

"Do not attempt to flee," said the foremost chrome officer, the plastic light atop its hat flashing with each syllable. Listay stepped in front of the chrome trio, barring them from May, Aimz, and Xan. "Scan me," she demanded. A blue light emanated from each of their visors and scanned Listay.

"According to Rhean records, General Listay under Rapite of Rhea is dead," the middle officer intoned. "Suspect," confirmed the two flanking officers.

"You're right, I'm very suspicious," Listay goaded them on. "Why don't you arrest me?" And all three of them did.

"Come on." May grabbed Xan's hand and dragged him toward the exit.

"Wait! Gloves." He collected the limp silk gloves that he had tossed in the tussle and re-sheathed his hands. "The gloves make the outfit," he said, wriggling shiny fingers at her.

May, with great difficulty, held back a contemptuous groan. "Where's Aimz?"

Xan shrugged. "Wager she snuck off with Yve. Again. Rude of her, don't you think? She knows how much I like Yve. I think it's rude. She could at least invite me."

Rather than waste her breath to tell him that Yvonne

was not here and Aimz definitely didn't sneak off with her,
May agreed and led him outside.

TEN

TRAVELING KISSING BOOTH

＊ ＊ ＊ ＊ ＊

Trying to force a three-hundred-pound Tuhntian wearing four-inch heels in one direction proved rather difficult for May. One hand grasped the bottle of Fraguntassle; the other, she had tightly interwoven with Xan's. His gloves, however, made escape too easy. Barely a block away from the venue, he pulled away, leaving her holding onto a limp, silky glove as he sauntered off to pluck something from the walkway.

"Xan, no," May whined, stuffed the glove in her coat pocket, and tried to collect him again. He looked at her, his mouth suspiciously closed. "What's in your mouth?" she asked.

He shrugged.

"What are you eating?"

He rolled his eyes and unfurled his tongue at her, a not-cigarette stuck to it. She plucked it off and held it up to shame him.

"Really?"

"I have to!" he protested. "They're not good for you, May."

She sighed, flicked the damp not-cigarette into a nearby receptacle, and grabbed his hand again. "I wasn't smoking it," she told him. "Wish I was," she mumbled. The monorail station loomed ahead, and May paused.

"Hey, look at me," she said.

He looked.

"Don't act weird in the monorail, ok?"

"Why—" He paused to stare at his glove flapping from her coat pocket, grabbed it with his teeth, and spoke around it. "Would I act weird in the monorail, specifically?"

She recovered the glove and pushed it into the recesses of her trench coat pocket.

"Please drink this." She tried to hand him the bottle, but the monorail pulled into the station, and this distracted him.

"Excellent. Monorail," he said. "Lots of beautiful people on the monorail!" He jumped into the open tube and May followed helplessly, finding him already accosting a dark indigo Tuhntian twice Xan's size. "Hey, you're cute. Want to make out?" Xan asked him.

"Xan!" May slung her arms around his waist and tried to yank him away. "So sorry. He's drunk," she said to the stranger.

The Tuhntian raised a tired eyebrow at May, slowly blinked, dropped the book he was reading to the seat next to him, and let Xan make out ferociously with him. May covered her eyes, partially to give them some privacy and partially because the sight of anyone—particularly Xan—making out made her queasy. The monorail, at last, jerked into motion beneath them.

Another passenger had gotten up from their seat to tap Xan on the shoulder sheepishly. "Is that free?" they asked.

Xan pulled away, eyeing them with a gleam of excitement. "Of course it's free! Love is always free!" he announced to the monorail car. "Anyone who wants a taste of this, form a queue, please!"

Horrified, May watched, or rather *listened*, for she refused to look, as he made out with half the people in the monorail, complimenting each of them on their excellent form, outstanding dexterity, delightfully cold hands, and so on.

Sitting, May swirled the Fraguntassle in its bottle, sniffed the potent wheaty brew, and took a swig for herself while she waited for Xan to finish off the line. At last, he settled down in the seat beside her. There were a great deal more smiles in the monorail then there had been a moment before, peppered with a handful of disgusted murmurs regarding the looseness of zuxing Carmnians.

"How about you? You want in?" Xan asked.

May groaned. "No," she said, resting her elbows on her knees, one hand cradling her face and the other barely holding onto the bottle of Fraguntassle.

"Oh," he sounded just slightly disappointed, then perked up. "Well, looks like this car's tapped out. Onto the next!" He made for the door which led between the cars. It very clearly read: Emergency Use Only. He pushed it open. May pulled him back inside and barred the door.

"Changed your mind?"

"No! You can't hop cars like a traveling kissing booth!"

"But I always do...did." He sat down on the plastic monorail bench next to her. "Tenses are hard, aren't they? Everything is happening in the now. Why do we use any other tense, again?"

"I don't know, you're the linguist, not me," May said. "We can talk about it if you drink this," she held out the Fraguntassle. He took the bottle and tipped it back, May hoped it was strong enough to not only fix his brain but to also kill any germs he might've picked up from the other passengers.

He handed the empty bottle back to her with an accomplished grin which faded, slowly, as he looked around the monorail. Half the passengers were gazing dreamily at him as if he had just—oh no. He *had*.

"Zuxing Blitheon's laser scythe, what in O'Zeno's secret swimming pool did I do?" he whispered, his fingers digging under his wig and pulling it off so he could grab at his own hair as he leaned over his knees.

May took the wig from him and put it on herself for safe

keeping. She tried to rub his back comfortingly, but a shower of sequins fell off when she did, so she stopped. "Nearly everyone in the car," she said. The monorail pulled into their stop and they got out.

The air swirling in Snoodark's Quarry was thick with a slimy, cold drizzle, as usual. The wig May had taken from Xan was long enough to wrap around her neck as an impromptu scarf, and she slipped his gloves on, wincing at the feeling of the glitter inside them scraping like sandpaper across her hands.

Their walk from the monorail to Largish Bronda was usually short and filled with good conversation, but now it seemed to stretch untold distances. They were already miserable, so May figured now was as good a time as any to ask a miserable question.

"What is the scourge?" May asked as Xan stopped to retrieve a discarded not-cigarette mechanism from a molding patch of yellow leaves. "Don't eat it," she warned him.

"Wasn't planning to," he lied, then put it in his pocket to eat later.

"Scourge. You and Aimz both have it, don't you? What is it?"

Suddenly, Xan remembered all the things he had meant to talk to her about, like the new zipnite enclosure at the market in the city. Or perhaps the upcoming art installation, a social commentary that was either for or against something or other. And she'd need to know about the Egg Experience which had just opened in the rougher part of town that would soon be either an art district or a red-light district; it was too early to tell.

He said none of these things, though.

He was working on not deflecting.

So he didn't speak at all.

"Xan?"

"Yes?"

"You don't want to tell me?"

"Oh..." Xan sung as if he were about to break into a sailor shanty which would explain it in a cheery, fun way. There was no cheery, fun way to describe scourge, but he tried.

"The fungi that Carmnia likes to eat—remember those? That cause the phosphorescence in Carmnian eyes? Well, the fungus is usually dormant, but under the right circumstances, it goes into...well, let's call it party mode. Because parties are cheery and fun. So once the fungus goes into party mode, it grows rapidly, feeding off brain matter until it's a proper rager in there. Lots of fun. Extremely cheery. Actually, a cool side effect is that the phosphorescence is so intense, fully scourged Carmnians can't sleep. Ever! Imagine, never sleeping." He laughed. "It's deadly and irreversible," he said lightly.

"Irreversible?" she asked. May refused to accept this. To her, there was always a way out. Always a fix. Always something that could make it better. "What about the Fraguntassle? That helped."

"Oh, sure, sure. Yeah. Alcohol helps!"

"We'll just keep you drunk for the rest of your life, then. Or until we find a cure," May assured him as they entered Largish Bronda. "We've still got some shermel in the cupboard, and tomorrow we can go back to the city and get more."

The reason they still had shermel in the cupboard was because shermel tastes terrible.

The reason they had shermel in the first place was that it's a key ingredient in what amounts to Tuhntian chicken noodle soup which Xan insisted on making for May when she came down with a space flu she had caught in the Pontoosa Adventure Hole in book two.

"Perfect. That will absolutely definitely work," he said. Xan peeled off his thigh-high white stilettos and shimmied out of the glitzy dress, letting it fall in a pile on the floor as he inspected the many greenish bruises he had gained. "Zuut, I'm wrecked! What...what did I do exactly?"

"You wrestled Aimz, ate not-cigarette butts off the ground, and started a traveling kissing booth in the monorail."

"Heh...Busy night." He folded his dress and removed the wig from May's head, looking for a clever place to hang it. The Big Mouth Billy Bass on the wall caught his eye, and he draped the curls over the fish's head. "I wrestled Aimz?"

"She wrestled you, actually. You didn't put up a good fight. There was a lot of glitter," she said, carefully laying down his glove atop the pile, trying to keep more glitter from falling out and contaminating the room.

Xan felt so heavy that when he sunk into the waterbed, he was surprised he didn't continue dipping into the floor below, down through the crust of Rhea, and into the planet's molten core where he could melt peacefully away. He buried his face in his hands, which were still covered in glitter and would be for the remainder of this novel. "How many strangers did I make out with?" he asked beneath his palms. May couldn't quite tell if he was hoping for a high or low number.

"Seven before I had to stop you from jumping cars."

"Yeah, that was my average," he said. May still couldn't tell how he felt about that. "How was the show? Before the...you know."

"I loved it."

"You did?" Xan flipped over, confused with his entire face.

"Yeah! I mean, I didn't really get it, but you looked like you were having fun. And Fuxoona is quite the charmer."

"They sure are." Xan laughed. "You know, it really felt like everything was back to normal for a bit there. I mean...I mean an old normal. Strange how many 'normal's you can have, right? Being alone in open space on the *Audacity* was normal. Racing with you was normal..." He paused and looked around at the still darkness of the hoverbus, deciding. "You'd think three seasons of this would make it normal but—"

"No, I agree. It's still weird." May yawned and stretched her arm out so he could cuddle up to her. She knew he wouldn't sleep, but if she started yawning at him, he would at least stop talking long enough for her to.

He caught the hint and shut up, but his mind refused to stop replaying scenes from all his past normals.

ELEVEN

FAMILY DROPS IN

* * * * *

"Scourged Carmnians are unpredictable."

"Guh?" May said, rubbing her eyes to dislodge the film of sleep as she coaxed her consciousness into wake-mode. A worried shadow hung over her, silhouetted in the icy gray light outside the window. Eventually, she pieced together that the shadow was Xan and that he was worried that he would do something unpredictable. "Everything you did last night was predictable as hell," she assured him.

"Is hell predictable? I honestly don't know, I've never been. I thought you said it was a mythical place. And sure, last night I was predictable, but I can't predict whether or not I'll continue being predictable in the future! That's the point of unpredictability!"

"Ugh, it's too early for this," May said, rubbing her eyes with her fists, convinced she had a piece of glitter in them. "You'll always be you."

"Okay, but consider, if you will, who am I?" He sat in the bag chair next to her. "Who are you? Who are any of us?"

"Jesus, Xan, the sun's not even up yet. Can't we wait to talk philosophy until morning?"

They would have to. Someone knocked on the door.

May tapped on Xan's BEAPER and opened the outside camera. Though it was dark and foggy outside, she could make out two figures. One was tall and thin, the other built like a small mountain. She would've liked to imagine it was Aimz and Listay, come to ask them to breakfast on the Merimip. But Aimz never used the front door. Front doors, she had said, were for strangers. Snipping the wiring around the plasma skylight and literally dropping in unannounced was for family.

Also, Listay probably wouldn't have a massive anti-matter cannon perched on her shoulder.

And they likely wouldn't have shouted, "This is the Scourge Authority!" Well, perhaps Aimz would. It seemed like the sort of thing she might do. Not around Listay, though.

"Zuut, zuut, zuut," Xan whispered, plastering himself against the wall. "What do we do?"

"I'll bluff. Tell them I don't know anything," she whispered, looking for a place to hide him.

"They're not gonna believe that. You look like the type who knows everything. And you're a bad liar."

"I'll consider that a compliment," she whispered harshly, helping him accordion himself into a cupboard and carefully shutting it.

"Just a minute," she shouted. "I'm naked!"

"Awful liar," came, muffled, from inside the cabinet.

"We don't care," one of them shouted. Of course they didn't.

"I do! Hold on!" May wished, for the thousandth time since leaving Earth, that she had been granted a flashy laser gun like most sci-fi protagonists. Even a real pocketknife that wasn't duller than the round end of a spoon would have been nice. There were no weapons to be found in the kitchen, either. The Largish Bronda Corporation proudly claimed their included range of sustenance-machines could prepare just about anything you stuck in them. They had no need for sharp, dangerous knives, unfortunately.

May composed herself and walked, or rather wobbled, across the waterbed to the door. There was absolutely definitely not a brain-eating-fungus-ridden-drag-queen-alien in her cupboard. It shouldn't have been that difficult to believe.

May never reached the door. Someone attacked her from above, pinning her against the waterbed. "Stay down," Aimz whispered in May's ear, for it was she that had pinned her.

An electrical buzz drowned out May's reply. A booming crackle shook the bus and everything went white.

"You're going to need a new plasmadoor." Aimz rolled off May and onto her back, grinning delightedly at the carnage as the bed undulated beneath her.

Xan extracted himself from the cupboard to survey his singed surroundings, a green, half-full bottle of shermel in his hand. "By Blitheon's holy inner elbow, what was that?" He handed the bottle to May, and she tucked it away in her trench coat.

"Plasma malfunction. Happens all the time...if you hook up the power source to a mini-rectifier and blow out the circuits, at least." Aimz flipped a thumb-sized contraption in the air, licked it fondly, then tucked it away in the neck of her suit.

"Are they alive?" May asked of the two armored figures gently smoking on the grass outside. Both were heavily armored and heavily weaponed.

"Probably." Aimz shrugged. "Hey zuxers, you alive?" she shouted out at them. They stirred in answer. "Yep, they're alive."

"And they want to arrest you for getting the scourge?"

"Oh, uh, not...not exactly," Xan said with an embarrassed laugh. "Quarantined, more like."

"Quarantined out of life," Aimz corrected. "Scourged Carmnians get disintegrated. No interrogation, no due process. It's just: 'Eyup, they gots the scourge alright,' a zap, a poof, and you're gone." She demonstrated the poof with jazz hands.

"How did you get so good at describing horrible things

in a fun, cheery way?" Xan asked.

"It's the jazz hands," she divulged with a wink. "Now shift it; we've got to get to the Merimip. Listay told me to collect you two and meet her there."

"Where's she?" Xan asked, clumsily pulling on boots and his mauve faux buffatalo coat.

"The cops took her in. Again. Terrible memory. Listay wants to take us to Fulogra on the mainland to see Yvonne. She's living on an apple farm with her lover and the apple-Earthling. You know, 'The dude that brought apples to the galaxy,'" she quoted the well-known slogan. "What's his name?" Aimz snapped her fingers as she tried to recall.

"August," May helped.

"That's the one! Know him?"

"I know of him."

"Small universe!" Aimz slapped her on the back. "It'll be a reunion! Except I'm with Yve's zombie ex (whom she murdered), Yve's with some random Rhean engineer and a scruffy old Earthling instead of Xan, and Xan's with...well, Xan you're not really going with anyone right now, are you?"

"I go where the crystals take me," he said with a shrug. "Which, as of late, has been nowhere. So no. No, I'm not. Yve never had trouble sharing, though."

"Listay wouldn't be into it," Aimz replied.

"She's a monogamist?"

"No, it's just that Yvonne killed her that one time."

A laser blast glimmered between them and toasted the opposite wall.

"Shift it!" Aimz shouted, pulling herself out of the open skylight, her legs kicking frantically below like a massive duck. Once she was free, she reached down to pull May up, then went back for Xan, but he was gone.

"Xan what are you doing?" Aimz shouted down through the skylight, May squishing in beside her to see for herself.

"Saving the fish!" he said, unhooking Big Mouth Billy Bass from the far wall, dodging laser blasts as he tucked it securely under his arm.

"Hold still!" shouted the tall agent.

"Sorry, can't!" Xan said. Spotting an opening, he dove between the agents, planning a sort of graceful somersault with a perfect landing right below the skylight.

Planning but not, to his chagrin, *succeeding.*

He rolled right into the waiting arms of the larger of the agents and was bound shoulder to wrist with a thick strip of constricting plasma before he realized his plan hadn't worked.

Growling her annoyance, Aimz swung back into the HoverBus, using the momentum to knock over the tall agent and using her sharp heel to crush the life support pack at the base of their helmet.

The agent ripped the helmet off, revealing puffs of pink hair which looked like pompoms framing her pale blue face. "We're trying to help!" she screamed.

"Help us die," Aimz said.

Dropping in after Aimz, May grabbed a heavy, ornamental lamp and flung it at the larger agent who caught it and, gently, set it down so as to not break it. While the agent was distracted, she pulled Xan to his feet.

"Wait, get Billy!" he protested, jerking at the plasma beam which kept him from reaching down for the fish.

"What's so important about the zuxing fish?" Aimz said from the door, wildly gesturing for them to hurry.

"It's ours, and we have to protect it! Look at the poor thing! Helpless. No legs, no thumbs, no moltsopial glands."

"I don't have moltsopial glands," May said.

Xan looked truly horrified at this revelation, but realized it was quite rude to judge another's biology. She couldn't help it. "And you get along just fine without them," he assured her shakily.

"Seem to be." May grabbed the plastic fish and shoved it into a pocket on her trench coat.

"Stop chatting and run!" Aimz pushed them forward as the scourge agents bounded over the waterbed toward them. "Get out, get out, get out!" Aimz shouted, but her words exploded.

Or rather, Largish Bronda's FlexiDimensional HoverBus

exploded over her words.

A wave of dry heat propelled the trio onward, nearly knocking them down as they fled with renewed speed.

"That was our home!" May shouted after Aimz who was nearly out of ear-shot ahead of her.

"Yeah, and now it's not. Things happen. All the time. Constantly, things are happening. That was one of the things."

May wanted to argue that point, but she wasn't an accomplished runner or an accomplished debater and, as such, she had neither the breath nor the wit to prove Aimz wrong. And besides, Aimz might have been socially wrong, but she wasn't technically wrong.

The distance between where Largish Bronda had been and where the Merimip currently was not the sort of distance someone in average health who goes to the gym thrice on a good week could comfortably run.

They were not the sort of people who got to a gym thrice on a good week.

And so, after a few minutes of running for their lives, they began briskly jogging for their lives, then urgently speed-walking for their lives, and finally, anxiously ambling for their lives.

TWELVE

HORNBALL

$$* \quad * \quad * \quad * \quad *$$

When at last they reached the Merimip, Aimz set about dismantling a section of the geodesic dome that created the greenhouse atop the Merimip as May worked at the plasma strip binding Xan's arms.

"Aimz, toss me the rectifier," May shouted between studying the mechanism for the plasma strip and the dark treeline where the pursuing agents might appear at any moment.

May barely caught the tiny chip between two fingers and awkwardly finagled it into the casing of the plasma strip generator.

"Isn't that going to-OW!" Xan yelped.

The plasma strip sizzled, sparked, and shorted out, the generator dropping away onto the soft, dewy grass.

"Sorry," May said. "But you're free now."

"Yeah, once I regain control of my muscles," he said, blinking one eye at a time as if his entire body was out of sync, then stooped to pick up the plasma strip generator. "Should we keep this?"

"Why?" May asked.

"Well, you know, in case Aimz or I...you know?"

"No. I don't know," May said firmly and flung the generator into the lake.

Xan knew she knew. He also knew that the heavily armored scourge agents likely survived the blast and were probably making their way toward them, and that was a bit more pressing than May willfully ignoring the danger she was in.

A rustling came from the tree line, and before Xan could decide if it was the agents or the wind, he scrambled up the Merimip's ladder. "Aimz?!" He knocked on the geodesic dome she had already broken into. She was working on the main ship hatch, now.

"Corral your puntls, mun, I got it," Aimz told him, then jumped through the hatch and into the ship. May and Xan followed her in, and she sealed the hatch behind them.

"Don't you have a key?!" Xan asked her.

She pulled the key out of her pocket. "Yeah, why?"

"Nevermind," he said. "We need to get out of here."

"Right. No sense waiting around for Listay, is there?" Aimz said, dusting her hands as if dusting off the entire relationship. She paused, looked at her palms, her face clouding with a sudden emotion which she just as suddenly whisked away as she patted May on the back. "Whatcha think, May? Can you larvea-sit two zuxed Carmnians in a boat? Not worried we'll cannibalize you, right?" Aimz's smile was unnervingly sharp.

Discreetly, May's fingers found the bottle of shermel in her coat. "I *wasn't*."

"That was one case!" Xan defended. "And she'd been living in the forest for decades before she emerged to eat people."

"Yeah, after she hunted down every creature in the forest. I heard she learned to weaponize stomach fluids and would spit acid at her victims to pre-digest them," Aimz said, enthusiastically.

"Eugh." Xan stuck his tongue out as if he couldn't bear to have it in his mouth anymore. "That's gruesome. Aimz, promise me we won't go feral."

"Oh don't be so posh. I hear gruflesnog tastes just like zipnite, and they're much easier to catch."

"I don't care what it tastes like—"

Knock, knock.

It was not a "Hello" knock.

It was not a "Monday" knock, either.

These knocks sounded more like they meant "Danger" or perhaps "Warning" or even, with a bit of imagination, "You're about to die, assholes."

"That was Listay?" Xan proposed.

"She lives here; why would she knock?" May whispered.

"Oh, she knocks," Aimz said between them. "She knocks four times because she's a snack." She laughed quietly at her own joke.

Knock, knock.

"Four knocks total! Gotta be Listay," Aimz said, then scaled the ladder to the hatch.

"That was two sets of two knocks!" Xan shouted after her, but she was already opening the hatch, already peering out, already realizing that it was definitely not Listay.

"Listay will catch up." Aimz said, sealing the hatch and scrambling to the cockpit.

"How? We're stealing her vehicle," May pointed out, scanning the cockpit and trying to figure out how it worked by watching Aimz pilot it.

May was of the opinion that there was nothing she couldn't pilot. She was wrong, and she knew she was wrong, but being of that opinion helped her feel a bit more stable in trying situations like this, and that's what mattered. She had always found it helpful to decide she was good at whatever it was she had to do.

The Merimip vibrated gleefully below them, lifting itself out of the water and hovering on the surface of the lake before jetting off through the Snoodark Channel toward mainland Rhea.

"She'll catch up!" Aimz repeated as if her insistence alone would make it true, then she grabbed Xan (who had been cowering helpfully behind her) by the wrist, yanked his BEAPER into view, and sent a message to Listay. Her own BEAPER had ceased working seasons ago, but she was almost always near either Listay or Xan, so she hadn't bothered trying to replace it.

Xan was getting tired of everyone using his BEAPER without asking, but he liked May too much to tell her, and he was too scared of Aimz to tell *her*.

"Alright," Aimz said, patting Xan's hand away when she was done. "Let's get to Fulogra. Yve's expecting us!"

"And she can fix us, right?" said Xan. "Tell me she found a cure."

"Her curves are the cure, mun," Aimz said with a wink.

"Hornball!" May said, snapping her fingers at Aimz. "Does she have a cure or not?"

Xan chuckled, repeating the Earthling insult under his breath so he wouldn't forget it. "Hornball."

"Of course not; there isn't a cure. If we get scourge-noodled on the way over, you'll have to fight us off." Aimz dug through the junk drawer (or, according to the label Listay had slapped on it, "The Aimz Drawer") and handed May a zapper. "Vooop!" she made a powering-up sound as she twisted the dial at the top from Pleasant Tingle to Zap+.

Finally, May had a gun at her disposal, but now she didn't want it. "Won't that hurt?"

"Oh yeah, sure. But the key is..." Aimz then produced a sharp metal bit from her pocket. It looked an awful lot like the sharp metal bit she'd lost on New Tuhnt, but it wasn't quite as rusted, which was a shame. "Once we're down, you need to stake us. Zapper wounds heal fast. Sharp bit of metal through the clacker? No chance."

"You want me to kill you?" she asked Xan directly, and he really wished she hadn't.

Rather than answer, he moved his mouth like he was attempting to start several different sentences, then silently begged Aimz to take over, held up a finger in a 'give me a moment' gesture, and went to the bedroom at the back of the ship, closing the door cryptically behind himself.

Aimz squinted after him for a moment. "Uh, yeah. If we get too rowdy, kill us. Never tried dying before, and it didn't work out too bad for Listay."

"If you insist." May took the zapper and the metal bit, stuffing them in her already over-full pockets, her coat sagging around her with the weight of everything in it.

"Really?" A fleeting glimpse of fear washed over Aimz's face.

"No! You know that's not going to happen. But I am confiscating these. If we are to duel, it will be hand-to-hand, like men, with honor," she said, attempting to lighten her own mood.

"Are all Earthlings as weird as you?" Aimz laughed, relieved that May wasn't serious about killing her because she wasn't serious about dying.

"Are all Tuhntians as weird as you?" May retorted, walking to the back of the Merimip. She knocked on the bedroom door, just once. She didn't understand the secret knock code everyone else seemed to know, and one knock seemed safest. "Are you decent?" she shouted through the thick metal door.

"Fair-to-middling," is what she heard, muffled, from the other side, and so she opened it.

THIRTEEN

POLYBLOTTER

* * * * *

May found Xan, arms and legs tied spread-eagle to the bed in a way which shouldn't have been possible on his own, reading a trashy romance holobook on his BEAPER, scrolling the holographic screen with his nose.

The average Earthling lives eighty, maybe ninety years, and because of this, they tend to get decent at a handful of skills with the intent of earning a living. And I promise this relates back, just hold on.

Tuhntians live seven-hundred years or more and, as such, get really, unutterably good at a handful of skills with the intent of earning a living. This meant that Xan was astoundingly good at tying himself up. He had centuries of practice. He might struggle to find his own hometown on a map, but by O'Zeno, he could tie himself to a bed.

"Comfortable?" May asked, sitting next to him.

"Not at all. But well contained! There is absolutely no way for me to get out of this bed without someone untying me and, since Aimz won't and you certainly—" May began untying the ropes. "W-wait, no, that was really hard to do on my own," he protested.

"It's a long trip," she said, struggling to undo his masterful knots.

"But what if I get scourged?"

"That's what the shermel is for." She nodded toward the green bottle which she'd set on the recessed Magno-E-Tic bookcase in the wall, the gentle magnetic force keeping it, and several neatly labeled holobooks, from jostling with the movement of the Merimip.

"Alright, but consider: how are you going to get me to drink it if I'm scourged? And what if Aimz goes off, too? There's not enough for both of us. I could try to eat you!"

"Wouldn't be the weirdest thing you've eaten." She went back to untying the shockingly snug knot around his wrist.

"I think it would be..."

"You eat bugs!"

"They're cheese flavored and come in a bag! That's not that weird! You're the only person I've ever met who's been weirded out by that."

"In all the time I've known you," she paused to pull at a knot with her teeth, speaking around it as she yanked, "you've never eaten me."

"I've also never been scourged."

"You have, and you ate not-cigarette mechanisms off the ground because you were worried about my health. You're not going to eat me." She finally pulled free the cording, and his arm dropped to the bed.

"Thanks," he said, rotating his freed wrist as May untied the rest of him. "Last time I was tied up like that, I couldn't feel my toes for two whole rotations! But, I was getting paid by the beoop, so I didn't mind it. And the Udonian who-oh Blitheon, that feels better-the Udonian who hired me...Chashee I think her name was? Or Shashtee? Shancy? Zuut, I thought I'd remember that one. Told her I would remember it, too, but, then again, I tell a lot of people a lot of things—"

May finished untying him as he continued monologuing about Chashee or Shashtee or Shancy. She didn't mind hearing about his exploits as a sex worker for The Agency, since he knew to spare her the graphic details. It was comforting, especially now, just to hear him chatter on as if everything was completely normal.

While he talked, she crawled onto the bed and began cleaning out her many pockets, making sure she was only carrying what would be useful to her. She spread each item out onto the bed, separating the bits of unidentifiable trash and lint from useful items.

Among the useful items were the lengths of rope she had just released Xan from, a small green dashpin, the metal bit Aimz had given her, and the zapper which she had turned down to a more reasonable setting: 'zippy.'

Among the not-useful: a sticky wrapper from a candy she didn't remember eating, a length of extremely thin string which pulled apart at the slightest tug, a single silk glove, and...May paused and held the last item she had found up to the light to inspect it. Useful or not? Iffy.

"Hey, did you...were you listening?" Xan asked, leaning into her line of sight.

"Yeah," she lied absently, staring at the thing clutched between her fingers. It was the *Audacity*'s anchor button, and it still glowed faintly green. It was still online. Still connected to the ship's teledisc a few thousand lightyears away. She kept it steady between the useful and not-useful piles, watching it as if the light might flicker off if she blinked.

Slowly, Xan took it from her and placed it in the useful pile.

"No point giving up, is there?" he asked.

May shrugged. "Not giving up. Just...letting go, maybe. Sorry, why did Chashee go into debt over a silver scale replica of an ancient Hooflatoo again? I missed that part."

"Oh, uh...she was a natural history museum fetishist."

"Ah, that checks out." May said, clipping the anchor button onto her coat and stashing the useful items and the shermel bottle back in her pocket. She put the trash into one of the drawers where she hoped it might disappear.

Putting trash in drawers with the hope that it will disappear is not an uncommon practice.

It is uncommon, however, for that trash to actually disappear. Unless you're dealing with a Flexi-Dimensional drawer built by the Largish Bronda Corporation. It's wise not to put anything terribly important in Flexi-Dimensional storage.

May leaned back and tried to get comfortable, but it was not to be. A scratching echoed from the roof, followed by clunks and cracks neither May nor Xan could identify as they both tilted an ear up to the ceiling. The lights in the cabin flickered a few times, then failed, casting the room into nearly complete darkness, the only lights were the glowing emergency strips sewn into the carpet and the subtle luminescence of the fungus in Xan's eyes.

"What happ—" May began, but the ship suddenly stopped, flinging May and Xan off the bed and into the wall with a painful thunk.

May cursed as she got to her feet and stumbled out of the dark bedroom into the dark hallway. She found the escape ladder with her face and cursed again as she climbed it, opened the hatch, and peered out into the soupy night. Rhea's moons lit the top of the ship well enough for May to pick out Aimz crouched atop the shiny black boat, peering over the edge.

"Zuxing polyblotter. Scram!" Aimz said, grabbing onto the handlebars which ran like a spine down the length of the Merimip's slippery black back. Attached to the side of the boat and holding onto an access door was something which looked to May like a hunched, furry, elderly gentleman. It chattered unhappily at her.

Aimz growled back.

Crawling onto the ship's roof, May peered around Aimz to get a better look at it. The creature's fur was clumped and matted with ocean gunk. It was balding in patches, revealing scaly gray skin which glistened nastily in the light of Rhea's three yellowish moons.

"Ugh, what is it?" May asked.

What it was, as Aimz had correctly surmised, was a polyblotter. One of a few species who had had the gall to leave the ocean, grow fur, arms, legs, and lungs, then decided to go back to the ocean like a student returning to live in their parent's basement after a miserable two years of business school.

Polyblotters are protected under Rhean law because they are the only known aquatic mammal that eats plastic, and this is usually a good thing. Usually. However, recent environmental campaigns had greatly reduced the amount of plastic produced on mainland Rhea and, as such, starving polyblotters had become a bit of a problem for vessels that rely on plastic parts. The Largish Bronda Corporation relied heavily on plastic parts.

The Merimip's engine casing was made of polyoxybenzylmethylenglycolanhydride, or, simply put, Bakelite plastic. A crunchy treat to a polyblotter.

Aimz did not tell May any of this, though. Instead, she said, "Snack," licked her lips, then launched herself at the creature which scampered over the dome of the greenhouse, dropping bits of plastic into the ocean as it went.

Failing to find purchase on the slippery boat, Aimz spun into a whirl of arms and legs. Her fingernails finally caught the wooden frame of the greenhouse and she got her feet underneath herself. Then, with gravity-defying ferocity, she scaled the greenhouse after the polyblotter.

"Aimz, let it go. We need to fix the engine," May said, but before she could get to the exposed engine on the top of the boat, something tapped her leg. She twisted around to find Xan eagerly looking up at her.

"You two alright?" he asked. "It's kinda dark down there..."

"Screeee!" went the creature. Aimz had it by the neck.

"Aimz, no! Xan, hand me something to throw," she gestured wildly at him to give her something and, moments later, he plunked a decorative pillow into her arms. "Something heavy?!" she clarified.

"You don't want to hurt it!" Xan said.

Though May wasn't sure this was true, she flung the pillow at Aimz, knocking the polyblotter out of her hands just as she was preparing to snap its neck. The creature scampered into the churning water below and disappeared.

"Go inside," May demanded of Aimz, pulling herself out into the drizzling night and toward the sputtering motor.

"I told you to scram!" Aimz leapt for the top of the greenhouse and barreled into May who had leaned over the side of the boat to take a look at the damage. May yelped in surprise. Her arm caught on a ladder rung, holding her onto the boat, as Aimz dangled from her waist like an angry sentient statement belt.

"What the hell, Aimz? I'm trying to fix it!"

"What'd she do?!" May heard Xan shout from the hatch, though she had slid too far down the side of the boat to see him.

"She's trying to kill me, get out here!"

"What?! Blitheon, Aimz, don't do that! Bad Aimz!" he said as he crawled out onto the top of the boat shakily.

"Get. Off. My. Ship!" Aimz said, trying her best to climb up May who had to use her free hand to hold her pants up.

"Take my hand." At last, Xan had appeared over the side of the Merimip, reaching down to help May up, but as he reached down Aimz reached up and he, clearly, had not attached himself in any way to the ship.

Aimz ripped Xan off the roof, and he ripped her away from May, plunging them both into the churning black ocean.

"Damnit." May clung to the side of the boat still, watching the spot where they had disappeared. She rearranged herself to make sure her elbow wasn't broken and leaned a little closer to the water. "Xan? Aimz?" she shouted into the depths.

Then the water's surface boiled, thrashing with flashes of orange and pink as Xan and Aimz battled to keep their heads above water, a difficult task for a Tuhntian. From her coat pocket, May extracted a length of rope that Xan had used to tie himself up with. Not trusting herself to tie a strong enough knot, she looped it around the lowest rung of the ladder and let it drop. It was just long enough to reach the water line.

"Xan, grab the rope!" she shouted. But briefly turning

his attention away from holding his own against Aimz to find the rope had proven to be a mistake. Aimz elbowed him in the face and kicked him underwater, making for the rope herself.

"Zux-off," Aimz told May wetly before coughing up a lungful of ocean water.

May climbed further down the side of the ship but pulled the rope up so Aimz couldn't get a hold on it. "Aimz, it's me. Earthmun. Don't you recognize me?" May said "You like to feed me alien drugs and get me into trouble."

Squinting up at her, Aimz seemed to be working through something and May forced herself not to distract Aimz by looking at Xan who was finally above water and paddling toward Aimz.

He launched at her and grabbed a fistful of pink hair at the top of her head.

"Get her mouth open!" May said. There wouldn't be enough alcohol for both of them, but Xan was decidedly easier to handle when he was scourged and, should *he* try to attack her next, Aimz was decidedly the better fighter.

Aimz tried to twist around, but he seized her cheeks and squeezed, forcing her mouth open. Uncorking the bottle with her teeth, May poured the drink down Aimz's throat, reminded of a forgotten memory of being ten and helping her father pill the old family cat.

Fortunately, Aimz enjoyed alcohol and didn't try to spit it out or foam at the mouth like the cat had. Xan let her face go but held onto her shoulders while she processed what had just happened. "Why are we in the water?" she asked, finally.

"Some parties just end up in the middle of the ocean, Aimz." Xan said, letting her go.

"Zuxing trok. Is he scourged?" Aimz asked as she grabbed the rope from May and began to pull herself up the side of the boat.

"No, you were." May showed her the empty green bottle.

Aimz smacked her lips, she could still taste the shermel. "First thing we do when we hit land is get some better alcohol. Did I try to kill you?" Aimz asked through a grunt as she pulled Xan out of the water by his collar, the faux buffatalo coat mopping up the side of the Merimip.

"Maybe. You thought I was something else, though. I don't think you were trying to kill me, specifically, at least."

Aimz twisted her mouth to the side as she thought, looking May over. "You need to tie me up," she said. "I don't want to—" she paused. "You need to tie me up."

"You're a feral one, Mazelmez," Xan said, wringing out his coat. "Zuut. This is Zilla's coat. Hope the saltwater doesn't ruin it..."

"Xan, you had that before you got the trunks. That's yours," May said. "You alright?"

"Best guess?" said Xan. "That android's got some messed up social protocols mixed into the software."

"Best guess at what? What android?" May looked around as if an android might suddenly appear on the bow of the Merimip.

"Sonan," said Xan as if it were obvious.

"Sonan's gone, Xan. Did you mean to say that in the last book?"

He opened his mouth, looked around at the empty expanse of dark choppy waters, looked at a dripping Aimz and a very confused May, then, at last, he answered. "Uhhh, yeah, I suppose I did."

"Yep, he's scourged now. The hullabaloo must've triggered it. Figures he'd get time-zuxed first." Aimz said. "The cerebral ones always do. His primal instincts are buried waaayy deep down. You're a zuxing nerd, Xan," Aimz told him.

"I know," he said, confused as to why she had to clarify that.

May looked miserable.

"Hey, un-pin it, Earthmun," Aimz patted May on the back. "Listen, Yve and I were working on a project back at university, right?" Aimz physically spun May around so she would stop watching Xan. "And the idea was, we were going to cure the scourge."

"Did you?"

"No. Well, obviously no. But we were young! This was

well before she was destroying planets and I was…" Aimz squinted, thinking. "In a stable relationship."

A tapping.

May and Aimz turned their attention back to Xan who was spread out flat on the roof, rapping rhythmically on the boat, listening with baited interest to the metal. He rapped again, listened again.

"Whatcha doing, buddy?" May asked, hoping she wouldn't regret it.

"Oh. You two were ignoring me, so I made friends with the boat. Bit of a language barrier, still working it out. Getting close, though! It's against the idea of self-cleaning food replicators having personalities, which I think is a bit backward minded, but I'm trying to see the issue from its angle." He held up a finger, listened, and laughed. "No, I've never single handedly reinstated a defunct political regime. Why, have you?"

Rather than attempt to explain to him that the boat was, in fact, insentient, May started to climb down to the open engine panel. "Get him inside. I'm going to take a look at the damage," she told Aimz. "And Xan?" May said before she disappeared over the side of the boat. He looked up at her. "Tie up your sister for me?"

He smiled broadly, delighted to be of service. "Gladly!"

May climbed down the ladder and studied the open panel, running a finger down a length of chipped, brown, plastic casing. Inside, some metal knob stuck out at an odd angle and jerked with pent-up energy.

From her pocket, she pulled out the metal bit and gently lifted the knob away from the casing. It began to work; the knob spun, and the main lights flickered back on, but the sharp metal edge of the improvised tool snagged and was flung out of May's hand, landing with apologetic 'bloop' in the Rhean Sea.

The knob was stuck again, and apart from the zapper (which May would only use as a last resort), all she had left was the anchor button. It was plastic. It was about the size of the chunk the polyblotter had eaten. It would have to do.

She pulled the button from her pocket, then wiggled the

piece in between the knob and the casing. It fit perfectly. The knob spun, the boat heaved forward, and May clambered for the ladder.

"Guess it was useful after all," she muttered and slammed the panel shut with her foot.

May dropped back into the boat to find Aimz tied to metal pole in the middle of the living room. A pole which May had not noticed before. She wasn't sure there was a good structural reason for it to be there, and she wasn't sure she wanted to know why it was there, so she didn't ask.

"She's all ready for you!" Xan said proudly. "What are you going to do with her?"

"Yeah, what are you going to do with me, Earthmun?" Aimz goaded.

May shook her head at Aimz. "Ugh, don't encourage him." She slipped into the cockpit and got the ship moving again. "Nothing, Xan. You did good."

"When do you think Milly will be back?" he asked her.

"Hopefully never," May said, then patted the seat next to her to get him to sit down. "Hey...you remember me, right?" she asked, wincingly, as he sat down.

"Of course! May, we've known each other for thousands of years, of course I remember you. We've raced rocket ships, infiltrated the Cosmos, summoned the Seam together..."

"Whoa, thousands of years?" May asked with a laugh. "We haven't done half of that stuff. Where are you getting this?"

"He's time-zuxed, I told you!" Aimz said from her pole.

May turned around. "You mean to tell me he can remember the future?"

"Yeah," Aimz said, as if this were obvious.

"That's not possible..." May was speaking more to herself than anyone else in the boat now. "Why did he ask if Milly would be back?" she asked Aimz.

"She will be," Xan told May. "Where are we going?"

"Look, May," Aimz said. "I know I exude an air of all-knowing confidence but I don't actually know everything. Time-zuxed Carmnians only have about a 20% accuracy rating when it comes to the future and half the time when you ask them about the future they start going on about the past. That's why it's called being time-zuxed. They're zuxed in—"

"Time. I get it," May said, cutting her off. "Twenty percent, huh?" she asked Xan.

"Huh," he agreed with her.

"So there's a twenty percent chance we survive all this?"

"No one survives anything," Xan clarified. "Even the so-called gods die."

That was not what May had wanted to hear from him. She tapped the BEAPER on his wrist and navigated to a holobook. "Just read your trashy romance story," she told him.

FOURTEEN

THE APPLE MAN

* * * * *

On mainland Rhea, the suns shone warmly, the breeze smelled of salt and slowly rotting wood planks, and it was difficult to imagine that just a few beoops by hoverboat away, the freezing island of NotTuhnt languished in the middle of a dreary sea.

Fulgora was an ancient-style town, a trend born after many hundreds of years of intense technological development finally made people realize that all they really wanted this new technology to do was to pretend it didn't exist. Rather than flashy, sleek hovercraft, the citizens drove run-down, rusted hovercraft. Rather than sparkling electro-roads, the pathways were paved with old fashioned, solar-soak dust which powered the holo-flame lamps the townsfolk used in place of the more modern atmospheric glow-spheres.

As soon as the ship docked, May climbed out, desperate to get on solid land, but the moment her feet touched the dock, someone picked her up and spun her around in a smothering hug that smelled of firewood and apples.

"August!" she said as soon as she realized that she

wasn't being kidnapped by an alien lumberjack. He set her down and smiled at her, one eye glistening with joy, the other glistening because it was made of metal.

"New eye?" she asked.

"Eyep. Yve felt bad about, you know, the Chaos thing, so she set me up with a new eye, new hand." He showed her the surprisingly natural hand which had replaced the old, stiff robotic hand Ix had installed on him. "New teeth!" He smiled and tapped a canine with his nail. "Looks like there's only one and a half humans out here now!" He laughed and squeezed her shoulder warmly. "It's good to see you, kid. Don't be a stranger, eh?"

"Oh, who's this strapping hunk of cyborg?" Xan asked, Big Mouth Billy Bass cradled in one arm as he sauntered up to August who side-eyed May.

"Xan, you remember August, right?"

"I'd like to," he said in a way which was ridiculously flirty and signified that he, in fact, still did not remember him at all. "Want to make out?"

"No, Xan," May said.

"Really?" August asked Xan, his eyes flicking momentarily to May as if asking her permission. He had always considered himself straight. Still did, actually, reasoning that he wasn't interested in Earthling men. Aliens, though, he'd come to realize, weren't men *or* women and as such, all were fair game.

Xan nodded eagerly.

"Oh well, I mean. I'm straight but, uh, sure!" August said with a shrug, and Xan pulled August into a long-lost-lovers style kiss. August was panting when he broke free of it.

"Whoa," he said.

"Yeah, I'm a professional." Xan winked.

"And I'm Aimz, professional adventure biologist. I don't want to kiss you now, but I might do later if you're up for it." Aimz held up a hand which August high-fived in a daze.

"How'd you get out of the ropes?" May asked her.

Aimz shrugged. "Xan always leaves an easy-out! The ropes were to make you feel better. Worked, didn't it?"

May grunted a begrudging affirmative.

"Hey, Appleman, got any alcohol?" Aimz asked August.

"Hmm?"

"He's scourged." Aimz tossed her head in Xan's direction. "Alcohol staves it off a bit."

"Right, that explains it." August laughed, embarrassed. He meant that, somehow, Xan being scourged explained why he, August, was suddenly attracted to him. Scourge has no such effect, of course, but August's logic was about as developed as that of the average goldfish.

He reached for a metal flask on his belt and handed it to Xan. "Hard cider. Made with my own two hands."

"I bet that's not all those hands can do," Xan said, then chugged the flask, then looked as if he'd really wished he hadn't said that. He slowly handed the flask back to August and wiped his mouth with the back of his hand. "Hello, August."

"Oh, we're back to introductions now?" August laughed, drained the last few drops from the flask, then secured it back on his belt. "Come on, let's get to the orchard. Yvonne and Ix have been in the lab since Listay BEAP'd us. They'll have a fit when we tell them alcohol's this mysterious cure! Well, Yvonne will. Can't imagine anything would give Ix a fit."

The vehicle August escorted them to could've been an old blue pickup truck had it not looked distinctly like a floating can opener with the brand name ThingHauler shimmering on its flank in holographic black. Aimz hopped into the front of the cab and Xan and May squeezed into the back.

"It's not a cure," Aimz said. "Just staves it off in the early stages. Still have a mushroom eating my brain."

"You don't sound too bothered," August noted.

Aimz shrugged. "Happens to all Carmnians eventually, and it's the worst thing that could possibly happen to me, so now that it has happened, I don't have to worry about when it will! The answer is now; it's happening now. That lets off a great deal of anxiety, actually. Also, I get to see Yvonne." She twisted around to Xan. "Yvonne!" She bounced in her seat.

Xan nodded. "Is Yvonne...really back to normal?" he asked August who was fiddling with the face scanner which would start the ThingHauler. It flashed a blue light over his features and dinged in recognition. The vehicle booted up with the whine of old machinery and set off down the thin, unpaved, one-way road which led out of the small fishing town.

"You know," he glanced back at Xan via the rear-viewscreen, "without knowing what's normal for Yvonne, it's hard to say. But she hasn't blown up a planet lately, so I think she's doing better." He touched a series of commands on the ThingHauler's control panel, and something which sounded like Motown played by a reggae band with synthesizers filled the cab.

May leaned her head on the window—an actual old-fashioned window, she noted, not a viewscreen—and watched the horizon, underscored by a field of red dust and purple rock formations which grew scraggly gray bushes like a teenager trying to grow a beard.

Suddenly, Xan's head was on her shoulder. "Alright, starshine?"

"Hmm?" She was in a trance, thinking about nothing as everything she wanted to think about swirled in a salty pool forming beneath her eyes. She wiped it away with her sleeve.

"What did I do this time?" He was soaking in sea water and had vague memories of befriending a boat with some pretty radical political ideas. Clearly, he thought, something interesting had happened on the trip over, but he didn't remember it well.

"Don't worry about it. You didn't try to eat me. The scourge makes you horny as hell, though, what's up with that?"

He shrugged, then twisted around until his head was on her lap and his legs were pretzeled over the rest of the back seat. "Lower inhibitions, I guess." He peered up at her coat curiously. "Where's the anchor button?"

She sighed and looked out the window again. "I used it to fix the boat."

"Oh." He dug around in the innermost pocket of his

coat and pulled out his own anchor button which glowed faintly green. "Want mine? It's still connected." He eyed the glowing green light with his own glowing green eyes, and May found the comparison a touch uncanny, so she grabbed the button, rolled the window down, and threw it out into the dust.

That was it. Her connection with the *Audacity* was officially severed. Even if she did happen to find it, she wouldn't be able to get in without breaking in. She understood what Aimz had said, now. The worst had happened, and knowing that somehow did ease her anxiety about it.

"I don't want to think about the *Audacity* anymore. It's lost. You're not."

"Uh...huh," he said at last. "You know, Yve is really a terrific person when she's not being possessed by an ancient evil. And August knows all about Earth! You two must have loads to talk about."

"You're trying to pawn me off," she said.

"No! Not at all. Of course not, starshine. It-it's just... eugh," he said. "It's only that...well...you see..." He began trying to express himself with vague hand gestures instead.

"What?" Her voice was sharper than usual.

"I'm just worried that you'll be lonely, that's all."

"Shh." She petted his wet hair and attempted to form it into its classic pompadour, but it had grown far too long. "I won't have time to feel lonely because I'll be busy helping you keep track of your various sexual partners, you massive precious butler."

A popular Tuhntian name happens to translate, in English, to "Precious Butler." However, re-translated from English to Tuhntian "precious butler" is an extremely rude euphemism for a prostitute. This quirk of the universe was discovered in book two for reasons which shall, forthwith, have no further bearing on the story.

It did, however, get Xan to smile. "That's a terrible thing to say about your best friend."

"It's just the truth," she said.

He chuckled and sat up clumsily in the tiny back seat.

"Yeah, no, you're right." He took her hand. "Promise me you won't be lonely?"

"You aren't going anywhere."

"Right, fair, okay, but just in case: promise me!" he insisted.

"Ugh, fine. I'll hang out with August."

"We're hanging out?" August shouted back from the front seat. Bits of conversation had made their way up to him, but until now it hadn't been any of his business.

"Yeah," May said.

"Sweet. It'll be nice to hang out with someone who knows who Bastian Schweinsteiger is."

May clenched her teeth and gave Xan a worried look. "Actor?"

August sighed. "Soccer," he said.

"I thought you called it football in Germany," May said.

"That's what I said, soccer."

"Translation chips," Xan reminded them both before this little skit went on any longer. It was curious, but somehow May felt she better understood the aliens she had met than most Earthlings. She put her head on Xan's shoulder. "I'm going to have to learn about sports," she mumbled miserably.

FIFTEEN

SUPERSONIC FUNGICIDE

* * * * *

The dusty landscape soon relented to scrub brush, then trees so dry and gnarled they looked like the feet of a 90-year-old ballerina, then trees that grew luscious yellow-orange manes and quivered erotically in the draft the ThingHauler made as it skirted by.

August still wasn't used to decelerating from the equivalent of nine hundred miles-per-hour, and the inertia flung everyone to the floor, waking May from a much-needed nap.

"Sorry 'bout that folks. Here we are!" August said, then exited the ThingHauler.

May carefully maneuvered out, shaking the pins-and-needles feeling from her legs which had been squished under her in the tiny backseat.

A glittering lake yawned for miles to their left; in front of them, a cabin replete with simulated rustic furnishings; to the right, a sleek white plastic-shelled machine with colorful winking lights and a tongue-like conveyor belt. It looked like the sets from the "Beverly Hillbillies" and "Forbidden Planet" had collided in a horrible back-lot accident.

Over-sized, winding trees cradled the house, but they were certainly not apple trees. All that grew from their twisting branches was downy green fluff and the occasional spiky yellow thing, like a pinecone, a pineapple, and a porcupine had met at a pine convention and hit it off.

May squinted at them, confused.

"Not like any apples you've ever seen, eh?" August said to her with an unwelcome elbow nudge.

"Eh, I've seen a lot of strange apples."

It was August's turn to be confused. "Those aren't the apples. I was kidding."

"I know. I was too."

"Oh. Right." He rubbed the back of his neck. "Those are just canopy trees; the apples are underneath them. Sun's too bright for the apples out here. Tried growing them in a cavern underground with fake sunlight, but the apples got depressed."

May understood. The Pontoosa Adventure Hole and her experiences Downtown had given her a healthy distrust of things which resided below ground. But there were also many things she didn't trust which were above ground. One of those things was now descending the house's wooden steps, wrapped in a pale-yellow patterned dress, smiling.

May tried to see her as anything but the goddess of Chaos who had tried to destroy Earth—and the dress helped a bit, but not much. The sight of Yvonne, even rid of the unmentionable look in her eyes, made May's back stiffen.

"Yve-onny!" Aimz squealed when she saw her and launched herself into the towering Rhean, nuzzling her chest affectionately.

Yvonne caught her with a startled huff. She'd gotten so used to striking fear into the hearts of all who approached her that this welcome came as a surprise. This was always how Aimz welcomed her, though. Or it had been, anyway. Before the war. Before the *Peacemaker*. But now the war was over and they were in an apple orchard and everything was alright.

Except, it wasn't alright. She was tempted to hold onto Aimz, pushing her face into her warm pink braid, but instead she pulled away.

"Scourge?" she whispered.

"Ah, you know. These things happen," Aimz said. "Fine right now, though! Alcohol helps."

"But it doesn't fix it," Yvonne said quietly.

"Don't be dramatic, Yve. We're fine. Better! Now that the proverbial timer has run out, yeah? Can't get any worse from here," Aimz said with a bright smile.

Yvonne shook her head. "In the name of Rheanoodal the Third, you're the only Carmnian who's ever taken scourge with a smile. It's good to see you, mun."

Xan had been lurking behind the ThingHauler. Not hiding, definitely. Definitely not cowering. But May was there too, and she *was* hiding a bit.

"Think she's safe?" May asked, peering through the ThingHauler windows at Aimz and Yvonne.

"Sure! Yeah! Of course. She's just Yve now. No Chaos. Not more than the regular dosage, at least. I mean, she did ditch me when the war started, broke my heart, called me all sorts of names. That did still happen."

"And then she beat you up, crashed a starship, and tried to end the universe."

He shook his head. "That wasn't her. Not even a little bit was that her. She's more emotionally damaging, less physically damage-wait no, now that you mention it she did like to run impromptu experiments back at university."

May nodded for him to elaborate.

"Oh, well, you know. She was a biologist and she believed in hands-on learning and, well, I was the only willing subject!"

"What did she do to you?"

"Nothing drastic. Just the occasional vivisection."

"Vivisection?!" May hissed.

"It was college; we were young!" He said it as if it had been a few keggers and one night stands rather than an invasive surgical procedure.

"And that was consensual?"

"Well sure! She's not a monster. She's sweet, actually. Just likes to chop things up sometimes to figure out how they work. That's science!"

May looked back through the ThingHauler's window at Aimz and Yvonne chatting.

"Well, we're going to have to face her eventually," May said and took Xan's hand as they rounded the ThingHauler and followed the party inside the house.

The house was moodily lit with candles that looked suspiciously like real wax. May removed her trench coat, hanging it on a deceptively rustic coat hanger and stopped at the nearest arrangement of candles to study them. The wax melted, dripped, then disappeared. Gently, she touched the side of a long candlestick, and her finger went straight through it. They were holographic candles, the image emanating from their holders. She smiled at the coziness of it; it reminded her of Earth and, perhaps for the first time since her abduction, she found she missed it.

Yvonne, August, and Aimz crashed into soft leather couches which encircled a faux fire pit in the middle of a large, wooden paneled room lit by candles and holowindows.

But May and Xan hesitated to cozy up anywhere near Yvonne.

"Go on, have a seat," August said, patting the leather cushion beside him.

Cautiously, carefully, like he was transferring a wedding cake from one cake stand to another, Xan slid down the arm of the couch and into the seat, eyeing Yvonne across the fire pit. May sat on the arm of the couch, determined not to get comfortable.

Yvonne cringed. "I'm sorry about the whole...Chaos thing. I didn't have any control over her, though. You know that, right?"

"Of course! All in the history books," Xan said, rather unconvincingly.

"Would you all please join me in the laboratory?" Ix suddenly made herself known. She had been watching them for a while from the shadows. She stood at the top of a staircase, her pale purple curls pulled back into a tight bun. "I have compiled a series of tests to run on the affected Carmnians," Ix said in a way that might have been called robotic, but robots were a great deal more expressive. "May and August, please stay here. You will not be necessary," she added, sensing that they were both already preparing to stand.

Xan groaned pitifully at May, and she patted his head.

"It'll be alright. August and I are just going to run off and have outstandingly wacky adventures while you're gone, I promise."

"You better," Xan said with a quiet smile and set Big Mouth Billy Bass down on the couch for May to keep an eye on. He trailed behind the caravan disappearing into the underground lab behind Ix.

Once they were out of earshot, August scooted a bit closer to May, pulled something which looked like a bag of marshmallows from the sofa, and offered her the open bag.

"Marshmallow?" he asked, grabbing one for himself and impaling it on a sticky metal skewer before thrusting the white cube into the fake fire.

May had a lot of questions. A) Where did he get marshmallows? B) Why were they in the couch? C) What the hell was Ix going to do to Xan down in the lab? and D) How would a holographic fire toast them?

Rather than try to decide which to ask first, she fished a marshmallow from the open package and skewered it, holding it in the flame which looked an awful lot like the Yule Log Christmas show. It could warm hearts, but not marshmallows.

After several minutes of sitting in silence, watching the marshmallows twist slowly in the cold flame, May finally said something. "Is this supposed to be doing something?"

August laughed, reined in his marshmallow, and ate it raw off the skewer. "No, I just wanted to see how long it would take you to ask. Three entire bloops!" He popped another marshmallow in his mouth and sighed thoughtfully as he chewed. "You know, I had to have

Yvonne re-invent these for me. There's nothing like a marshmallow out here! Nothing like an apple, either, which is why it's a good business to be in! What do you miss most? From Earth?"

May squinted at him. He was trying to befriend her with invasive questions. She knew this tactic. It wouldn't work.

"Nothing," she said.

"Come on! No family? No friends? Nothing? Not even steak?"

"No."

"What about your parents? I visited Earth, you know, just to check in on my oma. It's weird what's happened to it now they know about aliens. Visiting is a nightmare. You can't imagine the paperwork!"

May stood, handing August the skewer without eating the marshmallow. She wasn't hungry. Or, more specifically, she was so hungry she'd circled back around into not wanting to eat. "I'm going to check on Xan."

"Wait." August put a hand on her elbow to stop her from leaving. "Look, I know how Ix's experiments go. Trust me, you don't want to be down there."

That made her want to be there even more, naturally, and it showed.

"It's alright," August said. "Aimz and Yvonne are down there, too. They'll look out."

"Aimz is unstable, Ix is...I don't know, I just don't trust Ix, and Yvonne tried to kill me."

August laughed, popping another marshmallow into his mouth. "Ix is trustworthy, just terrifying. And Yve isn't anything like Chaos was."

May grabbed Big Mouth Billy Bass from the cushion and sat down, holding the mounted fish in her lap and stroking it absently as if it were a sleeping cat.

"What's with the fish?" August asked.

May shrugged. "Xan likes it."

August nodded, gave an old man grunt (that's what he called them, "old man grunts") and moved closer to May. "How ya holding up, kid?"

May raised an eyebrow at him. "What do you mean?"

"Well, aren't you and Xan...you know. Isn't he your

lover? This has to be—"

"No," she said. "He's an alien. I don't think we physically can. And he's... I don't know, not my type. I don't think I have a type." Then May's own curiosity got the better of her, and she said in a conspiratorial whisper. "You're not...with Ix, are you?"

August wasn't sure why she was whispering, it was nothing to be ashamed about. "Ix isn't into Earth men. Yvonne is, though. Frequently. I'm starting to have a hard time keeping up with her." Then he laughed at a self-depreciating joke he'd just thought of. The gist of it was that he was actually *not* having a hard time. He graciously spared May from hearing it.

"I want to check on Xan." She stood and made for the stairs.

"You do have a crush on him!" August accused laughingly.

"Ugh, no." May cringed visibly. She didn't care if he thought they were fucking, but a crush? That word gave her what psychologists refer to as the willies. "We're just partners. We look out for each other. You've got a crush on him, not me."

"Huh?"

"You told Xan you were straight on the docks, but you were really into that kiss."

"Xan's not a man! It doesn't count."

May raised an eyebrow at him.

"Does it?" August looked as if he'd just been given irrefutable proof that the moon landing was a sham.

Refusing to dignify him with an answer, May changed the subject. "Where's the lab?"

August stood with another old man grunt. "I'll take you," he said. "I wasn't kidding about Ix's scientific method, though. It takes a strong stomach."

Before they reached the stairs, Xan bolted up to the living room, cheerily smoothing back hair which dripped with something milky. "Fixed! Easy," he announced to the room before Ix, Aimz, and Yvonne followed him in.

He slung his damp arms around May and, unable to do much else, May patted his back hesitantly. Now she, too, was dripping with something milky.

"What is this?" she said, pulling away as soon as he let her.

"Uh, fermented hooflatoo milk. That didn't work. Neither did the centrifuge or the magnets," he counted off on his fingers. "But the sound stuff worked! The fungus hates sounds, apparently."

"The fungus hates sounds?" May asked.

"Not all sounds, just certain ones. It rather likes other sounds, apparently. Ix thinks it was triggered by some kind of sound in the first place! I'm saying the word 'sound' a lot, aren't I? Doesn't matter. I'm safe and sound! Everything's sounding good. I'm fine."

Aimz also dripped and smiled, but her smile was less face-eatingly huge, more of a quiet smugness.

"The ultrasonic treatments only delayed the growth of the fungus temporarily. You are not 'fine,'" Ix corrected, following, perturbed, behind everyone with a towel which she swiped across the floor.

"I'm fine," he said again, but quietly, just to May this time. "Let's celebrate! What do you folks do for fun around here? I..." He looked around the living room briefly to confirm his suspicion. "I don't see a TV. Don't you have a TV?"

"Celebrating is exactly what we shouldn't be doing," Yvonne said, slipping behind a well-stocked bar in the living room and pulling out glasses and armfuls of liquor bottles. "You two need to avoid anything that could set it off again. Anyone want to get drunk?"

SIXTEEN

THREE CRYSTALS A HEAD

✳ ✳ ✳ ✳ ✳

There's no better way to worry about something than by sitting on a wooden rocking chair on a creaking porch with a strong drink, staring pensively out over the lake.

So that's exactly what everyone was doing.

Aimz rocked slowly back and forth, worrying about Listay whom she hadn't heard from yet, worrying about Xan who wasn't taking the scourge very well, and worrying about herself—she was taking it *too* well.

May rocked beside her, worrying about her lack of purpose, worrying that Yvonne secretly wanted them dead, worrying that Aimz was going to eat her in her sleep, and worrying that the *Audacity* would get lonely out there on its own. She refused to worry about Xan right now.

Xan rocked beside her, worried too that the *Audacity* would get lonely. He stuck pretty securely to that one worry, but occasionally the creeping dread of scourge encroached on his pleasant melancholy. He mentally weed-whacked it. How lonely the *Audacity* must be, he thought. It's so cold in open space. Had he left the lights on? Such a waste of electricity. He was sure he had left the lights on and wished he lived in the kind of advanced society where lights automatically turned themselves off.

August also rocked and worried. He was worried mainly about the apple-stealing glotchburs. He'd seen two scuttling along the edge of the lake with twigs in their jaws, diving in and out, in and out like sewing needles, no doubt building nests deep in the muck.

Ix and Yvonne were both taking a break from worrying. They were in their workshop, working on a self-aware apple coring machine which couldn't stop apologizing to the apples it disemboweled. Yvonne consoled the machine while Ix wrote some sadistic subroutines into its code.

Eventually, the worrying got the better of August and he had to say something.

"Those damn glotchburs are building a nest, I bet," he muttered loud enough for everyone to hear, but not loud enough for anyone to feel obliged to acknowledge him.

The porch floorboards creaked under the rocking chairs.

A silver-eared horntaggler cuckooed in the distance.

Invisible buzzing things buzzed invisibly.

"Well, I think it's high time for a glotchbur hunt," August said, louder now.

The sound of creaking rocking chairs reduced by exactly twenty-five percent as Aimz put a foot down to still her chair. "Hunt?" she asked, a dangerous pink glow in her eyes.

"What are you, a parrot?" August teased. "Now that I've got you here, I might as well make you work for your stay. Who wants to go hunting?"

Aimz stood, downing the rest of her drink.

"Eugh, Aimz you're entirely too excited to maul small amphibians," Xan said. "Besides! Yvonne said to not do anything that could set *it* off."

"Yvonne's the decorative one who doesn't know what they're talking about," Aimz said with a wave of her hand, secretly hoping Yvonne wasn't within earshot.

"*I'm* the decorative one who doesn't know what they're talking about! Yvonne has no perceivable flaws, physical or otherwise, and you know that. I'm not hunting glotchburs." He set down his drink, but had no intention of abandoning it. "I say we find the nest, give them a convincing speech about respecting private property, and help them re-locate somewhere else. Oh! And we can send them a care basket full of apples to keep them over until they find a new food source. No, that's too much. We can negotiate a contract with them."

"They're pests," Aimz said in a pejorative warble. "They can barely spell, much less negotiate a contract. How do you hunt them? Lasers? Traps? Just chase after them and snatch them up? Can we dissect them? I haven't dissected anything in ages."

"You haven't dissected anything since university. You hate dissecting things!" Xan stood now, too. "You used to just scrape up samples of unidentified plant matter. It's like you're using the scourge as an excuse to be horrifying."

She squared her shoulders at him. "Xan, we're scourged. Horrifying is essentially our single personality trait now. I've accepted the inevitable, and if that involves learning to tear something to shreds with my mouth, then what's the point in waiting?"

"Right, yeah, only one hang up there, I guess. I don't *want* to go feral, Aimz! That's sort of the point, don't you think? Decades at university spent trying to get rid of scourge, and now you're giving up?"

"Not giving up, just letting go! It's happened, alright? It's too late. We failed. We're zuxed. And I've set my mind on enjoying it."

"Whoa, whoa," August said, getting between the two Carmnians and pushing them apart gently. "We're not killing them, and we aren't writing any contracts. We stun them with an InfraDin Stick, then bring them to the butcher down the road. He pays three crystals a head! Then they have a nice, long life on his glotchbur reservation."

"The butcher?" asked May.

"Yeah," August said.

"Keeps them in a reservation?" she clarified.

"I'm willing to believe that!" Xan interrupted.

"Of course he keeps them in a reservation. He might be a butcher, but he's really got a heart for the little guys."

The little guys August was referring to were, in fact, not little nor were they guys. Glotchburs are roughly the size of a watermelon, skinned in rubbery brown hide, replete with useless facial horns, and reproduce unisexually which means they are neither guys *nor* gals.

"I'm willing to believe that!" said Xan again with a smile. He realized that he was repeating himself and because he realized it, it was okay. He was fine.

"Let's get this over with," May said, ignoring her half-full cocktail glass which sweated on the porch at her feet.

SEVENTEEN

WAGER YOUR WALLY

* * * * *

August had insisted on a "boys versus girls" hunting challenge. This insistence had annoyed everyone for different reasons. It annoyed May because this meant she would be stuck with Aimz. It annoyed Aimz and Xan because the terms "boy" and "girl" didn't actually translate to anything meaningful in Tuhntian, and August had been forced to try to explain his ideas on gender to them, which he did with a great deal of awkward fumbling.

But they agreed to try it just this once. And so May twirled the InfraDin Stick August had given her, watching Aimz as she dipped in and out of the tree line ahead of her, and wondered what the likelihood was that she would have to use the stick on Aimz out of self-defense. The likelihood was high, but not unreasonably so.

"Zuut, these glotchburs are faster than they look," Aimz panted, returning to May, who hadn't cared enough to go sprinting after the flash of grayish brown glotchbur in the distance. Aimz grabbed the InfraDin stick from May's hand. "These things have an awful range, though," she said, studying it. "And they're not nearly as much fun as catching something and ripping it to shreds with your bare teeth, right?"

May snatched it back and resolved to keep a tighter hold of it. "Why are you asking me?" She started walking again and Aimz followed, more interested in her now than the escaped pest.

"What's got your taxi maxed, Earthmun? You look like you've spent the rotation plucking raldbugs off the flesh of an infested hooflatoo."

"What?"

"Annoyed," Aimz clarified. "You look annoyed."

"Sorry."

"Well, tell me! What's got you annoyed? It's obviously not the glotchburs." Aimz stopped her now and parked her hands on May's shoulders, forcing her to engage in conversation. "It's Xan, isn't it? You're horribly annoyed with him for getting the scourge and ruining your life."

The face May made at Aimz flirted between horror and outrage, but didn't have quite enough energy to make it to the full expression of either.

"I'm annoyed at you. You don't give a shit about what happens to anyone, including yourself."

Aimz squinted, then switched her focus to somewhere behind May and pretended to search for something she had just seen a glimpse of behind her. "Where's Bar Fight May? Bring her back; I liked her better. Bar Fight May!" she hollered down the line of trees ahead of them. "Where'd you go, you zuxine tchagg?" she called out to no-one. Bar Fight May was long gone.

"Those were strangers; it's entirely different! You've attacked your own aunt, Xan, and me, and you seem to be enjoying this. I thought you cared about Xan, at least."

Aimz shook her head so forcefully her hair whipped around her like a miniature pink tornado. "I care! I just care differently. He's my zoup-nog brother; obviously I don't want to see him worried about going feral. I'm trying to help him cope! I want him to at least enjoy the painful decline into an unrecognizable beast of the wilderness." Her eyes were rimmed with green when she pushed the curtain of hair out of her face to look at May again.

May stayed silent. Talking never seemed to get her anywhere she wanted to be. That's why she usually let Xan take the lead in conversations.

"Earthmun," Aimz said, as gently as she could manage. "It's easier to accept the chaos. Chaos is the natural order of life, and if you fight it, you will lose every time. I stopped fighting it and look at me!" Aimz walked backward now so May could literally look her over. Her hair hung like a curtain of seaweed around her dirty face, her t-shirt was stiff with dried saltwater, her limbs caked in mud.

She looked horrible.

But she was grinning with a *joie de vivre* May had only ever experienced at the finish line of a harrowing...*chaotic* rocket race. May blinked once, and Aimz was a glittering goddess basking in the ebb and flow of an uncertain existence. May blinked again, and Aimz was back to being a dirty alien with a death wish.

May shook her head and walked away, half-heartedly searching the shadows for movement.

Aimz jogged after her. "Hey, you're really trok at conversations, you know that?"

May ignored her.

"Listen, you can get off your pretty puntle, because you've given into chaos more than you think you have. Ditching a perfectly good planet to race rocket ships? If I had an intact planet like that, you can wager your wally I wouldn't be this far from it."

"I was stuck on Earth. Now I'm not."

"Now you're stuck on Xan," Aimz said with a laugh. "Come on, I'm not the only heartless tchagg here. What about your aunts? Left them on Earth without saying goodbye, didn't you?"

"My mother raised me, and I hadn't spoken to her in years before I was abducted."

"A lover, then? Relationship getting boring, you find an easy out?"

"Nope."

Aimz sighed, trying one final time to prove her point.

"Alright, houseplants! You got any houseplants you deserted back on Earth?"

May remembered Betty, the cactus, which sat on the mini-fridge in her old hovel of an apartment. "It's just a plant..." May begun, but Aimz thrust out an arm, stopping May mid-sentence.

Something in the distance had caught her attention, their conversation (which May had only just now accepted) forgotten.

"Blitheon, May, look at that! The glotchburs are in for a really *hot* time!"

EIGHTEEN

GLOTCHBUR STEW

* * * * *

The common Rhean glotchbur is a quiet, aquatic creature. It is content to spend its short life scurrying about, digging ditches that it knows it dug for a reason (though for what reason, exactly, it can never remember), and eating its weight in the fruits of other creature's labors. In this case, apples.

The only noise they are thought to make is a weak buzz which emanates from their slimy bull-frog throat and informs nearby glotchburs that they're ready for their daily humping.

This is why the scream of a terrified glotchbur is so chilling, and the screams of hundreds of glotchburs at once is altogether more horrific a sound than any human ear would happily hear.

The sound had come from the lake, and so that's the direction in which August and Xan ran. Before the lake came into view, a thick steam blanketed the orchard, forcing them to slow to a walk to keep from running face-first into a tree.

August coughed through the humidity, feeling as if he

were about to drown on dry land. "Where the hell did this come from?" he asked rhetorically. He knew Xan wouldn't know. Xan tried to answer, anyway.

"I don't know," he said to August. "May?" he shouted into the steam, cupping his hands around his mouth to amplify the sound. "Aimz?" he tried again, just in case she was within earshot and May wasn't.

"I'm right here," May's voice could be heard through the steam. She wasn't shouting because she didn't need to; she was just a few feet in front of them at the edge of the lake. The steam wafted ever upward until the scene cleared enough that they could see two blurry figures. One, Aimz, rolling on the ground, laughing so hard she was silently wheezing. The other, May, who stared down at her in quiet resignation.

The ground dipped away into a steaming mud-pit which burbled and smelled of beef stew.

"What happened to the lake?" August said, falling to his knees at the horrific sight of his once glistening, if glotchbur infested, lake.

"I—" Aimz wheezed between a chortle. "I—" she couldn't stop laughing.

May crossed her arms and shook her head. She was going to have to explain. She hated explaining things. "So, Aimz saw the Ray-Master Tree Trimmer parked at the edge of the lake. She said the glotchburs were in for a really hot time and ran off. I tried to catch up, but," May gestured to her legs, "short," she finished simply.

"So she used the Ray-Master to flash-boil the lake, and now we've got glotchbur stew," August extrapolated with a sigh, putting the rest of the event together.

"Yep," May confirmed.

Aimz was settling down now. She had stopped her mirthful rolling and was laying on her side, gazing out in ecstasy at the carnage she had wrought. "You're welcome," she shouted back gleefully to August who only whimpered. Xan put a comforting hand on his back.

Aimz dragged herself upward and shook off a few large clumps of warm mud.

May swallowed back nausea which might have been

inspired by the stench of glotchbur stew or the wet heat surrounding the lake. It could have also, possibly, been that she hadn't eaten in far too long. Furthermore, Aimz's erratic behavior had only solidified her suspicion that the scourge had not, in fact, been cured and was still looming over them like a deadly hot air balloon. She stood woozily, her feet sunk into the mud up to her ankles.

"Well," said August. "Close the lid, the monkey's dead." And he followed Aimz back to the house.

Xan squelched down to the shore where May swayed.

"I didn't see that coming," he said, reaching for her hand. "So at least I'm not time-zuxed anymore, eh?"

"At least," she replied as he dragged her from the mud and they trudged after Aimz and August.

NINETEEN
JAZZ HANDS

* * * * *

The air was thickly humid and smelled like the inside of an office microwave just after lunch time, reminiscent of food, but wildly unappetizing. They climbed the steps back up to the porch, creating a trail of watery silt.

"Okay," August said with a heavy sigh. "Everyone pick a bedroom. They all have showers and access to the wardrobe system, so you can put on something dry." He then leaned closer to May. "And Earth-style toilets."

"Thank God," May whispered. Why August said this, and, indeed, why May was so relieved to hear it, I will leave up to your imagination.

Aimz had already half undressed, leaving her filthy wet clothing in mournful lumps along the porch. Xan's mauve faux buffatalo coat had become a wet slap of a thing which mopped up his sides listlessly every time he moved. He draped it over a porch chair to dry and tried to open the screen door which led to the kitchen, only to find that the screen door didn't strictly exist. Not for people, anyway. It very much existed for the clouds of tiny bugs which, attracted to the nutrient rich silt that coated their legs, desperately wanted to follow them inside. He walked through the screen, the bugs stayed outside.

May whipped off her trench coat, which was now three times as heavy as it had been and wrung it out over the sink, then combed her hair back and wrung that out over the sink as well.

Then, tired of waiting for someone else to mention it, May confronted Aimz.

"The scourge is back, isn't it?"

"Pah-ha...what? No," Xan said before Aimz could get a word in. "That's just Aimz! Normal Aimz."

"It was the scourge," Aimz corrected. "And don't worry about lending us any clothes, August. You don't need clothes to wander off into the forest and become a folkloric beast." She was naked now, to demonstrate.

No one who hadn't grown up with Aimz was able to form a coherent retort to that, so Xan took it upon himself to shake out May's trench coat, wrap it around Aimz's shoulders, and give her the stern kind of look their Aunt Kalumbits used to pull off so nicely.

"Go upstairs and don't come down until you're clean and dressed and, preferably, of sound mind, alright, mun? You're not becoming a folkloric beast without me, and I'm not ready for that sort of celebrity just yet."

"What's wrong with you?" Aimz asked.

"Nothing. That's the point! Nothing's wrong with either of us. We're fine," he said in a tone which was meant to frighten the universe into making it so.

She gave him a sloppy scoff, pulled the trench coat further around herself, and stomped off to claim a room upstairs. For her benefit, he held the stern face until she was gone, then, for his own benefit, he let his face fall into a look of abject terror.

"Whoo," August said with a full-body stretch. "We had quite a day. Us Earthlings really ought to have some RnR, eh?"

"Zuut," Xan said, shocked. "I didn't know Earthlings could do that!"

"Rest and relaxation?" August clarified.

"Oh. Right, yes. That. He's right, May."

"Fine." May snatched Big Mouth Billy Bass from the couch and followed Aimz's wet footprints upstairs.

Xan followed her up the stairs visually but stayed physically stuck to the spot, wondering if he should go with her or claim his own room. The idea of time alone with only his thoughts for company distressed him, but August slapped him on the back in a friendly, heterosexual sort of way.

"Come on, I'll show you to your room."

* * * * *

The bedrooms in August's house looked slightly more normal than the rest of the house. Normal, in this case, meaning filled with whooshing doors and holographic floating screens rimmed in color changing lights and the constant quiet buzz of electricity.

This comforted May in some ways. It was better to be in an honest room than a room which was deceptively Earth-like, a rustic and cozy veneer over the pervasive technology.

Along one wall, a no-nonsense hard-vapor bed. Along the other, a no-nonsense SaniSteam shower.

She dropped Big Mouth Billy Bass on the nightstand and went over to the holowindow which displayed an idyllic day on the orchard, the lake glistening rather than boiling. If she were to pretend everything was fine, she wanted to make it totally and absolutely fine. She flicked through the holowindow settings until she found a video of the stars from space. Not a twinkle in sight, just steady points of silvery light like she remembered.

Satisfied with the new view, she began to undress, pausing as she heard August and Xan talking in the hall, then continuing, grateful that they hadn't come in. Privacy was not an alien concept to Tuhntians in general. It was, however, an alien concept to Xan.

After showering, May lay strewn across the bed, wearing one of August's undershirts, a worn flannel shirt, and ill-fitting boxer shorts which were a great deal more comfortable than the ill-fitting jeans she had tried on. She was unable to even consider sleeping. On the bedside table, bathed in a ring of light which looked uncannily like lamplight but which emanated from a thin floating disk, lay Big Mouth Billy Bass.

It is customary for the plastic mounted fish known as Big Mouth Billy Bass to sing snippets of two songs. The first being "Take Me to the River" and the second, "Don't Worry, Be Happy." And so, despite months of silence from the fish, it shouldn't have exactly surprised May that it began to sing now.

Still, it startled her, and she nearly fell off the edge of the bed trying to get away from it.

"Take me to-" it sang. "Take me to-" it sang again. "Take me to-"

"What? Spit it out!" May said, irritated.

Then, May's own voice echoed back to her from the fish's wobbling mouth, distorted through the worn speaker. "Carmnia."

May almost ignored it. Her options were A) acknowledge it and admit that she had heard it or B) pretend nothing had happened and wonder about it forever.

"Take me to...Carmnia," it repeated.

Yes, the fish had definitely spoken to her. The fish wanted to see Carmnia. Which, by all accounts, was incomprehensible to May. She had a lot of questions. She started with a simple "Why?" as she cautiously addressed the plastic mounted fish.

"To cure the scourge."

"Who are you?"

"Big Mouth Billy Bass," said the fish.

"No, who are you really?"

"I'm here to help."

"Why should I trust you?"

"It's your only option."

"Who the hell are you?"

"I'm a fish, you simpleton! Now take me to Carmnia, or let Aimz and Xan go feral."

May was sleep deprived, clearly. Obviously, this was a

new feature of sleep deprivation that she hadn't yet had the pleasure of experiencing. She grabbed the fish and opened the SaniSteam tube.

"Where are you taking me?" asked the fish.

"I need to sleep on it." May flung it into the shower where it clattered on the tiles.

"Wait! I'm your only—" The shower door shut, and the fish's voice was too muffled now to bother May.

She dropped face-first to the bed and slunk beneath the covers. Exhaustion seemed to redouble the amount of gravity on her body as she sunk into the mattress, but as her body stilled, her mind began its morning calisthenics.

Rather than sleep, she found her thoughts rotating like a wad of spun sugar in a cotton candy machine, every turn creating a sticky cloud of frustration. Doing something was always better than doing nothing, right? And here on mainland Rhea, she could do nothing.

Carmnia was a lead. Carmnia was something to act on.

She mentally wandered down the path of paying Carmnia a visit which ended, at various branches, in certain death. She wandered down the path of staying put, which ended, again, at various branches, in certain death.

Then, she remembered what Xan had said. "No one survives anything. Even the so-called gods die." And she realized he was absolutely right. That's just how the universe works. You live, you make good choices and you make bad choices, and regardless of how many good or bad choices you make, you die, and wasn't that just a clump of soured milk in her coffee?

Or was it? Was everything actually easier now that she knew the outcome? Death? If that was the outcome, despite anything she did to change it, then the point of existence must be...must be... Shit, she thought. She was still thinking. The same thoughts, too. This was the tenth, maybe eleventh time they'd spun around the cotton candy machine of her brain, and the sugary web had only gotten denser.

This was exactly why she didn't want to be alone with nothing to do but think.

Maybe she should find Xan. She was so used to having him around to drown out her incessant mental chatter. But her arms and legs were so heavy, they might as well have been cinched to the bed, so she axed the idea.

After a while, she almost thought she had fallen asleep, until she realized that, again, she had been chasing the idea of going to Carmnia and trying to suss out all the possible ways that option might end.

Sleep, sleep, sleep for the love of God, sleep, she thought. Thinking was not sleeping, she thought again and, instead, screamed into her pillow. Screaming was also not sleeping, but it felt better than thinking.

A moment later, a purposeful knock on her door. Four times.

"Come in," she said, tilting her mouth away from the pillow just enough to be heard.

The door wooshed open, and Xan entered wearing another of August's flannels, tied up at the middle, and a pair of August's jeans. May's trench coat was slung over one arm and the other held aloft a plate of something in a loaf.

"Heard you couldn't sleep," he said, draping the trench coat over the bedside table.

"From who?"

"The screaming was a dead giveaway." He sat down on the bed and offered her the plate of bread. "August told me to give it to you when you woke up, and that I definitely shouldn't eat it because it was poisonous and would kill me, but you know, I'm not sure I believe that? Worst that it could be is some kinda wheat and that won't kill me."

"Don't eat it," May said, dragging herself up to sit as if the hard-vapor mattress were a pit of quicksand sucking her in.

May observed the slice of bread, some kind of quick bread from the look of it, probably apple-based, given the business. She broke off a piece and chewed it, moaning at the sweet softness. "Sorry, it'll kill you dead," she said once she had swallowed.

His mouth twisted defiantly, and he tried to break off a

small corner, but May patted his hand away and moved the plate to the opposite bedside table.

"Alright, okay, zuut!" he relented with a light laugh and leaned back on the pale gray headboard. "Why can't you sleep? You're usually great at it."

With a shrug and a sigh, May put another bite in her mouth. "Thinking," she said around it.

"About?"

"Everything. You could make all the right decisions, and still, you've got to die one day, so what's the point in working so hard to make the right decisions when everything has the same outcome?"

The question sounded rhetorical, to Xan, so he kept himself from positing an answer.

"I was thinking about all the different types of things you can put in a stew. And also, is coffee a stew? Can you put coffee in a stew? Can you stew things *in* coffee?" he asked. "But your thing is better, admittedly."

"You're a few hundred years older than me. Don't you know what the point is by now?"

"Aha, ha...maybe. I don't think there is one. Not really, I mean. Not some big cosmic thing you could write out and then just be done with it. The point is just...it's just now. This moment. And then in a couple beoops, the point will be that. A few more beoops after that will be another point. The point is just all...this." He demonstrated "all this" by stretching his hands out and wiggling his fingers.

"The point is jazz hands?" May asked.

"Sure, yeah. The point is jazz hands."

"Well, that helps," she said, shifting back beneath the covers.

"It does? Jazz hands?"

"Yep." And it did. This time, when May closed her eyes, she actually noticed the soft coolness of the hard-vapor pillow, the gentle throb of her tired feet, and the slight dip in the mattress caused by Xan's weight beside her as she fell asleep.

TWENTY

FACE COFFEE

✳ ✳ ✳ ✳ ✳

"I'm going to see Carmnia," May, having slept on it, said immediately upon waking. She would've liked to say that she had a prophetic dream that told her it was the right thing to do. She would've liked to say that in the clear stillness of the morning the answer had come to her. In actuality, it was just the second thing that came out of her mouth when she woke up, the first being a bit of spittle which had moistened her pillow.

"Oh, that's umm...that's...uhh." Xan covered the confused silence in his brain with mouth-sounds. "Good morning, starshine?"

"Did you hear me?" she asked.

"I did."

"And?"

"I heard you! You're going to see Carmnia."

May shook her head and grabbed the half-eaten bread from the bedside table, inspecting it to be sure Xan hadn't snuck a bite. She finished it off.

"Are you going with me or not? It might be dangerous."

"I'm definitely not *not* going with you, but I also am not

going, because you're not going."

"You can't stop me," May said, putting on the trench coat which had dried, albeit stiffly, overnight. She felt the pockets and found that, miraculously, the zapper was still tucked away inside it.

"Wait, hold on. I missed an important part of this conversation. *Why* are you going to see Carmnia? That's what I should've said."

"Because..." May looked surreptitiously at the shower as if the doors might tear open and the bass would come bursting out singing, dancing, and mysteriously spotlit. This did not happen, and so May had to admit, "The fish told me to."

"Big Mouth Billy Bass told you to see Carmnia, and you're just going to listen to it? But when I told you to *not* see Carmnia, you didn't listen to me! Do you trust a plastic fish more than you trust me, May? Because, if you do, that's awful. That's really and truly terrible."

"No, I trust you! It's just that it seemed to know what it was talking about."

"Alright, but, consider: Trisy Yorgaslack seems to know what he's talking about on TV, but he sells reclaimed racing rockets for a living, and you know why Yorgaslack and Larvae's Reclaimed Racing Rockets has never had a bad review on the IFI? It's because no one who's purchased one of Yorgaslack and Larvae's Reclaimed Racing Rockets lives long enough to leave a review!"

"You don't have to come. I can't help Yvonne and Ix do..." She made a hand gesture to replace a noun she couldn't find, "on you and Aimz, but I can look for other options, so that's what I'm going to do. I *have* to do something."

Scales in Xan's brain balanced precariously as he thought. He stared out of the glowing holowindow to try to steady them before answering. The old familiar scene of open space wasn't nearly as comforting to him as it had been to May.

"I don't want Yvonne and Ix to..." He repeated her strange hand gesture, "on me, but I also don't want the Scourge Authority to vaporize me. I *do* want to make sure you're safe, and I've never actually met Carmnia before, so she has no reason to hate me. And I suppose...I suppose we're going to see Carmnia."

"You sure you want to come? I plan on finding Listay first, so I won't be alone."

"I'm sure. It couldn't hurt. Unless I get vaporized, and hey, even then only for a blip, right?"

"True," she said, her brain so focused on running through logistics that she had only half listened to him. "We better bring the fish," she said, watching the shower warily.

Showers are, of course, used to being watched warily.

Slowly, May pulled back the sliding shower door and found that Big Mouth Billy Bass was just where she had left it. The thing hadn't grown arms and legs and freed itself in the night. She wasn't sure why she had expected that it might, but she hadn't expected it to suddenly start a conversation with her, so all bets were, currently, off.

"We're taking you to Carmnia," May told it.

It did exactly what one would expect a toy fish with no batteries to do. Nothing.

Now May started to suspect that she had been hallucinating, and Xan, though he didn't dare say it, might have agreed. Until a mechanical whirr came from the fish and its mouth dropped open in an expression which might have been read, to the keen observer, as surprise.

In fact, the fish was shocked by this development. It had just begun to accept its soggy fate on the shower floor when May announced her decision, and it was having difficulty reacting properly.

"Good," said the bass, finally, fearing that it might lose their attention if it considered its next move too long. Then it shut its mouth. Talking used up a great deal of energy.

May stuffed it in the largest pocket on her trench coat. Only the bottom half fit, and so the bass rose awkwardly out of her pocket, staring at the sky, but it was secure.

"So what's the plan?" Xan asked as May shut the shower door.

"The plan is to figure out how to hot-wire the ThingHauler, hot-wire the ThingHauler, and get back to the Merimip which we'll take to NotTuhnt's police station to bail out Listay."

"That's utterly ridiculous, you know that?"

May paused at the door to the room, offended. "It's not *utterly ridiculous*. It's only slightly harebrained."

"Hot-wiring the ThingHauler, I mean. It's utterly ridiculous because I've got August's face!" And he did. When May looked back at him to see what the hell he meant, she was met by a holographic rendering of August's face emanating from the tip of Aimz's mugging pen.

"When did you get that? And why?"

"Eh, I had some time alone with August last night and had a feeling you might want a get-away option in case things got zuxed here."

"Really?" May didn't quite believe that he had that kind of foresight.

"No, we were just zuxing around with it," Xan admitted and flicked through several unflattering images of both their faces before shutting it off and stowing it in a flannel breast pocket. He had never worn anything with a functioning breast pocket before, and while he thought it was a terribly odd place for a pocket, he had quickly become accustomed to it.

"Good work, I guess," May said. "Can you tell Listay we're heading back to NotTuhnt?"

Xan raised his BEAPER. "Hey, Listay! How's NotTuhnt? Hope the weather cleared up a bit. Have they let you off, yet? Because if they have and you've noticed that the Merimip—"

"Get to the point," May whispered.

"Right, well, we're coming back, May and myself, to ask Queen Carmnia about the scourge. So just stay right where you are, and we'll come find you. Unless you're somewhere you don't think we'll be able to find you, in which case, please get somewhere we *will* find you and wait for us there. Just tell us where you'll be and stay there until we reach you, alright? That sounds alright,"

Xan confirmed. "See you soon, mun!" Xan sent the message and then put a hand on May's shoulder, the cheery timbre of the message he'd just sent dropping like a silken sheet. "I need coffee before we go. I couldn't sleep. Too bright."

What, thought May, had been too bright? Certainly not the room. The space-window twinkled with such minute points of light, it was nearly pitch black in there with the lights off. But as she turned to ask for clarification, she noticed something she hadn't before. The green bioluminescence of the fungi was a great deal stronger than it had been yesterday.

"Yikes," she said out loud, accidentally. "Sorry, Blue. Why don't you make some coffee? I'll find some alcohol for the road."

"What about everyone else?" Xan asked.

"What about them?"

"Shouldn't we let them know where we're going? So they don't worry. Or perhaps so they do worry. I feel like someone should be worried about this, and you certainly don't seem to be."

"They'll try to stop us."

"And rightly so!"

May sighed. "You don't have to come."

He rubbed his face with both hands as if he were trying to change into a different personality. One that wasn't too exhausted to go along with May's slightly harebrained schemes. "Alright. Okay. We won't tell them unless they ask. How's that?"

"Fine." May led them down the stairs and, with a forced casual ease, asked, "You sure you wouldn't rather hang out with August?"

"Eh, I've always preferred the company of people who are likely to get me killed. Makes me feel like I'm doing something important with my life."

"I can't tell if you're being sarcastic."

"You know…I'm actually not? As long as I get to complain about it, I'm up for anything. What is life if not the act of consistently defying death?"

The kitchen, like most of the house, had been styled

like a rustic Earth kitchen. A sprawling butcher block island flanked by dark wood cabinets. A bread box built into the cabinets was labeled with a metal Insinigator logo, the food replicator looked like an old fridge, and where most kitchens had a stove, this one had a rack of amber-bottled cider.

May's coat pockets were beginning to reach their limit, but she shoved a bottle of cider into an inner pocket, adding to the absurdly lumpy silhouette. She never thought about needing a bag until she needed a bag, and when she needed a bag, there was never one available to her. It was the BEAPER situation all over again.

Xan flipped on the food replicator and selected a large mug of coffee. As he watched the machine arrange the necessary molecules, a thought struck him. A thought which would culminate in this action: the moment the coffee was complete, he grabbed the replicated coffee mug from the bay, tilted his head back, and poured the entire cup directly over his face.

Fermented hooflatoo milk hadn't worked, but what evil was there that a good cup of hot coffee couldn't scare off? The answer was several. And, in fact, many kinds of evil can subsist on coffee alone.

Coffee ran down his shirt as he shook the liquid from his face which had gone from pale blue to bright green from the scalding. He blinked the coffee from his eyes. Nothing had changed.

"That help?" May asked, trying (and failing) to cram another bottle of cider into her coat.

"Too soon to tell!" Xan asked the replicator to assemble another mug of coffee, but May set down the bottle and slid between him and the machine before it was finished.

"Are you going to drink this one with your face?"

"Of course I am!"

"Xan—"

"My mouth is on my face, isn't it?"

The replicator dinged that it had finished. The door slid open to reveal a steaming mug of newly replicated coffee. May stood in front of it. He lunged around her, shoving her aside to snatch the cup and chug it.

"Get in the truck," May said.

TWENTY-ONE

PRTY DSH

* * * * *

The drive back to the dock was blessedly uneventful. They analyzed August's taste in music, concluding that he was around the right age for a mid-life crisis and the music he listened to absolutely felt like the kind of thing someone might enjoy when they weren't sure where the second half of their life was going. After concluding this, they both realized they didn't know where the second half of their own lives were going, and the music suddenly made a great deal more sense to them.

They discussed common Earth phrases which Xan was keen on further incorporating into his vocabulary. The phrase Xan had so commonly heard on TV, "Why I oughta..." May explained, was typically a threat. Xan explained that there are many things he ought to do and none of them involved threatening people, so he didn't see much use for that one unless he could change the implication, but May vetoed it all together, seeing as she had never actually heard anyone in real life say it to begin with.

"Where's the boat?" May asked as they parked the

ThingHauler along the dock and got out.

"There's a boat," Xan said, pointing to something much larger, pinker, and rounder than the Merimip Ocean Ship.

"That's *a* boat. Where's *the* boat?" May wasn't asking him; she knew he didn't know. She was asking the unfeeling cosmos that had stranded her on a Rhean dock with no boat. Rows of various watercraft bobbed along the boardwalk, but these were luxury craft, and their owners were all off doing the things which made them enough money to enjoy their luxury craft on the weekends.

They approached an egg-shaped floating attendant's kiosk with a service window and just enough room for one hover-stool and one under-paid young Rhean.

May knocked and the hatch whizzed open.

"How can I assist?" the Rhean teen said with so little inflection that May hadn't, at first, realized it was meant to be a question. He was looking at a holobook. Not reading it, as his eyes never moved from the middle of the digital page. Just looking at it.

"Er, hi. My boat's missing," she said.

Xan pulled her aside. "It's not technically our boat, you know. Sure, we bought it on our gem, but we gave it to Listay, so it's Listay's boat. We have stolen back the thing we purchased. Hold on, *is* it our boat? The great Udonian philosopher Fragahoo postulated that—"

"Tell me later."

"But—"

"Please?"

He looked like he might burst, but he forced himself to shut up anyway, and May turned back to the attendant.

"Black boat?" asked the attendant, eyes still trained on the holobook.

"Yes."

"Weird greenhouse thing on the top?"

"Yes!"

The attendant shrugged.

"Yes?" May pressed.

"Dunno," they said.

"You didn't see who took it?"

"Got impounded. Owner's dead, apparently."

To May, there was nothing more odious than the phrase "Let me talk to your manager." It had been used against her so frequently and with such vitriol when she worked at Sonic that she had made a pact with herself to never let slip the offending demand. But the sentiment was welling up in her. If this Rhean teen had a manager, May very much wanted to speak with them.

Perhaps re-phrasing it would remove the sting. The question "Is there someone else I could talk to?" seemed benign enough, even polite, if she kept her tone in check.

"Is—" She stopped, the words catching in her throat as the ghost of her former self rose up and strangled her.

"Hey!" Xan shouted from behind her. "Hey, May! I got us a ride!"

"Yeah?" She turned around as if she were a camera operator purposefully holding off the reveal, creating tension, creating suspense. When at last Xan came into view, he was attached to a rope ladder dangling from something which must've spawned from an ELO album cover.

A sun-blotting silver frisbee twirled above him, lights blinking in rhythms and colors precisely calibrated to create a sleek, futuristic effect. Its three levels rotated independently of one another like an electric three-tiered cake. Its license plate spelled out 'Prty Dsh' which, May surmised, likely meant they were about to be ferried back to NotTuhnt on the Party Dish.

Or perhaps ferried off to another, cooler dimension where seaports on alien planets didn't look nearly exactly like a small fishing town somewhere around New England.

A gnat buzzed into her open mouth. "You," she gagged slightly on account of the gnat, "you're sure that's going to NotTuhnt?"

Xan thrust a finger toward a marquee which wasn't, blessedly, spinning like the rest of the contraption. Squinting, May could just make out "NOTTUH" on the marquee. She chewed her lip.

"It's going to 'Nottuh'," she said, as she grabbed hold of the bottom rung of the rope ladder.

"Well, obviously the full marquee is meant to say, 'NotTuhnt', right? Clearly. I mean, that would be the logical thing, wouldn't it?" He sounded less confident now.

May snorted, beginning to climb the ladder. "Logically. But when has anything ever been logical?"

When they reached the platform where the line queued up, a boulder of a man greeted them at the entrance, and that's only a slight exaggeration. He was a Garveral, more mineral than man. "Tickets?" he demanded in a gravelly voice.

The only thing which gave him away as not exactly a hunk of granite was the crack in his face which opened and closed rhythmically, as if breathing, and his impeccably pressed tuxedo complete with cummerbund and a bowtie which nestled beneath the mouth-crack.

"Yes, please," Xan said.

Had the Garveral had eyes, he would've rolled them. Had he had lungs, he would've sighed. He had neither, and this made him particularly well suited to customer service jobs.

"I need to see your tickets."

"Can't we buy them here?"

"This isn't the Party Tray, boha. This is the Party Dish. If you don't have tickets, you're not getting in."

A line of people had formed behind them.

"Right, yeah, well we can purchase tickets, right?" Xan asked.

The line was beginning to make exasperated noises.

"This, again, is a Party Dish. You buy tickets at the Tray," the boulder said stonily.

"For the love of O'Zeno," muttered someone behind them.

"Let's go." May tried to pull Xan away by the elbow.

"Wait, wait, okay. Where's the Tray, then?"

"Zoup-nog," whispered the line.

"I'm not a zuxing information dome. Now get out of here and don't go climbing ropes you haven't paid to climb."

"We'll find a public teledisc to NotTuhnt; come on," May whispered just loud enough to be heard over the general hubbub of annoyance behind them.

Xan pressed his lips together in frustration but followed May back down the rope. Halfway, at least. The lower-level hatch gaped open, a soft blue glow pulsating from inside.

"Party Dish!" said Xan and, in a feat May didn't realize he was physically capable of, he sprung from the rope ladder, just catching enough of the edge to leave him dangling from the dish like a scrap of wilted lettuce on the side of a salad plate.

"Damnit." May whispered, dangling from the ladder as she watched him struggle.

"Hold," he grunted as he tried to lift himself into the ship, "on."

"Not much else I can do."

"Heh, this thing's slipperier than I imagined," he said, his boots flailing for purchase on the side of the Dish. The toe of his boot caught a piece of cracked siding and, cracking it further, he leveraged himself inside the Party Dish.

"Ha!" May heard, muffled. Xan reappeared inside the ship and held his arms out. "On in. Into the Party Dish," he cajoled her.

"Stop playing around. This isn't like you."

His shoulders dropped along with his smile, but his arms were still held out to her. "I'm going to pay for it," he assured her.

"Yeah, that's what I'm worried about."

"We shouldn't?"

"Defin—" A bone vibrating classic sci-fi sound effect extinguished her answer and the Dish, which had been hovering slightly above the water, hovered a great deal higher now.

The things which May shouted at Xan, eyes squeezed tight, fingers soul-bonded to the rope, don't need to be transcribed herein. I'm trying to keep the amount of "fucks" under ten, and I've just wasted one there. You'll have to come up with your own colorful language.

Fortunately, Xan heard none of it. Unfortunately, because neither of them could hear each other, and May refused to open her eyes, he was unable to communicate to her that he had the top of the rope and all she had to do was climb up one more rung, and he could pull her in.

He tried wiggling the rope gently to let her know he had it, but this only made her grip tighter and curses more creative.

So he tried to reel the rope in, but found his muscles weren't up to the task.

He reached down and, using his nose as a stylus, tapped his BEAPER which had (and always has had, before you ask) a megaphone function.

"MAY," he shouted via his BEAPER's megaphone (the megaphone which his BEAPER has always had). "CLIMB UP."

Carefully, she tilted her head up toward the sound and squinted at Xan holding onto the rope ladder above her. She was looking at Xan, but all she could see was the incredible distance from her feet to the vast ocean below as the Party Dish spun onward toward NotTuhnt.

"No!"

He couldn't hear her, but it was easy enough to extrapolate what she had said.

No further technology had been retconned into the BEAPER that would be of use, and so May hung there miserably as Xan tried to will the ladder to budge.

Until, high in the crest of the Party Dish, the pilot, who was high in both senses of the word, had the sudden realization that she had forgotten to reel in the ladder and rectified her oversight.

Outside, the winch shifted, groaning in protest of the added weight, then, knowing that no one heard its protest or (more to the point) cared, did its job, albeit pointedly slower than usual.

Once May was within reaching distance, Xan locked his arms around her and fished her into the luggage-stuffed lower tier of the Party Dish.

She had her feet under her for only a moment before wobbling to the floor, the nerves in her arms and legs twitching.

"Alright?" Xan asked.

"Uh-uh."

"Mun." He sat on the floor beside her. "You race a rocket for a living...what happened? You're not scared of anything."

"Heights."

"You...race a rocket. That's as high as you can physically get."

"But it's—" She wrested control of her arms again and made a kind of orb with her hands to demonstrate a rocket capsule. "It's inside. You're in something. Safe."

"Safe," he confirmed, putting a hand to her chest.

She stared at his hand, surprised. It was comforting, even if the way he was acting wasn't. "You're not supposed to be the brave one, Blue."

He dropped his hand and stuck his thumb and pointer fingers over his eyelids, rubbing fiercely as if he had been pepper sprayed.

"I'm sorry. I'm trying to be myself, I really am." He put his elbows on his knees and rested his forehead in his hands, staring at the floor despondently. "But who I am keeps changing. It's like trying to balance a ship without a gyroscope," he said.

The bottle of cider appeared in his field of vision. The bottle of cider shook gently at him.

He took it, drank from it, then smiled at May. "Much better," he said. It wasn't. But he said it anyway. "Got your legs back?"

May sealed the bottle, stashed it in her coat pocket beside Big Mouth Billy Bass, and made a show of patting her legs. "I think these are mine."

They stood and inspected their luggage-y surroundings.

"Have you ever been to a Party Dish?" he asked.

"Have you?" She didn't bother telling him that she hadn't. Of course she hadn't.

"Mmm, not sure. I've been to a lot of things which might have been Party Dishes. Let's check it out."

✳ ✳ ✳ ✳ ✳

The main floor of the Party Dish was not at all what May had been expecting. The lights were pinkish and brighter than daylight, and the entire room which stretched the length of the dish wore a soft white fur coat, pale fibers swaying grassily.

Lumps of floor and ceiling jutted out, creating tables, couches, stools, even several doughnut-shaped bars with columns of backlit glass bottles in the center interspersed with neon signs advertising everything the bored-looking bartenders were willing to serve.

Feather-like fibers tickled her shins in a way which felt uncannily like crawling ants. She shook her foot, only to have more fibers caress it when she set it back down.

The air smelled toxically sweet, and May got the sense that this was exactly what swimming through cotton candy would feel like.

A mechanical band played impossibly quietly from a fuzzy white stage, four pristine silver androids injecting as little soul as possible into four equally pristine shapes which looked more like oversized esoteric kitchen gadgets than instruments. Over the music could be heard the clink of glasses and murmur of meaningless conversations deadened by the plush coat of the room.

Fortunately for May, who was not much of a dancer, this party did not appear to have a dance floor. Unfortunately for May, Xan *was* a dancer and didn't care that there wasn't a dance floor.

He found an empty patch of fuzz and began to draw a great deal of attention to himself. A distraction was in order, and quickly, too. Before the confused stares of the quietly drinking onlookers turned into a call for security.

The perfect distraction blazed in pink neon above the bar: Hallucinogenic aphrodisiacal rice noodles. She had come across them before, but had somehow refrained from trying them. Hallucinogens had never been her drug of choice; they got in the way of work. Aphrodisiacs also had never interested her since she had never been nor desired to be in a situation where one would be warranted. Noodles, though, she could get behind.

Xan would either heartily disapprove and come over to tell her so, or, in this state, he might be eager to watch. Either way, he would stop trying to dance with the flustered waiter.

"Hey, I'm going to try the noodles. Want to watch?" she announced her intentions.

He paused in his pursuit and gave her a look which quickly morphed from excitement to concern and back again. "You sure? I mean..." He realized he was shouting to her across the relatively quiet room and cantered up to the bar where she had taken an obstinate seat. "I mean," he said again, in a reasonable tone of voice, "you know what those noodles do. I've built up a tolerance, sure, but zuut, the first handful of times I had them...Zuut."

May was reasonably convinced she could handle them. If they were anywhere near as strong as ZipZams or most alien alcohols she had tried, the effect would last her twelve minutes tops. Twelve minutes of horny hallucinations would mean twelve minutes of not having to worry that Xan would get them caught. She'd never been horny before, anyway, and she was curious about this apparently overwhelming urge to mate that everyone seemed so excited about.

"It'll be fine. My metabolism is a lot faster than yours."

"You would win a metabolism race, yeah."

"I'd win a lot of races."

"And you have! We were talking about noodles, though. Specifically, you eating them. Imagine me but younger. Did I have a mullet back then? Likely. Yes. Yeah, that was before the pompadour adventure." He spread his hands as if to smooth out a canvas upon which he was about to paint a picture of times past. "A crepuscular glow bathes the metropolis hub city on Eroticon-"

The bartender tendered a bar of dried noodles in a crystalline goblet before May, and she crunched off a corner of it, wincing as she chewed. Xan stopped reminiscing.

"You're eating them dry?"

May hadn't been aware there was any other option, but just as he said it, the bartender, with a captious glance, slid a carafe of hot water onto the table.

She set the brick down in the goblet and, still working bits of the noodles from her teeth with her tongue, doused the remaining noodles with the hot water. It was an eerily mundane ritual, pouring hot water on dried noodles to soften them. She had become so accustomed to the unexpected that she had neglected to expect the expected.

"Just testing them."

"What, for durability?" Xan asked.

Then, like a seagull to the face, the solution to the *Audacity* dilemma came to her. "Oh my God," she said. "I have it!" And, not finding anything suitable to write with, she began plucking limp noodles from the goblet and organizing them along the bar top.

"Have..." Xan eyed the noodles, then May's face which was nearly bursting with excitement. "Have what?"

"The answer! The *Audacity*—I know how to get it back!" Her hands magnetized to his shoulders, and she shook him, a ferocious gleam in her eyes as she tried to telepathically transmit to him her ingenious scheme. "I'll show you!" she said when her telepathy fell short. "The noodles. Observe." And she coaxed two long rice noodles closer to her across the bar, then draped a third, shorter noodle between them. Xan observed, as she had instructed, but failed to comprehend.

May paused, held up a finger to indicate that she was about to do something extraordinary, and plucked up the end of the shorter noodle to fold it over the longer noodle. She nudged it into position. "That's it!" She bit her lip, feeling as if she might blast off with the satisfaction of solving this impossible puzzle.

Now all they had to do was...was what?

"Now all we have to do..." she said, postulating that saying it out loud would serve to generate the rest of the sentence. "Is..." she said.

The hallucinogens in the bite of noodle she had eaten were already wearing off, and Xan could nearly see her fervor tumbling out like the last dregs from a spout that's been shut off.

"Solving unsolvable problems is what gets you randy,

then?"

May swallowed and looked at the abstract noodle art she had created. "Guess so."

She slid the goblet of noodles away, a bit disappointed that she, still, could not say she knew what it felt like to be aroused. Xan watched her intently, smiling as if he expected her to do something even more interesting now.

"What?" May asked with a shy grin.

He shook his head and sat up. "Oh, nothing. You were just so excited about the...I just hadn't seen you really excited about anything in a long time."

May gave a passive snort. "Nothing to be excited about, really, is there? Future looks pretty bleak from this angle."

"Try a different angle?"

She raised an eyebrow and made a big show of flipping herself around on the barstool, then dipped backward, observing the lounge upside down as she held onto the back of the stool. "Hmm," she mused.

"Less bleak?" Xan asked, following her lead and also inverting himself.

"A bit, yeah."

They hung like that for a moment, watching waiters shuffle through the tall fibers of soft carpet, studying the restless movements of legs under tables.

The legs of their bartender appeared, and they looked up at him, getting a stunning view of the inside of his impeccable nostrils.

"Would you like an escort to the sobering pools?" he monotoned.

They pulled themselves upright and the universe skewed uncomfortably around them both while the head rush settled.

"We're fine, thanks," May said, sending the bartender away as Xan habitually fixed her hair.

One of the band androids, bandroids, if you will, gave a polite little cough and turned up its volume slightly to make an announcement. "Next stop, NotTuhnt. On-boarding only."

"Damn," said May. "That's not going to make it easy to

sneak off."

"Shame. And it was so easy to sneak in!"

"A regular cakewalk," May agreed.

"Ah! Idea: if we walk backward out of the dish, they'll think we're walking onto the dish, right?"

May tried to picture that, then tried to figure out why he thought that would work, but found she couldn't accomplish either and shook her head at him instead.

"Why don't we let them kick us off? If the bouncer sees us, he's bound to throw us out again."

"Yes! Or kill us outright, which would rather quickly end all the other problems stacking up, now that I think about it."

"Oh yeah," May said, standing now and depositing a handful of crystals on the bar. "Why didn't we think of that earlier?"

"Classic us, always completely ignoring the obvious solution!"

They made their way to the door which read EXIT in sumptuous neon, assuming that any exit would do. And this one would but with a great deal more fanfare than they anticipated. As they pushed open the furry doors, an alarm sounded, and the lights which lined the corridors of the party dish flickered from cheery white to ominous Danger Diophalothene.

"Should we run?" Xan asked as they briskly continued to exit.

May shrugged. "The idea is to get caught." Still, it felt weird to be knowingly doing something wrong and not running. "When the bouncer shows up, make sure he wants us off at the next stop," she added.

"How?" Xan asked, still nervously walking down the corridor.

"Bother him, I guess. You're pretty good at that."

"I am?!" Xan asked, insulted.

"I meant it as a compliment, Blue!" May hissed. "You make a good distraction."

"Oy! What are you two doing back here?" The guest of honor had arrived; the bouncer was running, rolling, *avalanching* toward them down the hallway.

"Lost!" Xan said, nervously. "Would you believe it? We were just about to leave, but somehow we ended up right where we started. That's what happens when you don't give people clear instructions regarding where you'd like them to go when you tell them to get out."

"Why I oughta!" said the bouncer, grabbing Xan by the lapels and lifting him off the ground.

"May!!" Xan shouted back to her, excited. "He said it! He said the thing!"

"Oh my God, he did!" May laughed. "We've never heard anyone say that in real life before," she explained to the bouncer.

"But they always say it on old Earth TV shows," Xan further explained. "As if it's something people actually say. And you did! You're not from Earth, are you?"

The bouncer snarled grittily. "Shudup."

May and Xan caught eyes, stifling a laugh at his expense. "Sorry," May said, getting a hold of herself. "You can kick us out at the next stop."

"You'd like that wouldn't you?" He grabbed May by the front of her shirt and lifted her up, too until she was eye level with him.

"This guy's all concrete and clichés," May whispered to Xan who dangled beside her.

"May, you know you're really good at bothering people, too, when you want to be," Xan replied.

"Thanks. I hate people," she told him.

"That's enough," the bouncer rumbled at them. "Take a deep breath, pipsqueaks."

"Holy hell, how does he know all these tough-guy clichés? He must be from Earth," May told Xan.

"Gotta be."

Unfortunately, they were too busy mocking him to heed his warning and take a deep breath. The airlock opened and the bouncer did something that was strictly forbidden in the training manual. He tossed them both overboard, right into the Rhean Sea.

TWENTY-TWO

SERGEANT WUTHCK

✳ ✳ ✳ ✳ ✳

Listay nervously cataloged the spots on the back of her left hand and forearm again. There had always been twelve. There were still twelve. There likely always would be twelve. But she counted anyway. Counting freckles was about all she could do right now to distract herself from her anxieties as she sat waiting in a sterile office at the police station.

"Oh, oh, oh, look who it is! My number one favorite ghost," said the voice of someone who was not, in actuality, Listay's friend, but firmly believed he was.

"Hello, Officer Wuthck."

The owner of the voice lounged in the office doorway, cobalt face glistening with oil, bristly handlebar mustache flecked with crumbs, and thick torso torturing the snaps on his suit.

"Sergeant, now, my lav!" said Wuthck, patting Listay on her arm before sideling into the hover chair on the other side of the desk. Despite having no actual moving parts, the hover chair squeaked under his weight.

"Oh?"

"Well, it ain't too tough to scale the ranks when most of the force exploded, am I right?" Wuthck laughed at his clever joke and twisted a pinky in his ear to dispel a persistent itch.

Listay showed her teeth to him, then pulled the corners of her mouth up just enough that he saw a warm smile.

"Now, mun, what brings you to my humble office?"

"Same thing that has brought me here four times since I settled on NotTuhnt three seasons ago."

"Still dead, are you?"

Slowly, carefully, Listay breathed as if to prove that she was not, in fact, dead.

"If you would simply submit an E87-20," she said, "this wouldn't be a problem."

"Aw, nonsense! You're never a problem, Listay. I love spending time with you! Besides, I can't submit an E87-20 without a notarized E87-19. You of all people should know that."

Listay ground out an even wider smile. "But form E87-19 section 4 references section 32 of the attached form E87-20, which—"

"You don't have?" finished Wuthck with a mustache-bristling smirk.

"May I go? You can't keep me here if I've done nothing wrong aside from exist when the records say I don't."

"So soon? I've got a whole rotation I can keep you before I'm legally bound to let you go. Why not enjoy it? We can order take-out!" He yanked open a desk drawer and began shuffling through tiny cylinders which held digital delivery menus for the fifty closest restaurants to the precinct.

"I'm busy."

"You're dead! It's a bit late for being busy, don't you think?"

"May I please have my BEAPER back?"

"I tell you what." Wuthck held up a finger, a smile playing at his thick black handlebar. "You can have your BEAPER back and get out of here if you beat me at a round of Belvedere Masters." He pulled from his bottom-most drawer a set of thick, old-fashioned, plastic holodiscs and set them on the table, tapping them until they all flickered on, filling the space above his desk with thousands of tiny holographic cupolas and two avatars on the starting lanai at the bottom, one which looked like a tiny Wuthck and the other a tiny Listay.

"No."

"I'll let you keep score." He slid a smaller disc across the table and tapped it on, revealing a three-dimensional spreadsheet scoreboard.

A small whimper of desire sneaked past Listay's lips as she gazed upon the scoreboard. She couldn't turn down such a stunning spreadsheet and Wuthck knew it. She nodded, first conservatively, then with conviction. "Alright, one round. I start."

Wuthck put the toe of his shoe on the edge of the desk and pushed himself back in his squeaky hover chair with a victorious grin.

TWENTY-THREE

THE ZAPPER

✳ ✳ ✳ ✳ ✳

"Zuut, did we antagonize him too much?" Xan asked, frantically doggy paddling in the freezing Rhean sea.

"Maybe a bit," May said, wiping coils of hair off her face so she could get a look at the situation. The situation was, surprisingly, not awful. NotTuhnt was in sight and would only take a few bloops to swim to. "Come on," she said to him and began swimming toward the mainland.

It was oddly silent behind her, but she was so focused on getting out of the freezing water as soon as possible that this escaped her notice until her knees brushed the rocky ocean floor and she stood up.

"Xan?" she shouted out to the horizon, but he was not on the horizon, he was somewhere below it.

Now, May was not a good swimmer. Not by any means. And the thick canvas trench coat she wore hadn't been exactly hydrodynamic. But Earthlings, unlike Tuhntians, float.

"Xan?!" she called out, again, still scanning the surface of the water for him. Her shoulders drooped, the trench coat felt impossibly heavy. After exactly twelve seconds of feeling utterly sorry for herself and all the trouble she'd been going to lately just to keep the two of them alive, she shrugged off the trench coat and discarded it on a large rock.

"Alright, I'm coming in there," she said to the ocean, warning it. "And he better be easy to find," she said. "Because if he isn't and you keep me out here until dark looking for him I'm going to..." she considered her next words carefully. Not only was it difficult to threaten the ocean on account of it being much bigger and more powerful than the average human, it was also unwise to threaten something approximately twelve billion times as large as you. She did it anyway. "I'm going to lobby for whatever horrible toxic waste they produce on NotTuhnt to be discarded directly into the ocean. How's that sound? Bad, right?" She was stalling, now. That water was cold.

Fortunately, before she could work up the courage to go back in, Xan came out. "Blitheon's frozen ass nipples!" he said, draping over the rocky shoreline, doing a wonderful impression of May's soggy trench coat.

"What the hell, Xan? What's an ass nipple?!" She knelt beside him and turned him over onto his side. He was covered in a thick clear slime, and May hesitantly started sloughing it off, but he batted her hand away.

"Need that," he said, coughing up a lungful of water. "Oxygen," he clarified.

"Is that...normal?" May asked as he sat up, but he didn't answer. He was too busy licking it off his hands and arms while May stared at him, amazed that she still somehow felt more at ease around him than August.

It was, technically, normal. All A'Viltrial species, Tuhntians being included in that category, absorb most of the oxygen they really need from their skin. The lungs are mostly used for speaking, smoking, and blowing on food that's too hot. When totally submerged in water for extended periods, or in environments with unusually low oxygen levels, Tuhntian skin produces an oxygen-rich mucus coating. It's not something one does intentionally, nor in polite company, but Xan also found that, somehow, he was more at ease around May than anyone he'd ever known.

At last, he'd licked off enough to stop feeling quite so light-headed and took a deep breath, coughing up the last little bit of ocean water he'd accidentally inhaled.

"Sorry," he said. "You asked if ass nipples are normal? No, no they aren't. It's just a saying, don't worry. I've never met a species that actually has ass nipples," he assured her, stripping off the flannel shirt to wring it out.

"I meant the..." May studied the stringy mucus on her fingers. "You know what? Nevermind. You feeling ok?"

"Best I've felt in orbits!" He said with a wide smile. This, May knew, was a lie, but she let him have this one.

"Let's get to the monorail, then." May picked up her coat and wrung it out, but didn't put it back on. Xan was suddenly beside her, checking the coat pockets.

"Billy!" he said, happily, finding that the bass was still there. May handed the trench coat to him and he slung it over his shoulder to carry. He was used to carrying things for her.

A short plod away, they came to the raised monorail station, awash with other Tuhntians on their way to or from somewhere or other. It didn't really matter from whence they came, it mattered that there were a lot of them.

May stopped.

Xan stopped because she had.

"They're going to notice you're scourged," May said, tapping her own cheek bone to indicate that his bioluminescent eyes were the issue here.

"Easy." From a pocket of August's jeans, Xan pulled a familiar pair of pink, plastic, star-shaped sunglasses and popped them on his face, shielding her from the intensity of his scourged gaze.

"Are..." May squinted in disbelief. "Are those the sunglasses you got from Yusko's on Taeloo XII?"

Xan beamed as if the sunglasses held within them the feeling of the pink beach of Taeloo XII, the frothy cream sea, the warmth of Taeloo's twin suns, the ice cream.

"The very same."

"I didn't know you still had them. Why have you never

used them?"

Xan pulled them down to glance pointedly at the gray sky. The gray sky glanced obstinately back. "Never had an occasion to."

May also surveyed the porridgey sky over NotTuhnt. There hadn't been a single sunny day since Precious Butler dropped them off here. "Makes sense," May said. The sunglasses detracted from the scourge-glow but didn't eradicate it entirely. "Just don't look anyone in the eyes," May said.

"But eye contact is—"

"Don't look anyone in the eyes," May repeated, and when May repeated herself, Xan knew better than to push the subject.

"Why don't you have some cider?"

"Actually, I feel alright! I think I'm figuring out how to suppress it! You know, it's not too hard, really. Just cramming that bit down." They began to walk toward the monorail. "All I've got to do is focus on acting normal. Nothing that I wouldn't normally do or say, right?" he said, popping something into his mouth, which was something he'd normally do.

"What was that?"

"Oh! Berries." He held out his cupped palm which was indeed full of seethingly purple berries that very much looked not-edible. "Want one?"

"Where did you get them? Are they safe?" She paused to sniff them.

"Off the ground! And yeah, of course they're safe. I wouldn't be eating them if they weren't, would I?"

"Would you?"

He ate a few more. "Right, if they were poisonous, I might eat them myself, but I wouldn't in a zillion orbits be offering *you* any, would I?"

"Not unless—"

"Would I?" He smiled brightly at her with purple stained teeth. When Xan repeated himself, May knew better than to push the subject.

She sighed, grabbed a few of the berries to eat, as she was, after all, extremely hungry. She wished she had ordered something other than mind altering noodles on the Party Dish. But they were headed Uptown, and if there was one thing Uptown had, it was experimental museums, but if there were *two* things Uptown had, it was experimental museums and restaurants.

She took half a palmful of the berries and munched on the tart, bursting globules.

They arrived at the monorail station just as the next car rolled up, sidling into it as discreetly as possible and not daring to talk to each other, for fear that their conversation would give them away. After a tense and quiet twenty bloops, the monorail rolled to a stop near the UpTown police department, and they stiffly walked off.

Casually, so as not to raise suspicion, May nodded to Xan to follow her into the alley behind the police station. Once they were out of sight of the main walkway, she stopped him, pressing down on his shoulders until he was at eye level with her.

"Alright, here's the plan," May said.

Adrenaline had made May steady, which meant it was Xan's turn to worry for the both of them. They tended to trade worry as if it were a shared piece of luggage one could give to the other when they were too tired to keep carrying it.

He tried his best to hold eye contact with her as she disseminated the plan, but if he held eye contact with her, she would see the green glow of the fungus, and if she could see it, that meant it was real, and it was there, and it was growing, and he didn't know how to stop it, and—

He chomped down hard on his bottom lip. And it was getting bad again. He focused on May. Focused on May and the faint glow of green which he saw reflected in *her* eyes—and had it spread to her or was he just seeing his reflection and—oh, she was talking.

"Okay?" she finished.

He swallowed. He hadn't caught any of that. "I'm going to say okay," he said. "But know that I have no idea what I'm agreeing to."

May sighed. "Stay here. Do not interact with anyone. I'm going to get Listay."

Xan nodded. He felt so awful about not paying attention the first time that he had listened to every word with rapt attention this time.

"Got it. Wait, hold on." He watched the reflection of green bioluminescence flick around her eyes nervously. "No. One more time."

"You stay here," May said, pointing. "I'll get Listay." She gestured to herself.

At last, it had gotten through—"And where will I be?"

"Here!" May shouted, hoping she was loud enough to make it past the damn mushrooms in his face. "There's a zapper and the rest of the cider in my coat. Drink it."

"Drink the zapper?!"

Talking, obviously, was not getting May anywhere, so she dug through the coat which Xan had slung over his shoulder. She pulled out the fish, thrust it into his hands, then dug around, dug deeper, dug until pocket lint filled the spaces beneath her fingernails.

"A day. I had a goddamn zapper for a day, never used it, and now it's lost," May muttered. These were terribly unfair working conditions, she felt. "Just don't leave the alley." May reiterated before storming off.

TWENTY-FOUR

NATURE OF THE FISH

✳ ✳ ✳ ✳ ✳

The alley behind the station was pleasantly warm, buffered from the biting city winds by two solar-brick walls which sipped up what little sunlight they received and magnified it to heat the buildings. These bricks were extraordinarily hot.

Xan had the sudden urge to soak up a bit of that warmth for himself. He set Billy Bass down and smushed his cheek against the bricks, giggling as the radiation sizzled his skin.

"Stop that," said the fish.

"What?"

"Stop cooking your face, you foolish half-sentient."

He pulled away, confused, then realized a few layers of skin didn't pull away with him. He crouched to look at his reflection in the chrome siding of the refuse disintegrator. Half of his face was bright green and burnt from the radiation. Sighing, he sat on the ground and leaned his back against the wall, only realizing this, too, was a mistake when August's flannel shirt caught fire. He shimmied out of it, flinging it into a puddle in the middle of the alley.

"Zuut! That was Itkip's favorite top. They're going to be plivered when they find out."

"They won't mind."

"Well, sure," Xan said, topless, resting his face dejectedly in his hands. "They make you think they don't care. But they do; they're just being polite."

"That wasn't Itkip's top, it belongs to August. Itkip is dead. You killed them when you destroyed Tuhnt," said the fish. Xan wasn't sure why the fish was saying these horrible things, but he knew it was partially right.

"Yvonne destroys Tuhnt, not me!"

"So you're back up to that revelation. Who's May?"

He shrugged. "Friend of yours?"

"What's the *Audacity*?"

"That's...a cult classic novel?"

"No," the fish said curtly. "The *Audacity* is the rocket ship you stole, causing the destruction of Tuhnt. May is the horrid little Earth-creature who's been dragging you around the galaxy. She's the reason you lost the *Audacity*."

And suddenly a drawbridge which had been out of service in his brain started working again and folded itself back down, crumbling bits of the foundation as it fell back into place.

"That's not what happens." He rubbed his face, forgetting that he had severely burned it a moment ago, then staring at his hands, offended, when it hurt. "Not exactly. It wasn't May's fault, and it wasn't my fault, and I can't explain why it wasn't, but I do know that both of those things were neither of our faults. And, furthermore, how do you know any of this?"

"I know everything. Which is how I know that by the time you reach Carmnia, the scourge will have decimated your brain and there won't be anything left to save," said Big Mouth Billy Bass, its lips still twisted down in its natural fishy frown, but its voice had the ring of cruel satisfaction.

Xan had liked Big Mouth Billy Bass from the moment he saw it. It was a strange, silly, Earth thing and May had been so excited to show it to him that it had, in a round-about way, become his *raison d'être*. It was still strange, but the silliness had all drained out and been replaced with another s-word. Sinisterness.

"You don't know that," said Xan, hoping that saying this might make it true.

"I do. The scourge isn't just affecting your brain, it's consuming it. I'm telling you this because I can keep it under control if you let me in."

"In?! In where?!"

"Your brain."

Every question Xan asked of the fish had been answered in an unpleasant way thus far. It struck him that perhaps the key to ending this unpleasant conversation was to simply stop asking questions. It was just a plastic fish. He could ignore it. He was probably hallucinating the whole conversation to begin with.

He would just shut up. Easy enough solution, he thought. He was quite proud of it, actually. If he didn't ask questions, the fish couldn't answer them in horrific ways anymore. "Who are you?" he asked. "Zuut! Never mind. Forget I said anything."

"I am that which is, was, and is to come. I am beyond the imaginings of your frail and tiny mind. I am Awareness itself. The unavoidable end of all things. I am–"

"Chaos," Xan whispered. "How did you get in my fish!?" There he went again with questions he really didn't want an answer to.

"Sonan thought she deleted me by deleting the code I had added to her system." Chaos laughed now, waggling the plastic lips, her tail slapping the wooden mount luxuriously. "You can't delete a god. You can't *kill* a god. After Sonan deleted me, I latched onto your little eye-fungus and waited. Saved your life, even, when the *Innocuous* fell. I am not unfeeling. I can't possess an unwilling host, but plants, dead bodies, and electronics don't have a personal will to contend with, so I clung to your scourge until you brought me to Big Mouth Billy Bass," sneered the fish.

"Great! Then that's where you're staying," he told her.

"Safely inside the bass."

Xan typed a quick message on his BEAPER to Listay, a warning.

The fish flopped once, slowly; it looked like a flippant shrug. "Enjoy ruining the rest of your pet Earthling's short life, then. I'm a god," she reminded him for what felt like the millionth time. He knew. He got it. God. "I know *everything.* And I know that your little Earthling will feel obligated to care for you. No one can fix the damage that's been done, but if you let me in, I'll keep it from getting worse. I triggered it, and I alone can resist it, but I need your cooperation."

"You triggered it?" Betrayed! thought Xan, by the fish he'd fought so hard to protect from the Scourge Authority. He should've let Aimz blow it up with the rest of Largish Bronda.

Then the bass generated an obnoxious squeal. A familiar squeal. A tuneless, high-pitched whine. At its call, the fungi twirled in his eyes like a synchronized swim team, tingling, twisting, growing. He shut his eyes against the sound, but it didn't stop until the tone dropped to a new frequency, the same one Ix had used to quell the fungus at the orchard. Now he opened his eyes and saw the bass for the first time with an unreserved anger.

"Why?" he shouted at it. A cold rain began to drizzle on him.

"I thought it would be fun. It was. But I'm bored now, and I'm ready to get on with life, or rather, to get on with the systematic unraveling of all life. Carmnia has something I need trapped in her Folly. You will take me to it, and I will keep you from going feral. It's a neat little solution, don't you think?"

"No. Why won't you leave us alone? I know I zuxed up my life, but what the hell has May done to deserve any of this? Why won't you just stop?!"

The fish was silent.

The rain splattered, as rain does, turning the dirt in the alley to mud.

Xan looked up at the gray sky, let the rain sooth his burnt face, and realized he might as well be asking the rain why it wouldn't stop getting things wet.

Chaos didn't stop for the same reason he didn't. Chaos could not stop. Neither of them could. He and May had entered into a game of tug-of-war with nature and wondered why they were losing.

If it had been physically possible for Xan to merge with the puddle he sat in and slowly seep into the ground, he would've done so. He tried to, anyway and, for a while, he didn't say anything because what business does a puddle have talking to a plastic fish?

"There's always a reset, right?" he said, finally. "After every episode of 'I Love Lucy', things just go back to the way they were at the beginning. I mean. Sometimes things change a bit. Like when Lucy and Ricky moved to another apartment. Or when they had the kid. Things didn't go back to the way they were before exactly but...but mostly they reset. No explanation as to why Lucy wasn't arrested or how the mess got cleaned up or what happened to all the rest of the truffles. It was just suddenly okay again. Wouldn't that be nice?"

Chaos silently considered what he had said. "Yes," she said at last. "It would be nice."

"I wager you didn't plan to get stuck inside a plastic fish," he said with a light laugh as if they were best friends who had just had a fight and he was trying to make amends.

"Plan Billy was not my first choice."

"What was your first choice?" he asked.

Chaos opened and closed the mechanical fish mouth a few times as she tried to decide what to tell him. The truth, she supposed, at this point, couldn't do any more harm.

"Everything begins as Nothing, and Everything becomes Nothing. I am tired of Everything. I want Nothing back. Carmnia has the key to getting that."

"I...I mean, yeah Everything is a lot. Yeah. I get it."

"You *get* it?"

"Sure," he said. "I mean, zuut, I love a lot of the things inside of Everything, but there is a lot of Everything out there, and it gets overwhelming. If I could just keep a few things, though. Like May and 'I Love Lucy' and coffee and..." He buried his face in his hands and indulged in a single, heart-broken laugh.

"None of those things belonged to you in the first place," Chaos said. "They are the domain of Chaos, and I'd like them turned back into Nothing. Please."

He could feel the scourge penetrating further and further, wriggling its way into his head, sinking its roots into his synapses and twisting them apart. Desperately, he wanted someone in there with him, battling the invasive fungus. If that someone had to be Chaos, it had to be Chaos. It seemed easier to have a force of nature on his side, anyway.

"Yeah, alright." Xan rubbed his eyes and sat up straight, picking up the fish to hold in his lap. "You win this round. If you need permission to possess me, this is me giving you permission. Go for it."

And Chaos plummeted into him like a brick to the forehead, leaping from the fish and settling herself down, finally, in a body that had thumbs. Of all the things she didn't have access to as a disembodied being, the lack of thumbs always hit her the hardest. She worked Xan's thumbs now, making them dance as if she were handling an invisible video game controller.

The winning didn't last long for Chaos, however. She felt herself squeezed as though she were being forced through a tube of toothpaste into a darkened corner of his mind. Now it was only her and the scourge. No connection to the outside. He had shut her out, somehow. Repressed her into the mysterious basement of his mind.

The ability to repress things, which Xan had nurtured over a few decades alone in space trying not to think about what he had done, had proven a useful skill. He knew there was an extra box in the back of his head labeled "Chaos Goddess Consciousness: Do not open. Fragile. This side up. 87% post-consumer recycled cardboard." He stuffed it under the proverbial staircase and locked the door. He might have given a little ground, as a tactical measure, but he was not giving up yet. If he could respect Chaos's need to fight him, then she would have to respect that he needed to fight her back.

He had a thought about finger joints and sent it to Listay, hoping she would read it aloud to May when they were back together and that May would laugh.

TWENTY-FIVE

THE BELVEDERE MASTER

* * * * *

"Green twenty-eight, row five. Cap my cupola!" said Wuthck, punctuating with a swig of a llerke cider from an ice bucket his assistant had brought half a beoop ago.

"Zuut. I almost had that cupola." Listay sipped on her own bottle of cider. If she had to play a ridiculous old holo-game with a power-crazy police captain, she might as well enjoy herself.

"Message for ya'," yawned his assistant from the door frame. Bubble gum, as it is known to us, doesn't exist outside of Earth. Regardless, Wuthck's assistant chewed a pink wad of something which she consistently blew into hand-sized bubbles that popped so loudly they could be heard three rooms over.

"Oh, good! Good. Great," Wuthck finally sat up properly, smoothed down the front of his shirt, and set aside the bottle of cider. "What's the message?"

His assistant's head and shoulders wobbled briefly. "Dunno, didn't ask. They're out front." And she was gone, leaving only the sound of a popped bubble and the faint smell of what was certainly not bubble gum.

Wuthck blew an exasperated puff of air as she left. "I suppose I'll just go ask them myself," he said, loud enough that she could hear but not loud enough that she would care. "No sneaky cupola stealing while I'm out, eh mun?" He winked at Listay and left.

Listay, after a moment of silence in the claustrophobic office, decided she too could leave and did so.

She followed Wuthck into the hallway which was filled with the warm pink light of the setting sun as it filtered through the large windows at the front of the police station. Windows which were, in her mind, a ridiculous security risk. If she ever became officially undead again, she would have to insist they hire her. It was woefully under-managed.

Listay recognized the person at the front desk.

"May! What are you doing here? Where's..." She trailed off, not wanting to blow anyone's cover.

"Safe," May said.

"Know each other?" Wuthck asked.

"I'm here to pay her bail," May said.

Wuthck tsked. "Can't pay a bail that hasn't posted! Which is why we're in the middle of a Belvedere battle." His smile bristled beneath his mustache.

"Which is?"

"It's a game," said Listay.

"And she's losing, per the norm! Isn't that right?" Wuthck laughed and nudged her in the ribs. Listay replied with an annoyed puff.

"Oh don't take it so hard, General. I'll make you an offer, eh? The two of you against me at Belvedere Masters." The idea of the challenge brought a glimmer to his eye, and he gave May a good-natured wink. "Hope you're better at it than your un-dead friend, here."

"Three-time universal champ," said May.

"Really? I didn't realize the game was that popular." His mustache wriggled as he re-worked his idea of the world slightly.

"Never heard of it," May clarified.

"That's just how she talks," Listay told Wuthck. "She's from Earth, you see."

"Ah," Wuthck said with a touch of awe in his eyes.

"It's alright. Most Earthlings didn't catch on, either," she said. "So where's the game?"

"Just a few planets over on the swirling magma world of Helastico II," said Listay.

"Good thing I brought my magma boots," May said with a smile, and Wuthck, cautiously, as if the hallway might itself turn into magma, led the two of them back to his office where the game waited.

Wuthck cleared the game field, which he was mere moments away from winning, crashed into his chair, and opened another cider.

On the walk over, Listay had explained the details of game play to May, and May, as a result, now knew even less how to play it.

"So you gain an architectural flourish with every third capped cupola?" she asked.

"No, the architectural flourishes are distributed via a randomized algorithm which runs on every third capped cupola. Whether or not you get one is up to fate."

"No use strategizing, then, is there?"

Listay's face scrunched with grief. "None at all, I'm afraid."

"And I'd guess you've been trying to strategize."

Listay nodded sadly.

"Great."

There was only one other chair, so May sat on the corner of the desk and tried (and failed) to differentiate the three-dimensional playing field from a ball of tangled twine. She would have to rely on Listay's strategy, or, rather, she would have to rely on throwing off Listay's strategy to re-introduce the element of luck.

"Just because I want you to win so badly, you can start this time, General." Wuthck drank deeply from the cider bottle as if purposefully trying to cloud his own judgement.

Listay typed her move into the control panel and showed it to May for confirmation. There was no confirmation to be had. May tsked, shook her head, and changed one of the three numbers in the suggested coordinates.

"But I-"

"You were losing," May reminded her.

With no recourse, Listay sent the coordinates, and her figure moved to its new position. Wuthck moved his figure, and Listay suggested another move which May, again, negated. And then Wuthck moved, and then Listay tried to move only to be corrected by May again, and then Wuthck moved again and so on for what felt like a horrible eternity to Listay whose every plan was being ripped from her.

She barely looked at what May was doing now, just typed in something random and handed the disc over to May to be destroyed.

"No, this one's good."

"What?"

"That's a good move. Send it," May said.

Listay swallowed. "You're joking?"

"I'm serious! It's a good move. Go ahead."

Listay eyed her nervously, waiting for her to drop the punch line and tell her to change the coordinates. May smiled an encouraging smile, so Listay played.

Within four moves, Wuthck knew he was beat. His technique of absolute random choice could not compete with a carefully planned strategy seasoned with a pinch of chaos.

"Cap my cupola," said Listay as she claimed her first win against the police sergeant.

"Our cupola," May corrected.

"Fair win. Here's your BEAPER, General." Wuthck dug through his desk and tossed the BEAPER back to Listay. She quickly scrolled through her notifications. Mostly regarding sales on gardening tools, the latest conspiracy theory surrounding the mysterious salt field in the South, and several updates on her life-status which read 'No update to report.' One message stood out from the rest, though. Or rather, one set of messages.

All from Xan's BEAPER. Most of them were from Aimz (meaning most of them were lewd), but the last three were definitely Xan.

"Fish is really starting to zux with me, watch out for it."

"Scratch what I said about the fish." and "Have you ever noticed how finger joints only bend in one direction but your knuckles can bend all over the place? That's weird, right? What's the deal with fingers? What's the deal with joints, honestly? There's got to be a better way. I wager Aimz could figure out a better way to do the whole finger-hand-joint thing."

"Where did you leave him?" Listay asked May, knowing she would know who she was referring to and cautious about saying anything that might get the Scourge Authority set on them.

"Out back. We've got to go."

"Yes, I would say so." She turned back to Wuthck. "Well, Wuthck, it wasn't a pleasure and I hope I never see you again, buddy."

"Same to you, General. Stay away from the constables until you're on the right side of the veil again, eh?"

"I'll do my best."

The moment they were outside the police station's outdoor security system perimeter, Listay stopped May. "Where's Aimz, and why did you and Xan come back? Also, are you hungry?"

"She's safe at the orchard; Ix and Yvonne are running their experiments on her. I got a lead that Carmnia might have a cure, so I decided to come back to find her, and Xan tagged along. I left him in the alley. And I'm a little hungry, yeah."

Listay produced from one of her pockets a vegetable wrap she was keeping handy in case May needed food. May ate it gratefully as they rounded the corner to the alley.

TWENTY-SIX

LOOKING FORWARD TO NOTHING

* * * * *

There was, May had calculated, a seventy-five percent chance that Xan would still be in the alley where she put him. Not awful odds. In his right mind, there was a ninety percent chance he would stay put, but he was currently in his left mind, and that lowered the figure just a bit.

The hairs on May's arms prickled as they approached the alley, an electrical impermanence in the air. She dropped the figure to fifty percent. Something was decidedly wrong here, but it wasn't that Xan was missing. He sat cross legged in the mud, staring pointedly at the Big Mouth Billy Bass in his lap.

"Listay!" Xan flung the bass aside and launched at Listay to wrap his arms around her. "Good to see you again! I'll be honest, we're in desperate need of your help. Can't recall why. All I know is-Oh! Right, of course. We need your help finding Carmnia. The fish told us to. I mean...well...as it turns out the fish wasn't the fish, it was—" He froze as if paused by an invisible remote control.

"It was...?" May prompted.

He shook into play again. "It was what?" he asked.

"You said it wasn't the fish."

"Oh, right, heh." He laughed nervously. "Yeah. As it happens, we don't really need the fish anymore. I mean, I got the thing that was in the fish out of the fish."

"Xan." Listay locked her hands around his upper arms. "What was in the fish?"

He bit his lip and tried to keep Chaos down, but it was like trying to keep down expired shellfish. Rather than the green gleam of scourge in his eyes, Listay now saw something a great deal more unmentionable. May saw it, too.

"Well, aren't you looking *alive*, Listay," said Chaos, creasing Xan's face into a malicious grin.

"Excuse me?" Listay was fairly certain she knew what she was dealing with, but she hoped that being polite to the situation might make it go away.

"Listay, mun, don't you remember me? We used to be so..." Chaos forced Xan to lick his lips seductively. He had never been forced to do that before, and he had never hated doing it so much. "Close."

Listay flung Xan into the side of a refuse bin and bent its rusted metal handle backward, holding him there like a scientific specimen on a display board. May couldn't decide whose side she was on until Listay grabbed a busted bottle from the ally and held it to Xan's neck.

"Whoa! Geez! Don't kill him!" May got between the two and pushed Listay back. Listay eased up with May in front of her.

"That's not Xan," Listay said, seeing only the eyes of the creature that had murdered her.

"I've been smoking not-cigarettes on NotTuhnt long enough to know when something ought to be defined by what it isn't. When you were possessed, were you not-Listay? When Yvonne was possessed, was she not-Yvonne? When Sonan...no, forget Sonan. Point is, don't hurt Xan. It won't defeat Chaos anyway," May said, then peered back at Xan to look for some sign that she was right. He glowered unmentionably. May shivered.

"Listen to her, Listay. If you kill this host, I'll just find another one. You enjoyed our time together, didn't you?" said Chaos, lounging in the dent Xan's body had made in the side of the refuse bin.

Rather than respond, Listay motioned to speak with May in private.

"Alright. How did you defeat Chaos before, on Earth?" Listay whispered.

May opened her mouth to answer, but her mind was preoccupied with the seeping anxiety that Xan was well and truly lost, so it took a moment for her to recall that particular plot line. "Black-hole thing, when we destroyed the star drive. It was supposed to vacuum her up."

"M-hmm, and it didn't. How did we defeat her after that?"

"Sonan deleted her, I guess," May said. Listay had been there. May was starting to get the feeling Listay was being rhetorical, and she supposed she deserved it after her own rhetorical tirade a moment ago.

"So that rules out sucking her into a black hole and deleting her. How do you expect to defeat her this time? Because she always finds a way back."

"You're the strategist!"

"Chaos doesn't follow strategy. Chaos is like Belvedere Masters. The more you try to make sense of her, the less sense she makes."

May tried to lean casually against the brick wall, but jolted off it when the trapped heat sizzled her skin. Trying to look casual had failed, so she looked on-edge instead. "It's Xan. What's the worst he could do?"

"But it isn't Xan anymore; it's Chaos, and all she wants to do is destroy us."

"That's not entirely true," Xan interjected.

Obviously, his hearing was better than they had anticipated.

"Is that you or Chaos?" May approached him.

"It's me! It's me! Chaos knew you wouldn't listen to her, and I was able to put her away again. It's me."

May sighed, warring with whether or not to trust him. There was only one way of truly knowing who was at the reins.

"What was the first English pun I taught you?"

"Oh, that I'm a very cunning linguist," he said with a smile. "And it's true, I am."

May yanked the handle out of the bin and threw it aside, freeing him. "What's Chaos planning?"

Xan rubbed his bruised neck as he tried to work out what exactly he and Chaos had discussed. He knew it had been poignant. He knew it had been important. He knew it had made him feel that everything was somehow cosmically right with the world, even in the midst of everything being wrong. This is what he said:

"Right, so, you know how 'I Love Lucy' is always reset at the beginning? How no matter what sticky situation she gets into—quite a few of them literally sticky—everything is back to normal at the start of the next episode? That's what Chaos wants. She said Carmnia could do that. Or had the key to that or something. I don't know the specifics, but she said that Carmnia could cure me and then give Chaos the reset."

"Reset to what?" May asked.

"Nothingness?" Xan offered, realizing that it might not be the best hand to play in the debate.

May had to chew on that one. Nothing wasn't actually nothing, for in being nothing, it would necessarily be *some*thing. Or perhaps she just couldn't actually get her head around Nothingness, so she stopped trying.

"That's not good, is it?" May asked.

"It's not bad. It's just nothing," Xan said with a resigned shrug. "Maybe Carmnia can clear it up! I'm not as sharp as I once was on account of, you know, mushroom face." He winked as if it were an inside joke between them.

To May, it felt more like an inside tragedy, but she played along. There was no point thinking about how he once was, because there was no going back. They would muscle onward toward something. Or nothing.

"Alright, let's get to Carmnia."

While they walked, taking as many back streets and hidden alleys as they could, toward Snoodark's Folly on the edge of town, Xan thought it might be nice to talk to someone else who had been possessed by Chaos. Not

Listay, though. She was still mad at him. He messaged Yvonne.

"Any tips on suppressing an ancient evil trying to invade your brain? Or an evil fungus? Or anything? Any tips at all would help right now. Hear any good jokes lately?"

Her reply dinged in moments later, no hint that she was surprised to hear from them after they ran away, no hint that she was at all shocked by the return of Chaos. "Here's a tip: Chaos can be deceptively easy to control at first. She lets you think you've got the helm to get you off your guard. Here's a joke: Chaos absolutely destroyed my sense of humor, so watch out for that, too."

A brief pause, then.

"That's the joke?!"

"Oh, no I suppose that wasn't funny, was it?"

"Zuut, you weren't kidding."

"No, I rarely do anymore."

TWENTY-SEVEN

THE AGE OF GIFT SHOPS

* * * * *

It is a well-known fact that the establishment of gift shops marks a socio-economic turning point in civilization. When a society passes into the Gift Shop Age, it heralds an era of maximalism and sets off a chain of events so staggeringly wasteful, several subsequent eras are typically spent mitigating the volume of detritus created in the Gift Shop Age. In brief, these ages are referred to as the 'Storage Unit Age,' the 'Thrift Shop Age' and, finally, the 'Planet-Sized Ball of Trash Sent into Orbit For Future Generations to Deal With Age.'

A staggering percentage of the garbage a Gift Shop Age creates is plastic keychains.

NotTuhnt was no different, and gift shops had been in vogue for the past century.

One such gift shop belonged to Snoodark's Folly. The entrance was a brilliant concrete archway which had been carved into the shape of four handsome Tuhntians nakedly lifting a curving gnarled tree trunk laden with mushrooms.

Beyond it, sliding glass doors stated that the Folly's

hours were one to ten that day. May checked the time on Xan's BEAPER and wondered, as everyone does at some point in their life regardless of how civilized they are, if perhaps they would make an exception and stay open a touch later today on their account.

The doors opened, as if by magic, when they stepped on the control mat. May mused that just over a year ago, she would've been amazed by such technology, but now it seemed ordinary to her. She then realized that it seemed so ordinary because automatic sliding glass doors had existed on Earth since the 1960s.

They entered glistening rows of perfectly placed ceramic mugs, towers of neatly folded shirts, and aisle upon aisle of plastic name keychains. Immediately, as was his custom, Xan rushed to the X-names section, directly between the C-names and the Kiblot-names. May joined him, trying to figure out where M-names would appear in the Tuhntian alphabet. The answer, of course, was nowhere. M-names are not keychain appropriate.

"Zux it," said Xan, studying the line of keychains. "Who in the universe is named Xon?"

"Xon is," May said, searching behind the many "Xon" keychains to see if a "Xan" was mixed up in there.

Giving up, they looked over the generic keychains. 'Carmnia's alright' or 'Quanzar Bless Carmnia. She needs it' or 'Carmnians aren't complete trok lickers' were the more popular styles, nearly sold out. 'I survived Snoodark's Folly' and 'I believe in Snoodark' were also quite popular. Plenty of keychains which read 'I <3 a Carmnian' remained, however, and Xan snagged one.

"I'm going to get you this one for the *Audacity*'s anchor button!" Xan said, holding it up to her cheerfully, the metal bit which was meant to slip onto an anchor button dangling below.

The sound May made as she tried to decide how to respond was like the air being pressed from a sealed zip-lock bag. What good would it do either of them to remind him that they no longer had the *Audacity* or its anchor buttons? Exactly none. She went along with it.

"I don't know, Blueberry. Isn't it illegal to lie on a plastic keychain?"

"It's just a small fine."

"In that case-*oof!*"

The 'oof' was in reference to Listay slamming into both of them and stuffing them beneath a t-shirt display table.

"Scourge Authority," was all she said before dropping the tablecloth and plunging them into a darkness lit only by the green glow of Xan's eye fungus.

"Damnit," whispered May.

"Whom?" whispered Xan.

"Jellymint?" whispered a third.

A hand had been thrust between Xan and May in the darkness, two round jellymints sitting in its palm.

The pair screamed in unison and rolled out from under the table, their retreat halted by two armored legs. They looked up and, again, screamed in unison at a faceless Scourge Authority helmet.

"There you are!" the agent replied.

"Here I am!" affirmed Xan.

May swung her arm into the back of the agent's knee and used the momentum to roll herself in front of Xan. Listay took advantage of May's befuddling if ineffective move and stole the agent's ray gun, pinning them to the table and toppling a tower of tees.

Now the agent's Proton Fusion Ray 6000 was pointed at their own chest, and they raised their hands in surrender. "Whoa, hold on, I'm here to help," they said and removed the helmet, shaking out a waterfall of silver hair.

"Do you work for Carmnia?" Listay asked.

The agent threw their head back on the ruined pile of shirts and laughed. It was a warm laugh, familiar, a laugh that made the spots on their gray-blue cheeks squish up into their eyes.

"Well some might say that, sure. But no, really. I'm one of her consorts. Yulquitz!" They held out a hand to her despite one of her hands being occupied with the ray gun and the other smashing their shoulder into the table.

She let them stand up, but kept the ray gun poised, markedly ignoring their outstretched hand until they instead used it to casually scratch their head.

From the storage room, someone else in Scourge Authority armor, but un-helmeted, barreled out, joining Yulquitz.

"Hurmbert!" Yulquitz addressed him with a slap on his dinner-plate sized bicep. Yulquitz was not a small person, but they could have easily perched on the shoulders of the second agent who had the build of an industrial refrigerator. "Look!" Yulquitz pointed excitedly at Xan. "It's one of mine! He's got my spots; isn't that precious? Write that down, will you? Finally found a spotty Carmnian."

Hurmbert pulled a tiny pad of paper from his utility belt and plucked a pen from behind his ear to write it down.

"You know, I was beginning to think all my offspring had perished in the *accident*."

"Are you a Scourge Authority agent or not?" Listay asked.

"Both!" Yulquitz casually put a hand over Listay's, forcing her, gently, to lower the gun. They smiled broadly and clapped a hand to her back. "The Scourge Authority was disbanded on account of all of them being dead. But, if you've got scourged Carmnians, you need a Scourge Authority, so the other consorts and I decided we would do it our way rather than let the police set up a task force." They turned toward Xan and put a warning finger to his chest. "Never trust a task force, alright, larvling?"

"What is 'your way,' then?" Listay pressed. She had lowered the gun but hadn't turned it off.

"Glad you asked!" Yulquitz rolled out a white board from behind the keychain display, pulled open a dry erase marker with their teeth, and drew an arrow pointing to the only complete sentence on the board. "Step one deviates from the original authority's method in that we don't immediately kill a scourged Carmnian. Step two," they added a second arrow, pointing to nothing, then a hurried question mark next to it, "is being workshopped! We're thinking something along the lines of a welcome party. Something that says 'Yes, you're our prisoner, but in a *fun* and *cheery* way.' Turns out, it's a hard sentiment to celebrate. What color frosting do you use? I think magenta, but Prismuntial insists it's got to be peach."

"No, no, no," said a willowy Tuhntian with softly wrinkled skin who pulled herself from underneath the t-shirt table. "No cakes. Cake is too polarizing. Jellymints are the least offensive treat. Everyone loves jellymints. Jellymint, anyone?" she asked, holding out her hand, this time with exactly five jellymints in it.

Yulquitz rubbed their forehead. "MeMuddle, no one apart from you likes jellymints. We aren't trying to torture them. That's what the old authority did."

She popped all five jellymints into her mouth and chewed them thoughtfully. "Cake is still too polarizing," she affirmed.

"Alright, we'll scrap the celebration idea and come up with something different for step two, but step three is still the cure!" Yulquitz said, and drew a wobbling sort of amoeba shape on the white board, then paused, added some lines bursting excitingly forth from it, paused again, then drew a happy face in the center of it. They smiled at the joyful image of the cure.

"You have one?" May asked.

"Well, uh, no, not yet." Yulquitz's smile drooped, and they drew a massive 'X' over the happy cure. "We've been seriously considering one, though."

"Brainstorming," said Hurmbert, helpfully.

"Yes! That's the word. So far, our best guess has been fermented hooflatoo milk, right in the eyes. Sounds like a winner, right? I think that's a winner."

"It sounds great in theory, sure, but we tried that already. It doesn't work," said Xan. Something about seeing the happy little cure on the whiteboard then having it dashed into four pieces by the 'X' had unsettled him. It was an ominous doodle.

"I see," said Yulquitz, the undercurrent of jolliness ebbing for the span of a single word before surging back. "We've got plenty more ideas we can test now that you're here!"

"Why," May intercepted, "do you have a ray gun if you're not trying to kill anyone?"

"It's set to stun! Scourged Carmnians can be exceedingly dangerous."

"I'm not dangerous!" Xan said.

Yulquitz smiled fondly at him. "Of course you aren't, but you're one of mine. Prismuntial's are the worst. Don't tell her I said that, though. She's self-conscious about it."

"What do you mean by one of yours?" asked May.

"One of my brood! He's my precious little larvae broodling all grown up!" Yulquitz, seized with affection for their offspring, pushed Listay aside and pulled Xan into a smothering bear-hug. Xan let them do it, hanging limply in Yulquitz's arms until they at last released him and surprise attacked May, cupping their hands around her face. "Is this your partner?"

"I'm his case worker," she said, pulling away.

"Wait, I thought I was supposed to be *your* case worker," Xan whispered.

"Only on Wednesdays," she replied out of the corner of her mouth.

His voice went still lower. "May, we...we don't have Wednesdays here."

"Precisely," she whispered with a wink.

"They're friends. That's just how they talk," Listay assured a confused Yulquitz. "We're here to see Carmnia about the scourge." Listay glanced at Xan for a moment, considering whether to say anything about Chaos or not, but decided to tackle one issue at a time.

"Aw, don't worry mun." Yulquitz slung an arm around Xan's shoulders. "We'll get you fixed up. We've got a whole wall full of ideas. We've got a roomful of wallfuls!"

May suddenly remembered waffles. The last time she'd had a waffle had been exactly three years ago today, though she couldn't know it. It had come from Margery's Cafe, a mom-and-pop around the corner from her apartment. It had been lukewarm and flaccid.

"Any of those ideas involve injecting fungicide into my eyes?" Xan asked, dispersing May's waffle fantasies.

"Oh, yeah, sure, a few of them," said Yulquitz.

"No," May said. "We're here to see Carmnia about the scourge, not to experiment. Where is she?"

Yulquitz's seemingly unsquashable enthusiasm squished, and Hurmbert took over in a low, gentle voice.

"We haven't seen her in almost an orbit. She said she had family matters to attend to and disappeared. We assumed it had something to do with the scourge. You were part of her last brood, you know?" Hurmbert told Xan. "Even she was ashamed of how much the ophiocordyceps mushrooms she consumed had affected you lot. She insisted they were good for her health. Wouldn't even let me cook the zuxing things. I still think I could've sautéed the horror out."

"Bert, you can't sautée the horror out of everything," Yulquitz said.

"I sautéed the horror out of the smurbels."

"Mmmm," Yulquitz hummed doubtfully. "They still had a horrific aftertaste."

"That was the cilantro," Hurmbert said.

Listay stepped in to refocus them. "Where do you suspect Carmnia went?" Listay asked.

"No way of knowing," Yulquitz mused.

"Oh, she's back at the Folly," said someone who peeled back the curtain behind the register and slunk against the counter to remove her helmet and coif her voluminous pink hair back into its characteristic puffs. This was Prismuntial, but she made a habit of never introducing herself.

"What? As of when? Why?" asked Yulquitz.

She used Yulquitz's armored shoulder to check her reflection. "A couple rotations. Said her vacation home flooded. Or did it burn? Could it do both? It might have been both... Ask her yourself."

"You didn't tell me!" their voice cracked into a higher register.

"I just did," she said.

"Right, yeah, but you should've told me when it happened."

"Why?"

"Be-because I'm her head consort."

"You are not; MeMuddle is."

"Fine. Did you tell MeMuddle?"

"No," said Prismuntial with a delicate little shrug.

Yulquitz rubbed the space between their eyes, softening

the muscles that had tensed up. "Alright, let's go find her. Where in the folly, exactly?"

"Dunno. Wherever there's a drink, I'd wager. Keep this between you and me and," she paused to count the surrounding crowd, "the other five, but I think she's got a bit of a problem."

"She has a lot of problems, and we're about to bring her more. This one's got the scourge." Yulquitz nodded toward Xan who waved shyly.

"Yeah, I know; that's the one that tried to kill Hurmbert and me the other day. And you always said mine scourged the worst. Ha!" Prismuntial's laugh was like a single ring of a small bell.

There was no use, thought Xan, in trying to defend himself. He had been accused of much worse than trying to kill two Scourge Authority agents.

Yulquitz slid Xan an apologetic grimace then clapped their hands together. "I'll give the tour! Can't enter the Folly without a tour. Sincerely, it's extremely difficult to find the entrance. You three come with me, to the CarryCraft. The rest of you get this place cleaned up, just in case Carmnia wants to see it."

"She's never seen it!" Prismuntial whined. "Why would she want to now?"

"Because we're going to clean it up! She'll want to see it someday, and when that day comes, it ought to be sparkling. Off to it!" Yulquitz said, flourishing their hands until the other consorts slowly began to collect fallen t-shirts. Yulquitz turned around and grinned at May, Xan and Listay. "Follow me to the Queen!" they began marching out to the door at the back of the gift shop and the trio followed.

"I can see where you got your leadership skills," May whispered to Xan.

"Oh, yes, it's unendingly difficult to suppress them. But you seem to enjoy being in the lead so much, I have made a great effort to do so," Xan whispered back.

May snickered. "It's appreciated."

TWENTY-EIGHT

HISTORICAL INTERLUDE

* * * * *

Rhea I is a large planet with plenty of perfectly cromulent continents upon which to build cities. Temperate continents, continents with seasons, continents that are expansive and fertile and just generally far more suited to supporting intelligent life than the island upon which NotTuhnt was founded.

Snoodark the Damp, an ancient Rhean explorer who lived thousands of orbits before the civilization of NotTuhnt existed, wasn't satisfied with temperate climates and seasons and fertile lands. He lived by the philosophy that nothing good ever comes easy, and so he made his short life as difficult as possible in an effort to live well.

His search for a difficult life led him to the island where, it is said, he built for himself a mansion, stone by stone, with no help nor actual knowledge of how to build such a thing.

The mansion leaked, it was freezing cold in half the rooms and oppressively humid in the other half, it smelled like wet dog, required daily repairs, and proved to be about the most difficult thing anyone had accomplished on the planet of Rhea I since reaching complete environmental sustainability. It was totally unlivable.

Snoodark was thrilled.

This, thought Snoodark, must be good.

Every great philosopher goes through an ascetic phase. Some survive it, and some don't. Just a few short seasons after completing his masterpiece, Snoodark died of an easily curable lung infection.

TWENTY-NINE

SNOODARK'S FOLLY

* * * * *

Yulquitz, Listay, May, and Xan all gathered around the Carry-Craft which looked, to May, like a hovering golf cart. There was a thin bench in the front, a second thin bench in the back, and an aluminum roof which had partially rusted. It bobbed askew, the front left corner occasionally dipping to touch the ground, then lifting up slightly, then touching down again.

"Everyone in!" Yulquitz said cheerfully, hopping into the front seat. Convinced that Yulquitz was harmless, or at least meant well, Listay gave back their ray gun and sat beside them as Xan and May scrunched into the back seat.

Yulquitz twisted their thumb into the Carry-Craft's dashboard. It had two modes, Stop and Go, and nothing to steer with. Instead, it followed a line of wire embedded into the ground which sent it from the gift shop to Snoodark's Folly and back relatively quickly, despite the front corner which sparked as it dragged across the concrete.

As they approached, the folly loomed over the trees, and

Yulquitz gave the well-practiced, rarely used, tour speech.

"If you look to your right, folks, you'll see the tallest gable of Snoodark's Folly swooping majestically over the trees. This gable is not an original feature; it was built in NotTuhnt orbit 137. The construction was overseen by Carmnia's extremely attractive consorts who felt it just looked more dramatic to have something appear over the trees. The upper levels are completely unfinished inside, as no one typically wants to stay in the folly long enough to make it up there.

"One of the many unusual facts about Snoodark's Folly is that seventy percent of the structure exists underground, making it the only private connection from Downtown to Uptown on the island. A service entrance was built at the edge of Downtown for Carmnia's many servants, butlers, and attendants who reside in repurposed shipping containers below our very feet. Consorts like myself are free to live in the above ground structure. We just don't want to. Which is why we spend most of our time in the gift shop."

May tapped Xan's arm to get his attention; he was watching the trees whizzing by with great interest. "Hey, do you think Milly works for Carmnia?" she whispered.

"No. Why, do you?"

"Have you been listening to the tour?"

"Oh! Uh, yes. Yeah. And you think Milly works for Carmnia because..."

"Milly lives Downtown in a shipping container complex. Yulquitz just said that's where Carmnia's staff lives."

"Right, yeah, but Milly's never worked an orbit in her life. She's a layabout! Kinda like me. Or I suppose, since she raised me, I'm like her." He curled his lip, disgusted at himself for taking after Milly in this respect.

"If she doesn't work, how does she get gem?"

Xan puzzled on it. Aunt Milly had always just had money; he never questioned why or how, exactly. It just existed. And she spent it wildly, too. Vacations, food, tchotchkes, more food... "I don't know, actually."

Their conversation was cut short as the Carry-Craft screeched to a halt in front of a massive arch which appeared to be carved into the shape of several tall, naked beings groping each other.

"And here we are!" Yulquitz said, turning the craft off but remaining seated. "The arch was commissioned in NotTuhnt orbit eighty-two as a testament to Carmnia's mass sexual appeal. The banner above the arch, though now faded, once read 'Carmnia: The Zuxine Queen' and represents the period of Queen Carmnia's life which historians refer to as the Great Mid-Life Crisis. Notice the cluster of mummified—"

"Cease this blithering and get on with it!" Xan said in a tone of voice he had never once in his life taken. It sounded like he was doing a marvelous impression of Gloria Swanson in Sunset Boulevard. Chaos had never been in control of a body quite this theatrical, and she had to admit she was enjoying it. She made him grab the railing between the back and front seats and glare at Yulquitz.

Yulquitz looked hurt. "Is that a symptom of the scourge?"

May shook her head. "It's a side plot. He's also possessed by a chaos goddess."

"*The* Chaos goddess, Tiny Human May. The singular and most powerful. I am the Beginning and the End and Most of the Stuff in the Middle. Everything except IKEA. I demand to—remember the time Lucy needed five hundred dollars for some charity event and she and Ethel dressed up as caricatured aliens for a publicity stunt to earn the money? At first, I was so offended. I mean, yes, sure, I've got a long nose, but zuut it's not *that* long. And they were just talking gibberish! Didn't even bother to learn a second language for the part. I watched it a few times; right, no, I lie, I watched it seventeen times, and eventually, I realized it was actually a masterful parody. Lucy really hit center mark with that one. The headpieces were a bit extravagant, but zux it if I didn't have an outfit near identical to hers for an act I used to do with Itkip—"

He went on.

No one was brave enough to stop him.

They all watched, mesmerized, loitering in front of the

yawning arch to the gardens as Xan dove into a flashback, tied it back into another episode of 'I Love Lucy,' ricocheted into an explanation of ancient neo-Panseen verb agreements (and heated noun disagreements), settled into a light musing on the validity of limericks in literature, ended with, "Great, she's zuxed off." and then breathed.

"You out-monologued Chaos," Listay said in fearful awe. "That's genius."

"Yeah. Yeah! I guess I can move 'incessant chattering' out of character flaws and into the special skills category. Neat!" He smiled broadly for the first time in a while, and May joined him. She needed something to smile about.

"Good work, 'genius,'" she said in a tone that was so mocking it circled back around to being affectionate.

"Thanks!" This was the closest anyone had ever come to calling him a genius in a way which wasn't entirely mean-spirited, and he appreciated it.

Yulquitz finally dismounted the ailing Carry-Craft.

"Right, well, that was odd. Now, everyone out, and please stick together as we enter the gardens. The hostas can be a tad bite-y, and the last time I was here alone, a rogue fern got fresh with me." Yulquitz led them through the encroaching garden on a narrow stone path to the entrance of the folly. No door appeared there, just a solid wall of rust-colored, fleshy tendrils which curled around each other.

"Just walk straight on through the creneli mushroom barrier, please; it won't hurt you," Yulquitz said, then chose a section of the fleshy wall which appeared to be slightly looser than the rest and pushed through it, breaking off chunks of the mushroom which fell to the stone steps and slowly bled a sticky-white goo. Listay pushed her way in, but Xan's BEAPER dinged just before he had the pleasure of breaking through the mushroom wall, and he and May stood outside the structure to read the message.

"Do not attempt to remove the fungus manually," was all it said. It had come from Yvonne's BEAPER, but it sounded more like something Ix would say.

"Wasn't planning to. What happened?" Xan whispered into his BEAPER; he didn't want Listay to overhear. They waited, but there was no reply.

"The mushrooms won't hurt you," Yulquitz said, popping their head out of the creneli wall. "Well, these won't, at least. Other mushrooms will, but not these. Come on in!"

Upon entering the Folly, two things became clear. The first was that more spiders than people called the folly home, and the second was that there was a mold problem. The entire interior blossomed with spores. The only life this place seemed equipped to nurture was vegetal. If Carmnia was, in fact, here, she wasn't exactly living in Queenly comfort.

A heavy silence hung in the Folly, the kind of silence that falls in a forest when a predator is nearby, and an even heavier darkness hung from the rafters high above.

No one moved.

No one breathed.

"Snoodark's Folly," Yulquitz trumpeted cheerily, "is the oldest standing structure on the island, and its age is placed at between five and six hundred orbits." They shattered the chilling spike of foreboding which had penetrated the party. "It's longevity is often attributed to the organic matter which has replaced much of the original material and created a living architecture which grows like a skin atop the original building's bones. A self-sustaining ecosystem in the exact shape of the original Folly. This natural historic perseveration retains the Folly's characteristic shape with little need for upkeep."

Their voice seemed to be absorbed by the soft growth on the foyer walls as they led the group to a bay of telediscs circling the foyer's centerpiece, a gray-green topiary which depicted a haughty-looking blob. "Excuse the state of the Queen Carmnia topiary, if you will. Since Carmnia left, we haven't bothered to pay the gardener, and since we haven't bothered to pay him, he hasn't bothered to work."

Here Yulquitz paused, awaiting the polite chuckle of a group of tourists acknowledging that a joke had been told. The polite chuckle didn't come. Yulquitz frowned, considering whether or not to repeat it. Deciding against it (for fear that the group would, once again, ignore his quip), Yulquitz ushered them to the teledisc bay. "If everyone will please stand on one of the telediscs, we will begin the tour from the top of the Folly and work our way down. One adult to a teledisc, please."

"We don't want a tour; we want to find Carmnia," May told them quietly so as to not embarrass them in front of the others.

"Right, sure, but the best way to do that is to search the entire Folly top to bottom, innit? So enjoy the tour, larvling!" Yulquitz patted her back and stepped on their own teledisc. The group fizzled away.

THIRTY

HORNTAGGLER

* * * * *

The party remerged in a thick, gravity-less blackness. Oxygen-less, too. There was nothing. No light, no air, no mass aside from the four beings lost in the darkness.

One of the beings had bioluminescent mushrooms in his eyes which illuminated the other three beings. Xan looked to Yulquitz, sharing just enough light to allow Yulquitz to fiddle with their BEAPER until a proper environment whipped around them, settling with a splat like a wet towel.

It was still dark but purposefully so, as if this darkness had been tastefully placed there. Two massive chandeliers dipped from the ceiling which bowed in the middle of the long room, and a steady drip of mysterious fluid, too rank and thick to be merely water, created a stalactite pointing to a stretched dining table that was polished to a fine shine by the constant dripping. Candles flickered in rows of candelabras along the length of the table, glinting off gilt damasks in the wallpaper which seemed to have grown across the wall organically. Upon closer inspection, the candles were actually tapering lumps of mineral which spurted ignited gases from their tips, closer to delicate, miniature volcanoes than proper candles. It seemed as if Mother Nature had seen someone design a Baroque dining hall and decided she could do it better herself.

May, who hadn't been expecting the oxygen to suddenly disappear, and who rather needed oxygen to support her breathing habit, gasped in gulps of heady air.

Yulquitz and Listay, who had kicked the oxygen habit several evolutionary phases back, watched her with curious concern. Xan was used to it and rubbed her back in a way he hoped was comforting.

Noticing their stares, she tried to downplay her struggle, quietly slurping in as much air as she could. The air was thick with humidity and mold spores, and this in no way helped her in her quest to re-oxygenate herself.

"Where are we?" is what she tried to say. It came out more like: "*Wheeze* are *wheeze.*"

But Yulquitz had a sharp mind and filled in the blanks. "Oh, that's easy! We are perpetual beings made mortal to learn the lesson of impermanence."

"I-wha-no," May stuttered. "'*Where* are we?' Not 'what are we?' Although, I have to say, your answer is a lot better than-" May jazz-handed at Xan.

Xan looked horribly offended. "Yulquitz is my dad! They're a great deal older than me. Of course they've got more of a handle on what life's about."

It was Yulquitz's turn to look horribly offended. "Not a great deal older, no! Why, I was only two hundred and a quarter when I had you."

Listay, having died and felt it was nothing particularly special, was wary of philosophical questions and turned their minds, instead, to something more pressing. "Why did the telediscs glitch?"

"Now that *is* strange," Yulquitz said, fiddling with settings on their BEAPER, then looking up at the caving ceiling as if they could see through it to the other side. "That is very strange," they mused again.

"Is it stable?" Listay asked, also watching the ceiling which creaked as if in reply.

"Oh, very! Hasn't collapsed yet, has it? No. No, it hasn't.

The thing which is strange is that this isn't our intended destination. We're a floor below the highest floor in the dining hall. The telediscs up there rejected us. Must be out of order."

"We'll take the stairs, then," May said, heading for the massive pair of doors at the far end.

"Whoa, whoa." Yulquitz grabbed her shoulders and held her back. "If the telediscs are out of order up there, Carmnia certainly isn't there either. Besides, the upper floor is…"

He trailed off, staring again at the ceiling silently as if waiting for it to spring to life.

"Is what?" May asked.

He looked back down at her, distant concern still wandering across his face. "Creepy. No matter, though! Here we are in the Grand Dining Hall! In the original Folly, records indicate that this space may have been an exercise room, which would explain the chains embedded in the walls at regular intervals."

"That's one explanation," Xan agreed, eyeing a thick rusted chain that grew from the wall and dangled half-way to the floor. He had never exercised intentionally, so far be it from him to say what did and did not look like an exercise room. Still, this did not look like an exercise room.

Again, the ceiling creaked as if it were about to collapse under its own weight and, though no one admitted to concern, the group half-jogged to the far end where the ceiling was highest.

"Right, no one go upstairs, okay? Stay together as a group. Everyone stay together, and don't go upstairs," Yulquitz whispered, then grabbed hold of the touch-bar on the massive doors which unlocked and dissolved away. This led the group into a windowless hallway, and once everyone had exited, Yulquitz twisted the touch-bar back into place, and the doors reappeared. The tour-guide grandeur returned to Yulquitz's manner. "The next stop is the Marsupian Lounge across the hall. Queen Carmnia spends most of her time at the Folly drinking in the Marsupian Lounge, so I think we've a good chance at getting a look at her in there!" Yulquitz said as if Carmnia were an elusive critter they were hoping to spot.

The hallway, though lined in gilt crown molding and hung with stuffy paintings of important historical Carmnians, gave one the impression that they had been swallowed by an enormous snake. The walls, softened with organic growth, had worn away such that the metal structure of the building could be seen, wrapping like ribs around them as they traveled, single file due to the constricting nature of the hallway, toward a swirling holodoor at the far end. The holodoor swirled because the humidity in the Folly had seeped into its casing and rusted the mechanism so that it spluttered and swam as it tried, and failed, to retain its solidity.

But that wasn't what made the hallway so unsettling.

It helped, certainly. But what clinched it was this:

A rhythmic thumping. Growing, quickening.

The group looked about before all agreeing, silently, that the thumping came from the staircase opposite the holodoor.

Yulquitz moved between the group and the oncoming sound, aware that it was either Carmnia or something horrifically dangerous. Quite possibly both.

Listay stood, ready to assist, behind Yulquitz. May and Xan enjoyed their relative lack of responsibility and slowly backed down the hall. Not enough to utterly desert Listay and Yulquitz to their fates but enough to give the clear impression that in a fight or flight situation, they would pick the latter.

A curious cuckoo preceded the next creaking step.

"Blitheon's stars, she escaped the aviary," Yulquitz said in an appalled whisper and began to push Listay back.

"Who did?" Listay hissed.

"Chuzoople, Carmnia's prized horntaggler. She'll kill us."

"Who, Chuzoople or Carmnia?" asked May.

"First Chuzoople, then Carmnia."

They were now all pressed against the busted holodoor, but it refused to open.

"God, it would be embarrassing to be killed by

something named Chuzoople," May said.

"Not at all," Yulquitz said. "It's difficult to be embarrassed when you're dead, and Chuzoople is the nastiest horntaggler in the aviary. That bird's responsible for the deaths of twelve of Carmnia's attendants and the resignations of all the rest," they added, an air of practiced tour-guide cadence weaseling back into their hushed voice.

A horntaggler isn't so much a bird as it is a sensation of dread wrapped in stringy muscles and decorated with neither feathers nor fur but fine downy 'furthers' which fluff out around its neck like a doomful feather boa.

Millions of orbits ago, the horntaggler briefly evolved hands but quickly backtracked, leaving the creature with six vestigial arms which ended in useless, clawing grey fingers. The species has never lived down the shame of this horrific misstep and has nearly embarrassed itself to extinction.

The creature appeared at the end of the hall now. Its mass expanded to fill the hallway, feathers unfurling into the crepuscular yellow light to reveal its weapon of choice, a sharpened bone bayonet protruding like a periscope from its beak.

"Graw?" Chuzoople asked, politely, it thought, for someone whose home had been intruded upon.

Rather than answer, Yulquitz pulled the ray gun from their belt and jammed it into the holodoor casing, severing the diodes with a single explosive blast.

"Graaww!" Chuzoople shouted at the intruder who had wrecked its lovely swirling door. It lunged toward Yulquitz bayonet first, underdeveloped fingers waggling gracelessly beneath the majestic canopy of its wings.

Yulquitz, in good tour guide fashion, waved Listay, May, and Xan through the holodoor first, but Chuzoople had no qualm with Listay, May, or Xan. They hadn't shot at its door. Yulquitz ducked under the initial attack and the creature's beak lodged itself in the wall.

"Arm yourselves!" Yulquitz shouted as they crawled out from under the beast, narrowly avoiding its thrashing talons, and somersaulted into the Wine Lounge. They rammed their body into an oozing credenza and slid it toward the doorway, leaving a trail of pink sludge.

May grabbed a near-empty bottle of shermel and slammed it on the counter to give it a jagged broken edge. Xan chose a splitter which sounds like a terrifically gruesome weapon but is, in fact, a kind of spoon constructed specifically for the task of splitting the toxic foam from the delicious liquid in a wildly expensive Porzalctu. It was therefore only threatening in that wielding one might give your opposition a fleeting feeling of fiscal inferiority.

Listay took one of the three decorative antique swords which hung on the wall. She observed May and Xan's choices with curiosity as the four of them gathered behind the bar, but the moment she imagined either of them with a sword, she understood the wisdom of it.

With a sucking plop, the horntaggler freed itself from the wall and made it clear that a credenza was a poor sort of defense against its boney bayonet which rendered the furniture unrecognizable with a single blow. A menacing cluck boiled in the creature's throat as it pushed through the sharp remains of the credenza and did a visual sweep of the lounge.

"How good is that thing's sense of smell?" Listay whispered to Yulquitz, trying to determine whether or not they had a chance of it just wandering away.

"Oh, it's terrible," Yulquitz assured her. "The bony protrusion through its beak absolutely destroys the horntaggler's ability to pick up a scent. They do, however, have exceptionally keen ears."

They looked up to find that Chuzoople had, in fact, heard them quite clearly and was hovering above the bar, eyeing them like an irresolute eyeing a buffet.

"There you are! We were just talking about you, buddy," Xan said, hopping up behind the bar as if a favorite customer had just walked in and asked for the usual.

By this, the horntaggler was confused. It reared back, briefly reconsidering whether it was the predator or prey as it watched Xan's face, trying to work out in its tiny brain if that was a smile or a baring of teeth.

"Aw, look at those little hands," Xan continued, holding out his own hand to the creature.

"What are you doing?" May whispered urgently, hoping he would have a coherent answer.

"Shake?" asked Xan, and lunged at one of the creature's many poorly formed hands with his own, grasping it tightly and wiggling it around a bit.

"Gar-raw?" asked Chuzoople, by which it meant: "Whom, me?"

The soft clatter of metal against metal distracted May from her concern for Xan's well-being. Yulquitz was gone; Listay was hunched over a hole in the wall just large enough for a body and gesturing wildly at May to follow her and, presumably, Yulquitz into it.

May looked again at Xan who was deftly mixing various liquids in a tumbler, staring the beast down as if daring it to attack the person who was making it a drink. The beast did not, it would seem, dare.

"Right, now try that," said Xan, setting a fluted glass in one of the creature's malformed hands.

Listay gently set the metal cover down, but Yulquitz was right behind it and held it up so he could see out of the opening as Listay crawled over to May and grabbed her hand in an attempt to physically lead her away from the danger. Earthlings, for such a fragile species, seemed to have an underdeveloped sense of self preservation. But she, too, paused to watch as the beast stared, transfixed, at the cocktail it had been given.

Time stretched like saltwater taffy on a pulling machine; it became stringy, it glistened, it smelled overwhelmingly of manufactured strawberries.

The horntaggler attempted to bring the glass to its beak and failed due to the weakness in its twig-like forearm. It attempted to bring its beak to the glass, but found its neck didn't quite stretch that way. Everyone watched. Had the horntaggler noticed this, it might have been embarrassed. Then again, the creature had no real sense of societal norms, so it might not have minded.

Maneuvering a downy wing under the glass, Chuzoople at last brought the cocktail to its beak, just close enough that its barbed tongue could flick out and lap up the concoction.

Time was still stretching, pulling itself thinner and thinner until its tensile strength gave out and the strand snapped, heralded by the creature's teeth-grinding roar.

The spell broken, May seized the back of Xan's shirt, and Listay seized May's hand, and the whole conglomeration stuffed into the air vent moments ahead of a wildly clacking, foaming beak.

"The shermel must've been off," Xan said, bewildered as he crawled backward through the vent, away from the unhappy customer.

"Oh, that's not shermel," Yulquitz called back to him. "Carmnia used to give that to interns who asked for a glass of water." They gave a single heartless laugh as if to excuse Carmnia's antisocial behavior as an endearing foible.

"What is it?" Listay asked.

The war-cry of the creature ended, punctuated with a hearty flop.

"I've no idea. But I do know we won't be bothered by Chuzoople again. Clever stuff, Xan! You must've gotten that from Carmnia," Yulquitz called to a horrified Xan.

"I was fixing her a drink! I thought we could maybe have a chat to the effect of 'Hey, we're really not all that bad; how about you don't kill us?' I was loosening her up! Difficult to kill someone who's just made you a cocktail, I thought. A bit rude. Figured at the very least she would feel silly for overreacting."

"It worked," Listay said by way of congratulations. "Now let's get out of these vents."

THIRTY-ONE
PIÑATA ROOM

* * * * *

Yulquitz kicked open the next grate they came to, and the group emerged in a hallway which flickered under orange light and the exaggerated warmth of faux torches set in faux cast-iron sconces illuminating faux frescos which depicted Carmnia's faux heroics.

The first scene which assaulted their sense of reality was one of an abstract and formless universe, like great colored amoebas wriggling inside a wobbly bean held in Carmnia's vast blue fingers. Her face was arranged in a way no living person had ever actually seen her face arranged—in a gently blissful smile, full of warmth and love for, presumably, all of existence. The inscription beneath this scene read 'Before there was anything, there was Queen Carmnia, and this was good.'

"The Hall of Truth," Yulquitz said, sweeping their arms out to either side in the flickering hallway. "Commissioned in NT two-thirty-six, in order to 'set the record straight,' according to Carmnia."

"What record?" May asked, pocketing her bottle shank and moving on to the next fresco which pictured Carmnia reclining, disinterested, prodding at the bean which contained all things. Below it read, 'Queen Carmnia grew weary of the Nothingness she dwelled in. Thus, she personified the formless mass of the Universe and went down into it and became the suns and the planets and that which crawled among them, and this was good.'

Yulquitz shrugged. "*The* record. Her creation mythos. She wanted it known."

"And you believe in it?" May asked. She had assumed, despite personally knowing a goddess, that everyone out here in the enlightened universe didn't actually believe in mythology. She had assumed wrong.

"Sure I do! I mean, to an extent, sure. Vaguely." Yulquitz smiled a smile which said they believed it because that was what they were expected to do and that this, like everything else Queen Carmnia had done, was good.

"Oh look!" Yulquitz shouted before they could further backpedal on their answer. "This one's fun. 'Queen Carmnia,'" they read the text, "'became lost in existence, and for eons, forgot from whence she came, and this was good!' That's good, isn't it?" Yulquitz said cheerily.

The scene they referred to showed Carmnia again, multiplied in a thousand ghostly outlines scattered with stars. It looked as if it had taken a lifetime to paint.

At the end of the hallway, past one last fresco, massive gold-gilt double doors blocked the path, but they were too far to make out the nature of the carvings which danced across it.

"Alright!" Yulquitz chirped. "Onto the Piñata Room. I do hope she's not in there, but we ought to check."

"What about the last painting?" May asked. Yulquitz was standing in front of it so she couldn't see. She ducked around them.

"Oh, uh, don't worry. It's nothing," they said.

"'Queen Carmnia shall one day rise to power again, and on that day, all existence shall violently collapse into itself and be held once more in the palm of her Queenly Hand, and this is good?'" May read. The question mark at the end was her own.

"It's nothing, really." Yulquitz said. "The ultimate

Nothing." They laughed nervously. "Come along. She's not in this hallway, is she? Well, in spirit, perhaps she is. Bodily, she's not."

Xan stared into the face of Carmnia in the final scene, and a shiver of recognition hit him like an arrow to a bullseye at the center of his being. May joined him, putting a hand on his shoulder. "Come on," she said. He stayed.

"The horrible thing about mushrooms is that their root system can be thousands of times larger than what's on the surface. So, you know, you *think* you know what you've got there, and you *think* everything's all sussed out, and then you start to dig a little, and you realize this thing has taken over entire forests, entire planets, even. And there's no digging it out without destroying a whole civilization."

He paused, and May thought perhaps he was done, so she prepared to reply. He was not done.

"I fucking hate mushrooms," he said.

May nodded, approving both of his use of the word "fuck" and his sentiments regarding mushrooms. She waited for him to start talking again, but after several moments of silence, she patted his back. "Agreed," she said. "Let's go."

"Wait." He showed her his BEAPER, above which floated a message from Yvonne. "Aimz is lost," it read.

It was followed by Xan's reply, "Lost how? As in gone? Missing? Dead?! Be specific!" and no further communication.

"That's vague," May noted. "Are you going to tell Listay?"

"That we're receiving cryptic messages and her lover may or may not be dead? Probably not."

"Probably not," May confirmed and they followed Listay and Yulquitz to the massive gold-gilt door at the end of the hall which was slowly being patinated by a thin, powdery mold. The door was carved with Carmnia's distraught visage wielding an enormous baton, her body poised to swing at what appeared to be a sea urchin dancing from a string.

Below, a plaque read in a font so decorative it was nearly illegible, 'The Piñata Room.'

Yulquitz paused, their hand on the door. "I only ever found her in here once after Queen Rapite sent her a nasty message about her hair. It is said that breaking the Piñata will summon a great and primordial power, its true name beyond fathomable language, but we know it as The Seam. So let's hope she's not in there, eh? That would be a bit of a mess, wouldn't it?" Yulquitz laughed as if they had just told a spooky campfire story to a group of frightened girl scouts and were trying to now lighten the mood.

They pushed open the heavy door to reveal a windowless room. The words 'Break Piñata in Case of Catastrophe' danced in colorful letters, projected onto a cloud of water vapor above an enormous papier-mâché fish which hung from the ceiling on a line so thin that it appeared to be floating, its fine paper fins undulating in the umami scented draft of the mansion.

Something pinged in the back of Xan's head. It was Chaos. Polite, he thought. Too polite to be Chaos, right? But the scourge didn't ping and, as far as he knew, his own mind had never done that either. But there it was, undeniably, the moment he had seen the papier-mâché fish floating in the empty room. This was it. This was the reason they were here.

"Stop me if this sounds plivered, but I really think we ought to break open that piñata," he heard himself say.

It seemed like everyone else heard this too, because they all looked at him as if he had suddenly burst into song and begun recapping the story so far.

Yulquitz, fearing they had lost control of this tour, was the first to deter him. "Now, we must remember we are guests in Queen Carmnia's home. Please refrain from damaging the historical surroundings and summoning primordial powers. I realize I must sound a touch hypocritical; I did, after all, blow up a doorway. But as the Queen's head consort, I do have some rights here, and I was only acting out of the interests of group safety."

Listay moved between Xan and the piñata. "If that

piñata really does contain The Seam, you don't want to meddle with it. The Seam is the center of the universe. Who knows what they could do?"

"That's the reset," Xan said. "The Nothingness Chaos was talking about. It's what she wants, and I'm starting to think it's our winning wager." Then his tone shifted, and he addressed May as if he were about to suggest a fun outing. "Besides! Piñatas are great, right? In the event that it's not full of a primordial universe eating entity, it will be full of cheap candy. Who wouldn't want to get at that?"

Yulquitz and Listay couldn't dissuade Xan, so they both looked at May, silently urging her to take their side. The fish piñata looked at May, but from it, she could glean no advice. "I'm not giving up, Xan," she said at last, grabbing his hand. "We need to talk to Carmnia. Can you fight Chaos off a little longer?"

"I could fight her off forever, but..." He was beginning to wonder why he ought to. Beginning to doubt whether she really was all that horrible. Then he began to wonder if thoughts like that were how Chaos had snagged Yvonne and, for May's sake, he shut up. "You're right. Carmnia. I've always wanted to meet her, anyway. Only the wealthy and well-off ever get a chance to meet their own Queen, and I've never heard of a wealthy or well-off Carmnian, so I imagine I'll be the first! She's in the mud baths, by the way."

No one reacted to that revelation the way he had expected them to. No one reacted at all.

Perplexed, he pointed to his head. "Chaos told me. She's cooperating."

"That's great, mun!" Yulquitz clapped Xan on the back, hoping to dispel the tension that had strung the room round. "Saves us a great deal of time, too. The courtyard's the last stop on the tour. Unless, of course, you folks would like to arrive there naturally? See the rest of the Folly first?" After a brief and poignant silence, Yulquitz continued. "Or let's not! Right onto the courtyard, then. Just skipping the rest of the tour..."

THIRTY-TWO
A MURDER

* * * * *

Chaos had been correct; Carmnia was in the courtyard stewing in a mud bath. They found her coated in fine beige mud, lounging in a round and Queenly pool, looking so much like every statue and stone carving they had seen of her thus far that, at first glance, May actually believed she was made of stone.

The courtyard hosted several of these mud baths, but none as richly decorated as Carmnia's, which lay in the center surrounded by golden waist-high statues of hurgles —evolutionary cousins to the flamingo who had developed space travel long before the Earth was replete with shrimp. The rim of the bath was gilt in gold, the tap which fed the bath was gold, and the magnificent puff of hair, the only bit of Carmnia which could be clearly seen, was gold, as well.

Bubbles of mud laboriously rose from the pool, paused, then burst with steam.

"Carmnia?" Yulquitz hazarded, bravely walking around the pool while the others remained on the far side. Yulquitz tapped her muddy shoulder.

As slowly as a mud bubble inflating, Carmnia filled her lungs with hot, humid air, her chest rising until it looked as if it might burst, too.

Carmnia forced all the air out of her lungs in a guttural, miserable, primal sigh. She did not open her eyes. She knew it was Yulquitz.

"What?"

"Uh, Carmnia, it's me, Yulquitz."

"And?"

"Well, aren't you happy to see...er...hear me?"

May, Xan, and Listay had gathered uncomfortably at the opposite edge of the pool, but Carmnia's voice had drawn Xan forward, his forehead wrinkling in thought.

"Not particularly," she said. "What do you want?"

Now, Xan strode forward with purpose, pausing only to snatch a rolled towel from the beak of one of the hurgle statues. He whipped the towel open, knelt beside Carmnia, and wiped the mud from her face.

"Chrismillion on Trilly under Carmnia of Tuhnt," Xan sat back on his heels, letting the towel drop to the concrete. "What in Blitheon's name are you doing here?"

Her eyes opened. She screamed like a hundred glotchburs fleeing a boiling lake and clambered from the bath.

"You're Carmnia?! I never noticed!" Xan squeaked. "Why didn't I notice that?" His voice grew faster, higher. "That seems like something I should have noticed!" He was barely audible now, like a busted squeaker toy.

It is worthwhile to mention here that the average meat-brain is really astonishingly bad at recognizing faces out of context. This is why most actors are so easily able to convince the layperson that they are, in fact, several different people rather than one person putting on a wig, some makeup, and occasionally a well-practiced accent.

Xan was now experiencing the same shame which comes from suddenly realizing an important side character in a movie you've watched dozens of times is the same actor in that commercial you can't seem to escape.

"She looks nothing like her statues," May whispered to Yulquitz who had quickly gotten out of Carmnia's way to avoid a torrent of mud.

"When she posed for the statues, she still had a team of stylists at her command."

"What happened to the stylists?"

"She had them all killed for perpetrating an unflattering caricature." Yulquitz cringed. "But nicely! Not killed, really. Put down. She had them laid to rest."

"Yulquitz, my love," hissed Carmnia between her teeth, pulling Yulquitz closer to her by the hem of their shirt.

"Uh, yes Queen Carmnia?" they said with a nervous warble.

"I thought you and the other consorts were handling the scourge situation. I was *told* you were handling it. By *you.* Does this," her eyes flicked to Xan then back to Yulquitz, "look like it's been handled?"

"Well, no, but...well, you see, the consorts and I have been working on the problem, but we, uh, don't really know exactly what causes it. They suggested that perhaps you might have some insight into that on account of—"

"It's the mushrooms, you *know* that. *Everyone* knows that. I told you to fix it, not lay the blame back on me!"

"Right, yes, of course, but—"

"But nothing! Your task was to either cure it or dispose of the infected, and since you have obviously failed to accomplish the former, you must proceed with the latter."

"D...dispose of?" Yulquitz asked. "You want me to kill him?"

Listay and May stepped in front of Xan, but Xan wasn't worried.

"Alright, Milly, you can get off their mark. I know you can't help me. I'll just leave."

Milly shook her head slowly. "Not at all, mun. Now your Aunt Milly hates to see you like this, you understand." She turned her blazing red eyes onto him, and he shrunk back. They had never been loving, never trustworthy, but now there was outright disgust in them. It was as if he were a once favorite chair, but the stuffing had started to come out in places, and it creaked when you sat on it. She had, mentally, put him on the curb the moment she saw the flash of scourge in his eyes at the burlesque show.

Yulquitz was the overly friendly neighbor who had noticed the chair, thought perhaps it had been taken to the curb accidentally, and tried to bring it back.

"By putting them down, you see," she said to Yulquitz now, "we are doing them and the community a favor. There's no curing the scourge. Kill him."

"No! I mean...well, obviously no!" Yulquitz said.

Seizing the beak of a nearby statue, Carmnia pulled it from the bird's face, revealing a long golden blade which rose from the bird's throat.

"I'll do it myself, then."

Xan backed up defensively, and May wrapped her fingers around the neck of the broken shermel bottle in her pocket. Chrismillion had her back to May, and slowly, carefully, so as not to alert her, May moved toward Chrismillion, focused intently on the middle of her golden curls. Everyone knew exactly what May was doing and refused to look at her for fear that Chrismillion's attention would be drawn.

"Milly! You raised me! Well, I mean you were around while I was being raised. Why are you doing this?"

"Listen to me now," Chrismillion said, and since she was the one holding the sword, everyone did. "There's a perfectly good explanation as to why I posed as a simpleton to raise you and Aimz." May paused just a few steps away from her, thinking Xan deserved the explanation before she walloped Milly.

"I'm sure there is," Xan said, hands up, trying to back away without startling her. "What...what is it?"

"I wanted to!" she cried. "You can't imagine how lonely it gets once the larvae are adopted out to their caretakers! It's not my fault you and Aimz were impossible to handle. *Particularly* Aimz. I was a wonderful caretaker!"

At this, May raised the bottle from her pocket. She was within striking distance. She raised it higher. She looked to Xan, her one-person ethics committee, and waited for the go-ahead. Xan's focus had been trained on Chrismillion up until now, but he could tell that May, a blurry figure in the background, was waiting on his word.

Subtly, he shook his head. Even more subtly, his eyes met May's. And that was a mistake. Chrismillion noticed. She spun around, sword slicing in a semi-circle around her.

Metal clanged against glass; May had blocked the sword with the shoulder of the bottle. She smiled, having not realized she could do that. Perhaps she could hold her own in a sword fight, after all, she thought.

She thought wrong. That had been a wild stroke of luck. While May was busy mentally congratulating herself for being so effortlessly cool, Chrismillion was busy plunging the little sword into the space between her third and fourth ribs.

May dropped the glass shank. "That was quick," she said, looking down, confused, at the metal protruding from her. Chrismillion retracted the red-polished sword and gently pushed May into the bubbling mud bath.

Surging forward together, Listay and Yulquitz wrestled the sword away from Chrismillion while Xan dove into the mud after May.

"Wow, uhm," said Yulquitz, holding Chrismillion's muddy, heaving shoulders. "Okay, Carmnia, larvling, let's get you cleaned up." They turned to Listay. "I'm going to get her cleaned up," they repeated. He began to lead Chrismillion to the showers, but she wriggled an arm under Yulquitz's and unsheathed the ray gun without their noticing. Listay snatched the gun from her, twisted her arm around her back, and pressed the nozzle between her shoulder blades.

"Does the Folly have a holding cell?" Listay asked Yulquitz.

"Oh, well, that's not really necessary is—"

"Holding. Cell." Listay turned the ray gun on Yulquitz now. "Or I'll put you both away for murder."

Yulquitz nodded sadly and led Listay through the courtyard to a staircase. Before they disappeared down it, Listay looked back at the mud bath and the two mud-covered globs on the edge of it.

"Try to keep her from bleeding out!" Listay shouted at one of the two blobs, hopefully the one that was Xan. The blob she had shouted at raised a hand in recognition, and Listay shoved the Queen down the steps, followed by an apologetic Yulquitz.

* * * * *

You're welcome, May thought, floating in a warm, thick darkness which slowly dragged her down. Why had she thought that? It didn't seem like the kind of thing she was likely to think. *Now can we smash that damn piñata?*

Oh.

Her thoughts were not her own. Her own thoughts, at this moment, were more along the lines of *Fuck Chrismillion, who does she think she is?*

Chaos agreed, though.

May was being dragged in another direction now. Up. Up was not as comfortable as down had been, but whatever was dragging her up was adamant, and so she let it.

She breached the surface of the mud and, though she had the natural inclination to take a deep breath, found that her lungs refused to inflate.

"May, talk to me," Xan said as he dragged her onto the courtyard tile.

"Your aunt is a bitch," May wheezed, coughing up a mouthful of bloody mud, rolling onto her elbow to spit it out.

This, though it was true, surprised Xan. He had fully expected her to be dead. Listay was shouting something at him in the distance, and he waved to acknowledge her.

"Zuut, I'm sorry about her. She does that sometimes."

"Murders people?!" May asked.

Xan shrugged, tilting his head. "Well, we could never prove anything, but we always just kinda assumed. She's got some issues."

"Issues," May repeated. "That's 'issues'?"

"More to the point, are you okay?" Xan opened her trench coat and began to wipe the mud from her shirt, searching for the point of entry. Her entire shirt was stained red under the beige slime of mud.

She knocked his hand away before he could get too freaked out by the blood. Leaning back on her elbows, she stretched out her aching rib cage with a wince. "I'm fine, thanks to Chaos," she grumbled.

Xan prodded around in his own head and found that Chaos had, indeed, left. But she could only possess a willing host, and May was certainly not willing. Unless... Xan shivered. May and Listay would have a lot to talk about. He grabbed a towel from the towel-holding hurgle and wiped the mud off May's face, then his own.

"So, Carmnia was a bust," May noted, seizing another towel to wipe off her hands.

"Sure, but do you know how expensive this mud is? Our skin is going to look incredible after this," Xan said, combing the mud through his hair. "At least Milly was direct this time. She used to make up the wildest excuses. 'I've got an emergency hair appointment at the Marscaral Palace,' she'd say. Or, 'One of my attendants just got eaten, I have to go,' she'd say. Or—by O'Zeno, I'm incredibly thick, aren't I?"

May pat his arm. "It's alright, Blue," she assured him and began twisting the mud through sections of her curls, feeling she might as well make the most of the situation, too. "What are we going to do, now?" she asked, though she doubted he would have an answer.

He was silent for a long while, watching bubbles rise in the mud, linger, then pop. Rise, linger, pop. Rise...linger... "Have we considered," Xan said, "letting Chaos win?"

"What, giving up?" May asked. "After all this?!" May pointed dramatically to her chest and the unpleasant looking hole in it.

"Why not?" Xan said, wincing.

"We can't just give up! That isn't how it works. We're the good guys. We don't give up. We fight, we win, the end," she said, crossing her arms, determined to take command of her own life story.

"What end? Nothing ends. You can't win or lose if there's no end," he said.

May thought perhaps the scourge had really gotten to him without Chaos there to buffer it.

"Of course there's an end," she said. Then, she had to sit and think about it a minute longer. "Death is the end. We've been through this."

"Well...sure," Xan said. "But there's no winning or losing. Not really. We win one round, we lose the next, and on it goes until..."

"Until you stop playing the game," May suggested.

"We have no way of saving ourselves now," Xan said. "We have nothing to save. We've already succumbed to Chaos."

May watched the quietly burbling mud bath for a while. Watching the bubbles form, grow, and burst over and over again. No one, truly, was out to get them.

The scourge was just a thoughtless disease munching away at a tasty brain. Chrismillion, a hapless screw-up terrified of her own creations. Sonan, a computer on a mission. Even Chaos herself just wanted to do her job. To rid the universe of the agony of being. To end all suffering once and for all.

They had been fighting nature all along.

May sighed. "You're right, Xan," she said at last. "Most piñatas *are* full of cheap candy. I could go for some of that right now," she said.

"Then let's go get some!"

THIRTY-THREE

ZOMBIE HIGH FIVE

* * * * *

Beneath the courtyard, in a slat-lit basement cell block, Listay sensed that someone was about to make a terrible decision.

"Yulquitz, watch her. Don't let her out," Listay said, handing the ray gun back to Yulquitz despite her reservations.

"Good thinking! You go check on the kids; I'll hang out with Carmnia!" Yulquitz said, cheerily.

This did not increase her confidence in them, but she bolted up the stairs and into the soft light of the courtyard to find Xan and May both trying to yank another statue from the concrete floor.

"What are you doing?!" she shouted, breaking into a sprint.

"Getting a bird for May," Xan grunted, throwing his full weight into pulling the creature from its post.

Listay put a hand on May's arm. "You need medical attention!"

"Oh, no, not really," said May. "Zombie high five?" She held up her hand, waiting. She felt giddy with the realization that everything was well and truly over. Or was it Chaos in there making her think that? Likely both, but it didn't matter. She felt at once vanquished and invincible. Dead and alive. Hopeless and ecstatic.

Listay felt there was something very wrong with her. She refused the high-five. Xan continued to tug at the hurgle bird.

"Why does May need a bird?" Listay asked, thinking that perhaps asking something concrete might get her a more reasonable answer.

"We're going to smash the piñata," Xan said.

It had not.

"And summon the Seam? You can't do that!" Listay's tone shifted suddenly, as if she were talking someone down from a bridge. "You're not thinking clearly. Why don't we sit down and talk about this? There are still options."

Xan's BEAPER dinged an alert, and he wiped the mud off it to allow the message to float in the air above his wrist.

It was from Yvonne's BEAPER.

It was not good news.

"Blitheon," Listay whispered. She could read the holographic message, though it was backward. It was just three words.

"You've been in contact with Fulogra?" Listay's voice was distant as if some other entity were puppeting her from far away.

Xan couldn't put sentences together yet, so May stepped in. "Off and on. We didn't know anything important until now. We didn't want to worry you."

Listay nodded, looked as if she were about to say something, then nodded again as a pair of tears raced down her cheeks, cutting two glistening lines down her face.

Unable to stand the sight of someone crying, particularly when he felt like crying himself, Xan swept Listay up into a hug, petting her hair.

May stood by awkwardly, entirely unsure of what to say or do in this situation.

"Hey guys!" Yulquitz called from across the courtyard, saving May from having to deal with uncomfortable feelings. "Carmnia is *really* sorry, and she wants to apologize to everyone."

"Not now!" Listay shouted back to him, her grief ricocheting into vitriol with ease. But it was too late. Chrismillion rose, unbound, clean, and dressed in a white, fluffy robe, her hands raised in surrender.

"I," said Chrismillion, then paused as if her voice were being broadcast around the near empty courtyard and she needed to give it time to reverberate properly, "Queen Carmnia," she paused again, "apologize for any harm—"

"Stop!" Xan said, releasing Listay and approaching Chrismillion. "Aimz is dead, and you nearly killed May. I don't want an apology from you. It wouldn't make a scrap of difference. You acted in the only way you knew how to act: as an antagonist to those who trusted you. Even the zuxing god of Chaos is honest about who she is and what she wants."

Chrismillion's acquiescent expression hardened. "Fine. I'll be honest. I am your Queen, and I want you to disappear," she said, then stole the ray gun, again, from Yulquitz. This time, though, Yulquitz noticed. They launched at Chrismillion's arm, deflecting the blast into a distant marble pillar which shattered, collapsing half of the surrounding colonnade.

Listay snatched the ray gun from the errant Queen's weakened grasp and with a single blast she untethered the hurgle bird statue Xan had been trying to dislodge. It clattered to the ground in front of May and she picked it up, slinging it over her shoulder.

"Go," she told Xan. "Summon The Seam."

Xan nodded, kissed her gently on the forehead, a crazy kind of half-smile on his face as he and May ran back to the piñata room.

THIRTY-FOUR

UNFATHOMABLE JELLYMINTS

* * * * *

For the first time ever, May and Xan found themselves running toward something not because they were being chased, not because they were running out of time before something horrific happened, but because they were excited to get there. Whatever fearful mystery the fish piñata held couldn't possibly be any more terrible than what they were currently going through, so sheer curiosity had won out.

"Hey, Chaos," May shouted, looking up as if she could see into her own brain. "We're doing your thing now. Happy?" After a brief silence, May laughed, and Xan asked what Chaos had said. "She says, 'vindication is a sweeter and more satiating fruit than happiness,'" May relayed.

Bits of mud flung from their shoes as they jogged out into the foyer and through the ceremonially lit hall which led to the piñata room.

The bass floated in its haze, the words "Break Piñata in Case of Catastrophe" shimmering above it. They studied the tissue-paper scales of the enormous creature with interest, savoring their last moments of here-and-now.

"Who do you think made it?" Xan asked.

"It's always existed," May said. When Xan tilted his head at her, confused, she clarified, "Chaos says that it contains the center of the Universe, which means that it's always existed. I was paraphrasing. She used more insults and expletives."

"Why does Carmnia have it?"

May listened to the voice in her head for a moment, scrunched her face, and shrugged. "Because she's a greedy zuxing zoup-nog tchagg. And I think that's the first time Chaos and I have ever agreed on something! Making progress, right? Ouch!" May ducked away from nothing.

"What?"

She rubbed her scalp, looking around suspiciously. "Chaos thwacked me in the head. She wants us to get it over with."

They had a universe-ending piñata to destroy.

May bounced the head of the bird statue against her shoe, getting a feel for the weight of it.

"Thank you," she said to Xan.

"For what?"

"Everything," she said. "Everything except the canned corn."

Rather than risk speaking, he nodded and pulled her into a tight hug, savoring the way her back felt under his palm, the enclosing warmth of her arms, the softness of her hair in his face. "I love you, May," he said.

"I know, Blue." She patted his back.

Chaos almost made a snarky comment in May's ear, but she had finally learned not to meddle in matters of love and devotion.

May took up her bird statue and swung at the bass.

A wave of glitter poured from the fish, threatening to fill the room as it ferried May and Xan back toward the doorway. As it settled, May realized it wasn't glitter, exactly. It was stars. Suns. Billions of tiny points of light hanging in a heavy darkness all around her. They tickled where they touched her skin until she realized it was less of a tickle, more of an extremely small burn.

"Ugh!" shouted the stars which filled the room before compacting into a single, bright entity in the space where the fish had hung. "This reality is so much smaller than the last one. You're supposed to be expanding, not shrinking, you twits."

May averted her eyes. Not out of respect or awe or anything, just because it was physically painful to look at her.

The Seam, The Unfathomable Everythingness of What Comes Between The Beginning and The End, was miffed. "What?"

"Bright," May said, unable to look at her.

The entity dimmed by 50% and May hazarded a peek at it. "What do you want? It's..." The entity paused to look at her wrist where the edge of all Creation slowly moved outward into the great Nothingness. "Yikes, it's only 6 am. Y'all! What could you possibly need me for? I was in the middle of an intense game of bridge with Time, and I swear if I lose to him again, I'm turning this entire Universe around."

May was distressed. Not because she was in the presence of an entity who could read universal time off her wrist, but because said entity looked and sounded exactly like her fifth-grade teacher. "Mrs. Nina?"

"No, you twit! I pulled an image from your memories. I've tried universe and universe again to present myself plainly, and it's always the same reaction: hysterical shriek, instantaneous soul ejection, and blamo, you're a puddle of flesh. Do you have any idea how unpleasant it is to squeegee melted mortal flesh off the ground? The answer is very, very unpleasant! Now, what do you want?"

"Uh, well," Xan began.

"Let me talk," Chaos said with May's mouth.

The Seam narrowed her eyes at May, giving the effect of two twin suns squeezing under the horizon line. "Chaos, is that you?"

"Yes."

"In *another* body?"

"Yes."

"You didn't get stuck in that ridiculous fish again, did

you?" The entirety of the Universe stifled a laugh, and it felt like an earthquake.

Chaos answered by making May give The Seam a silent and humorless glare.

"This is why we don't lose track of our immortal flesh bodies, Chaos. You only get one!" The Seam leaned over Xan now, speaking in that pejorative, cheerful voice one uses for children they are fed up with. "Has Chaos been picking on you?"

Xan nodded, feeling a little embarrassed as if he were tattling on a school-yard bully.

The Seam sighed, and Xan got the feeling that a supermassive black hole had just patted him on the head. "Chaos, I will reunite you with your immortal flesh body, but first, you're going to have a one-eternity time-out to think about what you've done. Now, I need to get back to our bridge game. Time waits for no one. Jellymint?" The Seam held out her hand, revealing two bright green jellymints on her unfathomable palm.

Xan and May both took one and, gingerly, ate them.

THIRTY-FIVE

IMMEASURABLE EMPTINESS

* * * * *

There followed an immeasurable period of immeasurable emptiness.

Imagine nothing.

Total and complete non-being.

Now scrap that and try again because you've imagined far too much.

It was as if the Universe's plug had been pulled and everything contained in it drained away and then the container itself followed those contents down, but the direction "down" was *also* gone. Not even the vacuum of space remained.

What remained could not be put into words, because it does not exist.

The impossible exceptions to the above statement un-drummed their non-existent fingers on non-existent mahogany office desks as they un-waited for something not to happen.

These were the immortals, and they were one fewer this time than they had been the last, though it was difficult to tell because they did not, in any meaningful way, exist.

These non-entities, after some incomprehensible amount of anti-time, began to experience a something. This something felt an awful lot like boredom.

Soul-sucking, bone-twisting, eyeball-bleeding boredom seeped across time spans immeasurably long and fields of space immeasurably wide until that boredom finally gave itself a name. A name which, for lack of a better approximate, we'll just say was The Seam.

And from there, the rest is history.

THIRTY-SIX

HISTORY

* * * * *

During the final age of the War of Reversed Polarity, in the darkest booth in the farthest corner of the seediest sub-bar in the city of Trilly on the continent of Further Masedon on the planet of Tuhnt in the system of Flotluex, Xan stared at his wrist.

More specifically, at four red, digital words that scrolled in the air just above his BEAPER.

He took a tingling swig of his third Electro-Blitz.

It was an alert from the Tuhntian government. 'Mandatory Draft in Effect.'

Xan wondered if perhaps destroying his BEAPER and pretending he had never received the message would work. He closed his eyes to escape it, but was met with the afterimage of the scrolling text. 'Mandatory Draft in Effect,' but this time in green.

He rubbed his eyes, trying to wipe the image away, and slid down in the seat, pursing his lips as his coat bunched up behind him. It would make no difference, but he wanted to look as absolutely put-out as possible. The Universe would know, he thought, and that was enough.

Unfortunately, the Universe is a touch nearsighted and didn't notice.

Wait, he thought. *Wait, hold on,* he added, mentally.

He had suddenly remembered great swaths of things which he hadn't previously remembered.

Why was he back here? Was he dead? Was this one of those 'life flashing before one's eyes' moments? No, those weren't supposed to last this long, were they?

He looked at the condensating Electro-Blitz in his hand. The Electro-Blitz he knew he'd just drunk from on account of the tingly after taste.

But that wasn't right. He hadn't had an Electro-Blitz since...well, since now. Here, in the sub-bar. He couldn't remember the name of the sub-bar, but a large glowing mirror behind the bar told him he was in Gulate's Glugger. So this wasn't a memory, it was actually happening.

He felt perhaps he should scream. An uncomfortable, quiet, "Ah," squeaked out.

The reset.

He wasn't sure exactly what had happened. He was fairly certain, however, that at this very moment May was several decades away from existing and that thought gave everything a background radiation of anxiety.

Millions of light years away, on a planet called Earth, Napoleon was furiously scrubbing at a spot of tarnish on his favorite spoon.

Xan stared at the entrance to the sub-bar, apprehensive of what was to come. Any moment now, Admiral Ranken Warders, the person who had, under the influence of Chaos, absolutely obliterated Xan's life, would walk in and tell him to steal the *Audacity*.

Any moment.

Annnyyyyy moment.

Perhaps, thought Xan, this was a case of a watched pot never boiling, and so he looked at his drink instead.

Nothing continued to happen aggressively at him.

And then Aimz happened aggressively at him.

She'd slipped in while he was studying his drink and bulldozed him into the wall beside his booth.

"Hey, zoup-nog, got your draft message yet?" She beamed at him. Being drafted into military service wasn't exactly the sort of thing you beamed about.

"Whoa," she then said, frowning as memories from another lifetime suddenly smacked into her brain. She re-observed her surroundings. The sub-bar, Xan's mullet, Yvonne stiffly sliding into the booth across from them, the Electro-Blitz she had grabbed from Xan out of habit.

She chugged the Blitz. "What on Blitheon's purple grass happened"

"I've been waiting seasons for your timeline to catch up to mine," Yvonne said. "Our consciousnesses have been returned to the moment before Chaos entered our personal timelines which, for me, was when I took the helm of the *Peacemaker*. For Xan, it was when Chaos possessed Rankin Warders to convince him to steal the *Audacity,* which is why I met you here. Aimz, you must've been looking for Xan, and your timeline changed when you didn't find him here."

"So Tuhnt exists again! Oh, and whatcha think, scourge back to normal?" Aimz spread her eyes wide with her fingers for Yvonne to study. They were, indeed, returned to a dull pink glow, no longer an unhealthy neon.

"Normal as you'll ever be, Aimz," Yvonne agreed with a smile.

"That's great, honestly, but what about the others? Where are they?" Xan said.

Aimz shrugged. "Probably back to where they were before Chaos zuxed with them, just like us. I was coming in to tell you about the draft!"

"Yeah," said Xan. "Maybe a touch too enthusiastically. Do you want me to die?"

"No, zoup-nog! Yve snatched you a cushy desk job in communications! Turns out your degree wasn't entirely useless after all."

"Great." He tried to smile, but couldn't even pretend he was happy about anything right now.

"And don't worry about the others!" Aimz continued, summoning the bartender over. "It can't be too hard to find Listay and Ix, right? Six more Electro-Blitzes for the table," she told the bartender. "We beat the scourge!" The bartender looked as if he had heard this before.

"May doesn't exist yet. She'll never be abducted by Chaos, and I won't be floating listless about the Earth, and we're never going to meet, but I still remember her. Why do we remember things that aren't going to happen? That's horrible!"

"We were essentially at the center of the next big bang. As this timeline wears on and replaces the old one, we might forget," Yvonne said, hoping this might comfort him.

It had done just the opposite.

"Can we stop it? I'll write down everything I remember; I'll write a book! Zuut, why didn't I think of that before? This is some wacky stuff we just lived through, someone *should* write a book about it," Xan said, oblivious.

"You might not believe it, even if you wrote it yourself," Yvonne said. "It's also entirely possible that we will remember everything from both timelines."

"Eugh, that's horrible, too!" Xan said, burying his face in his arms.

Yvonne shut up now, realizing that there was nothing she could say to comfort him, because there was nothing comforting about the situation.

"Hey, she's not dead," said Aimz. "She just doesn't exist yet. If you remember her later, you can go abduct her again!"

"I didn't abduct her! Yve did it."

"Chaos did it, not me," said Yvonne.

Xan flopped across the filthy bar table, his arms hung dramatically over the side and his nose pressing uncomfortably into the tacky resin of the tabletop. "Do you remember when you abducted her?" he asked the table.

"Again, not me. Listay would remember."

"Listay!" Aimz shouted. "Zuut, does she remember me? Will she be a zombie still? I hope so."

"She's already caught up to us." Yvonne said. "Difficult to keep her from coming after you the moment she remembered, too. Not a zombie."

"That's right. You never got the chance to kill her in this timeline."

"Chaos. Chaos killed her. And then brought her back."

Aimz sighed, seriously considering if she was still interested, but Yvonne had already messaged Listay the news that Aimz and Xan were caught up with them, and the moment Listay stepped into the sub-bar, Aimz vaulted into her arms to kiss her.

Xan followed them outside. The blizzard had died down as quickly as it started; the sky was clear. He looked at the moons and tried to comfort himself by saying that May might be looking at the same moons right now. This was impossible for several reasons, not least of which that May didn't currently exist.

"Fuck," he said.

THIRTY-SEVEN

FUTURE

✳ ✳ ✳ ✳ ✳

May pulled a thick rope of smoke through her cigarette and into her lungs and immediately coughed it out. This wasn't *not* a cigarette. It was a real Earth cigarette, and she was smoking it on the cold concrete steps outside her apartment and watching an empty street. The traffic light at the intersection nearest her flickered through its rounds: green, yellow, red. The morning stirred with the occasional chirrup of an early bird followed by the complaints of birds who much preferred to sleep in, but now they were up, thank-you-very-much.

She was on Earth. She was at her apartment complex. She was smoking into the early morning. She had emotional whiplash.

If all had been going according to plan, she was about to be abducted. All, it seemed, was not going according to plan. There was no Gremlin, which, May assumed, meant that Chaos had been dealt with.

That was good.

She smiled.

There was no Xan.

That was bad.

She frowned.

And, since Xan was not here, there was no one she could confide in about this either.

Trying to suss out what, exactly, The Seam had done to her made her feel dizzy. Or perhaps it was the cigarette. She took a long drag from the cigarette and felt a little better, so it wasn't the cigarette.

With a universe-weary groan, she lay back against the stairs, letting the icy concrete divot her arms. She gazed up at the stars.

"Fuck." She closed her eyes and did not see the blue afterimage of the *Audacity* that she had grown accustomed to. These eyes had never seen the ship. "What now?" she whispered.

Back to Sonic, she thought immediately.

She'd rather get run over by an AMC Gremlin.

But she had bills to pay again and the millions of crystals she had amassed racing no longer existed, and even if they *did* exist, they would be next to worthless on Earth.

It occurred to her that she ought to think it had all been a dream. That's what someone in a book or a movie would say.

"It was all a dream," she said out loud, testing the sound of it. But she knew it wasn't. She wished it had been. Dreams are so easily forgotten, but she couldn't shake the feeling of zipping through the universe in the *Audacity*. The freedom, the excitement, the mountains of crystals.

"I'm going to bed," she said to no-one. She had become so used to announcing these sorts of things to Xan, but now she lived alone again. Alone with her pet cactus, Betty.

She tapped out her cigarette and pulled herself up from the cold concrete steps, leaning her weight on the wobbly cast iron railing, flakes of black paint coming off on her palms when she did. She hadn't missed that. In fact, she couldn't think of one thing she had missed about this place.

She slumped onto her busted dumpster-rescue couch and tried to force herself to fall asleep, hoping that perhaps she would wake up back in the *Audacity*. Through the criminally thin apartment walls, she could hear her neighbor's TV. It was faint, but there was no mistaking the brassy melody of the "I Love Lucy" theme song.

What Yulquitz had said echoed in her mind. "We are perpetual beings made mortal to learn the lesson of impermanence."

"I get it," she told the universe, miserably. "Thanks. Impermanence, learned. Check that off the list." She smushed her face into the lumpy couch cushion, trying to find some comfort in Lucille Ball's muffled shenanigans. "I would've preferred it if the meaning of life had been jazz hands."

THIRTY-EIGHT

FIX-IT FIC

* * * * *

May awoke to yet another unpleasant text message from her manager at the Sonic, Kathy. "Wat on gods green erth did u do last nite..." was what it said. It had been two years now since she had gotten stranded in space and five months since she had gotten re-stranded on Earth.

May wiped the crust from her eyes and tried to fluff her hair into place. She missed having her own personal stylist, and she desperately missed the alien hair products.

"Cum in erly?" her phone asked.

Why not? Thought May. Why. The hell. Not. Until classes started at Maple Leaf Meadow Wood Aviation Academy, she was at the mercy of Sonic. Once classes started at Maple Leaf Meadow Wood Aviation Academy next month, she was at the mercy of her student loan provider. Someday, with a little luck, she might be at her own mercy again.

"On my way," she replied to Kathy and opened the mini fridge to a single egg, a handful of ketchup packets, and a bottle of Sriracha, which was one of the few things she had missed about Earth. She cursed her past self for not having the foresight to pick up groceries for her future self and began the long walk back to Sonic. There was food there.

Her Civic was still about as useful as the average lawn ornament, and so she had to walk. Her first student loan check would not be going to books, that was certain. It would be going straight into the Civic.

As she approached the Sonic, Kathy greeted her at the rusty back door, along with the familiar smell of old kitchen grease and food-waste.

"Girl, what kind of freaky stuff are you into?" Kathy asked, hands on her hips, head tilted at a daring forty-five-degree angle.

"Just the usual," May replied.

"Well, keep it outta your work. There's a tall fella in blue makeup and spandex asking for you, and he's bothering the customers."

Pushing past Kathy, May bolted through the kitchen, leaving Kathy outside and wondering whether she could write someone up if they weren't clocked in at the time of offense.

Of course, Kathy had been mistaken. There was no fella. There was only Xan, perched on the back of a red and white booth, chatting with an elderly couple who had offered him a few of their French fries in exchange for his gripping tale.

"That's her!" He pointed a limp fry in May's direction, stuffed it in his mouth, and rolled off the back of the bench. The elderly couple gave an arthritic clap.

"Oh, isn't that nice?" said the wife.

"Charming," agreed the husband.

They wrapped around each other like two wet noodles intertwining, Xan wiggling from side to side as if that would keep his soul from shooting out of his body with joy. "May!" he told her enthusiastically. He finally let her go, and then went back in to cup her face delightedly.

"Xan!" she managed between smushed cheeks.

"May!" he repeated, releasing her. "Blitheon, I could kiss you." He hoped it had come across as rhetorical. It hadn't.

May laughed. "I know, Blueberry. It's okay, go on."

"What, really?"

"Yeah, why not? You look like you're gonna burst."

"Oh, really, I'm fine, I just—" His smile was so wide, it squeezed tears from his eyes, so she offered up her cheek to him, pointing to it teasingly. He gave in and pressed a kiss onto her soft, round cheek.

"Next?" She offered him her other cheek to even it out. "Okay, last one until we're separated with no hope of ever seeing each other again." She tilted her forehead toward him and he gave her a third and final kiss. "Feel better?"

"Enormously. Thank you."

"Anytime, Blue. How did you get here? Is the scourge gone? Are you okay? How long has it been for you? What's with the accent? And what are you wearing? You look..." She stepped back to observe his suit, double breasted, velvety, lined in something which looked expensive, and most shockingly, decorated with three splendiferous medals. "Fancy. You've got medals now?"

"I do!"

"Hey y'all!" Kathy stood at the kitchen door. "You're making a scene! May, can you come to my office?" Kathy had a clipboard-full of forms in her hand and was rhythmically tapping it with her long, non-regulation, fake nails.

"No, because I'm fired," May said, grabbing Xan's hand to drag him outside.

"You mean you quit?!" Kathy shouted after her.

"I never quit!" May said.

"It's true, she doesn't." Xan confirmed to Kathy. "Nice to meet you all!" Xan waved goodbye to the elderly couple and then Kathy as he was whisked away.

May pulled him to one of the outside tables, and he sat down across from her.

"Is my English accent really that bad?" he asked in a bad English accent. "It was awful to learn. No one speaks English, but I knew you wouldn't have a translation chip, so I had to try!"

"It's fine. I'm just happy to see you!" It was better than fine; she had a million questions, and now Xan was at a disadvantage in the language department, so she pushed ahead. "How's the…" she quieted, as if the Scourge Authority were still after them and might pop out at any moment from behind the callbox. "How's the scourge?"

"Better! Well, normal, at least. Aimz and Yve figured out what-uh-heh…sound level? Sound thing. Sound type. Eugh." He winced in frustration. "It isn't a Lucy word!"

"Frequency?" May helped.

"Yes! That's the one! They built a thing that stops it from growing." He tapped his temple where the tiny sonic implant was dutifully keeping watch over the fungus with a constant, nearly imperceptible whine. Nearly imperceptible. He was used to it by now, but the first few seasons had felt like a terrible case of tinnitus.

"So you're fine? The Seam reversed the damage?"

"It never happened! Listay thinks The Seam zuxed up somehow because anyone who had known Chaos personally remembers the other timeline. Our consciousnesses got sent back to the moment Chaos entered our lives."

"But that was ages ago for you," May said.

"A hundred and fifty orbits ago, yeah."

This was not a length of time May could comprehend. Not least of which because she still only had a tenuous grasp on the length of an orbit. She knew it was a long time, though. Nearly a hundred and fifty years. "And you remember me? After all that time, you came back for me?"

"I *missed* you," he said, holding her hands across the table.

"For a hundred and fifty orbits? I barely remember the people I knew in high school and that was…" She counted, then cringed. "That was only a decade ago."

"Yes, I've missed you for a hundred and fifty orbits! How long has it been for you? I tried to get here right when Listay said the Earth abductions started, but I'm not terribly good at navigation, and I had the ship going just a tenth of a degree in the wrong direction for several hundred light years, and honestly, that was quite the detour and I–"

"Five months," May interrupted. "I've missed you for five

months."

"Blitheon, it'll be nice when you have a chip again." He paused, looked around as if he had just noticed that they were on Earth. "Well, if you want one. I—oh zuut I never thought of that. Do you want to stay here?"

"Well, let's see..." She began counting on her fingers. "Saturday is my gallery opening at the Met, Sundays are always yoga and brunch with the gals, oh! and on Monday I'm being knighted by the Queen of England."

Xan squeezed her hands gently to stop her. "Seriously, can you come?"

"Friday, I've got a dentist appointment for something I'm pretty sure is going to be a root canal, which I can't afford. If you can take me to a free space dentist, I'm in."

"Root canal?"

"God, it must be nice to not know what that is," she said. "So what are the medals for?"

"Look!" He snapped off one of his medals and showed it to her, beaming. The center medallion depicted a field of glistening stars and illegible markings which looked like they might have been trying to tell her something wrapped around it.

"It's, uh..."

"Zuut! It's in Tuhntian isn't it? Right. It's..." He chewed his lip for a second as he searched for the English words. "Eugh. It's a thing which says that I'm band leader of a ship. Band leader...not band leader but..."

"A captain?"

"Yes!" Xan said, delighted that she had understood him. "Yve got me into interplanetary communications and, as it so happens, I'm fairly good at talking!"

"I hadn't noticed."

"Right? I'm usually the strong, silent type. I have hidden talents," he said with a shrug.

"Guess you do!" May laughed. "So how did you get here? Do you have a ship? A crew? Oh my God, Xan, do you have a crew?" The idea of Xan in any kind of command position confused and troubled May.

"A ship, yes. A crew, not anymore."

"But you did?" May nearly shouted.

"Eh..." He cringed leftward. "Well..." He cringed rightward.

"Come on, it can't be anywhere near as bad as stealing a rocket ship and getting a planet destroyed," May said. He didn't answer quickly enough. "Wait did you do that again?!"

"No!" He said quickly. "No, I just am trying to think of the words," he said. "I'm good at talking, in Tuhntian, at least, right?" he said.

"Uh-huh."

"And I accidentally got on the good side of an Admiral, Admiral Warders, believe it or not! Remember him?"

"Uh-huh..."

"And so he gave me a command position, among other positions, and I sorta had a fleet for a little while."

"Seriously?!" May asked.

"Seriously! I did not use it, though. I sent them all home indefinitely with pay. Evidently they weren't too pleased with that deal, because a few rotations later I was suspended. Honorably! Honorably suspended."

"And they gave you a ship when they suspended you?" May asked.

He smiled, but shook his head. "Here." He handed her a ship's anchor button attached to a keychain which May couldn't read, but from the heart shape in the center of the text, she deduced that it said "I <3 a Carmnian."

"What kind of ship did they give you? Can I pilot it?" she asked, studying the button for clues. He didn't reply. She had seen the words painted in a magnificently spacey text, zooming proudly across the small green disc. Her mouth opened, perhaps to allow more oxygen to flow to her brain as she tried to make sense of the Tuhntian letters.

"Is this..."

Xan nodded.

"Wait, this says..."

He nodded more enthusiastically.

"You stole the *Audacity* again?"

"Wha-no! No, I didn't steal it! It was about to be–" he paused, his hand circling. "Close the show? Stopped?

Canceled?"

"Decommissioned," May suggested.

"Yes! That one. I had some friends who had some friends and, well, I bought it for you."

"For me?" she said, a bit teary as she clipped the familiar anchor button to her Sonic polo.

"Yeah! And this. Finally." He unhooked the extra BEAPER he was wearing and gave that to her, too. "Why did we never get you one before?"

"Because it was more fun using yours."

"For whom?"

"Me! You would sit there for hours just holding your wrist out while I browsed the IFI. It was hilarious. And how is your English grammar better than mine? 'Whom?'" May teased, snapping on her own BEAPER and testing it out.

"Grammar is fun!"

"Your mom's fun," May said, grabbed his hand, and teleported them both to the *Audacity*.

"You met her; she's really not," Xan mumbled as they remerged on the ship.

"Wow," May said, stepping backward off the teledisc. She hadn't been aboard the *Audacity* in over a year, and she had never been aboard this version of the rocket, but the main room was exactly how she remembered it. The same couch, the same coffee table, and junk-yard-rescue retro TV.

"Couldn't put back the..." He swirled his fingers spookily.

"Mysterious wormhole," May filled in. "How did you get that in the first place?"

"No idea! That's why I couldn't put it back. Plus side, though, we've got bedrooms and a proper basement now!"

"How did you afford this?"

"May. I have a *job* now. A real one. An actual, every rotation job. I took the next hundred orbits off to spend with you, though. A 'Maycation.'" He beamed with pun pride. This was the first English pun he had invented, and he was quite fond of it; his co-workers, however, had not been.

"A hundred orbits? I'm not going to last that long," she said, imagining herself racing rockets as a dilapidated old woman. She liked the idea, but was certain he wouldn't go for it.

"Yeah, I know. I planned in grief orbits." He hadn't been expecting to be reminded of her relatively short lifespan. The specter of impending doom put a bit of a damper on their reunion.

"Hey," May said, pulling him back from the brink of a downward spiral. "Don't worry about the future. You told me that the point is what's happening now, and this," she stretched her hands out and wriggled her fingers. "This moment is all jazz hands."

An End

THIRTY-NINE

AUGUST GETS ALL THE APPLES

* * * * *

In Germany, on Earth, about two hundred years after a woman named May June July became a missing persons case, a Rhean Ultra-Luxe Aether Cruiser accidentally crushed a fifty-year-old apple tree as it parked in the Apfel Family Orchard.

The cruiser's winged door slid open, moving in a way that only really expensive vehicles can move. Ix stepped out.

"Ix, if you're wrong about this, we're going to have to mind wipe someone, you realize that? Mind wipes aren't cheap."

"I am not wrong," Ix said back to Yvonne who pulled herself from the Cruiser a touch less elegantly, stretching out the long journey from Rhea. "Do you see his dwelling?"

"You're looking directly at it, mun. Just walk forward."

She began to walk, but was stopped by sound of a slamming screen door and the distant shouts of "You!" from a voice which was either furiously angry or furiously happy.

August, unmarked by the ravages of time, ran toward them. It was still difficult to say what emotion he was feeling, exactly, but whatever it was, there was undoubtedly a lot of it.

"You!" he shouted again, about six feet away.

"You," he said, finally. This time he was definitely angry.

The moment he was within reach, Yvonne grabbed him, and Ix put a gun to his skull behind his ear. This was not a typical greeting for either of them. He felt a sharp stab, a bit of pressure, then, finally, Ix sheathed the gun and Yvonne let him go.

"Damnit," he said, rubbing the back of his head.

"August, Yvonne and I have reason to believe you may be immortal, which is why we have come to check on you. I have installed an S59 translation chip on your auditory cortex for our convenience."

August looked like he was about to do a livid sort of jumping jack. "Two *hundred* years? *Two hundred years?* Humans just replicate apples, now. Do you have any idea how hard it is to keep an apple orchard in business when everyone wants replicated apples? I've seen generations of people live and die without aging a day myself," he shouted.

"You are shouting," said Ix.

He ignored her. "Dogs have evolved a rudimentary form of language; do you know how creepy it is that dogs can now *tell* you that they want to hump your leg? Soccer players are genetically modified super-humans which ruins the point and...*and,*" he stressed, looking as if he were near tears, "bluetooth connections still don't work reliably. They cannot *fucking* get it right!"

And then the tears came. Ix was never great with tears, so he buried his face in Yvonne's chest, and she sighed, patting his back as he wept.

"I told you we should've come sooner. Two hundred orbits is a lot to these little fellas," she whispered to Ix. "Relatively speaking, it's been about a thousand orbits to him. No one should have to live that long. That's horrific."

"Uh-huh," he sobbed.

"It's alright, August. It's alright," Yvonne soothed.

"Everyone who met Chaos has experienced slower aging
—"

"Completely halted aging and spontaneous cellular reset," Ix corrected.

"Yes, that. You remember Xan and his Earthling leaving the orchard to find Carmnia, yes?" Yvonne asked.

August pulled himself together. The orchard...he looked around. Not this orchard. The orchard he had on Rhea. Yes, he remembered. Vaguely.

He nodded. "Who's Carmnia?"

"A Tuhntian Queen; she doesn't matter. What matters is that Xan summoned an entity who restarted the Universe and, as Xan recalls it, put Chaos in a 'time-out' for this go-round."

"Yeah, I gathered that!" August said, gesturing to his expansive orchard, the one he had inherited and tended for the past two centuries.

He had not, actually, gathered that. In fact, he had for many years assumed that he'd gone mad and checked himself into an asylum. A few years after that, he realized he wasn't aging properly and checked himself *out* of the asylum to avoid suspicion. Then the real trouble began a few decades later when he came to the conclusion that he wasn't just not aging properly, but he wasn't aging at *all*, and suddenly the decades he imagined he had spent on planets other than Earth weren't so mad after all.

Something, clearly, had gone wrong.

What, he had no idea. And closure had not been forthcoming.

"So why am I not aging?"

"We are unsure, but we thought it would be appropriate to check on you. How are you feeling?" Ix asked. The shouting and the tears hadn't tipped her off.

"Not great!" August said. "I mean, physically I'm fine, sure, but you two forgot about me for two centuries. Didn't you miss me?"

"Of course we—" Yvonne began.

"Not for long," Ix interrupted.

Yvonne nudged Ix in the ribs. Ix sighed at Yvonne. "Yes, August, we missed you. I missed you. We believed it would be to your advantage to allow you to complete your natural human life on Earth. That was before we realized you might have been stripped of said natural life. I am happy to see you, my friend."

August got a little misty-eyed again. Two centuries of work, and Yve had finally got Ix to play nice. "Aw, thanks Ix. So what do we do now? I can't believe it, but after two centuries, I'm ready to see the stars again."

"Now, the Death Quest!" Yvonne said, joyfully, grabbing an apple off a nearby tree and *not* rubbing it clean before taking a bite. It was worth a shot.

"The Death Quest?!" August repeated.

"Yes! Nothing left to do, really. Eventually, we will want to die, and as immortals, that's the one thing denied us. So Ix and I have been posed the question: how do you kill an immortal? and, by Rheanoodle the Third, we're going to answer it."

"Sounds fun."

"The pursuit of death is a serious—"

"It's gonna be fun," Yvonne agreed.

GLOSSARY

Length

Qal: A wee bit.

Horbort: Slightly longer than a meter

＊ ＋ ＊ ＋ ＊

Time

Blip: Slightly less than a second.

Bloop: About 50 seconds.

Beoop: About 45 minutes.

Rotation: Varies by planet, but lasts exactly twenty beoops in space (based on the rotations of the planet Estrichi).

Season: Varies by planet, but lasts exactly fifty rotations in space (based on the rotations of the planet Estrichi).

Orbit: Varies by planet, but lasts exactly six seasons in space (based on the rotations of the planet Estrichi).

Quilfraudoron: One infinity.

Quifeee: Infinity infinities.

* * * * *

Insults

Positor: "Dick". Short for "ovipositor".

Poslouian-slug-grass-eating-coward: Xan

Precious Butler: Prostitute (offensive). Also Xan.

Taagshlorph: A piece of slimy, wilted leafy green.

Tchagg: A jerk. Also the term for the musk gland of the common glotchbur.

Zoup-nog: Idiot.

Zingnat: Idiot (affectionate).

Ovi-booster: One who boosts another's ovipositor, a suck-up.

Jultido: A sucker, an easy mark. Common Anat term.

* * * * *

Endearments

Boha: Buddy, friend, mi amigo.

Mun: Comes from the cute fuzzy critters that like to chew up wires on spaceships.

Lav: Gender neutral pejorative term like "kid". Short for "larva".

Larvling: Another form of "larva", more respectful than "lav".

Zuxine: Sexy.

✳ ✳ ✳ ✳ ✳

Other

Splice in the duct: Like a "kick in the pants", referring to the oviduct.

Twa-don: Short for "Twagolohoontz dontargel" which essentially means "Twagolohoontz is leaving the building". Twagolohoontz was a famous Tuhntian comedian who would end every show with this phrase.

Trok: Casual term for the radioactive waste the Rhean government dumped on Tuhnt, creating the wastelands.

Unpin it: Relax. Referencing the physical restraint or "pins" used in cheap rocket races to make sure rockets don't start too early.

Porscinunct: A vow of truth. Invoking this word means you have to tell the absolute truth.

Serpentine palbeatus: Disease characterized by the compulsion and mysterious ability to slither.

Gloxalatal: Biology. Part of an A'Vilrial voicebox which produces clattering sounds which translate as either "Q" "Ch" "Ck" or "X." This is the reason May can't pronounce "Xan" and Xan can't pronounce "Fuck."

Zuut/Zux: Noun/verb. A sexual act specific to the A'Vilrial species.

$$* \ * \ * \ * \ *$$

Species

Anat: Not actually humanoids! But they may appear to be. Anats are predatory creatures from Pan who have the ability to closely mimic their prey.

A'Viltrian: A'Vilrial race. Not extinct, but highly evolved. They don't play well with others, but they love to release futuristic technology into the galaxy and see how the lesser beings take it. Andolon was their planet of origin, but they are beyond the need of a planet as most of them live in a more subtle dimension.

Bewlahoo: Primoid race. Very large, feline-humanoids from the Primox system. Their language is Bewlahooon. Yes, there are three "o"s.

Filporthean Weet: Also not technically humanoid, though they may embody a humanoid. The weet is an entity that puppets corpses, keeping them partially alive. Most weets are beneficent, but all weets are deeply feared. Their natural form is as a pink sentient fog found in Tuhntian wastelands. The Filporthean Weet is a single weet, the most prolific one on Tuhnt.

Garveral: Primoid race. Large, tough-skinned, slow, and long-lived.

Panseen: Panen race. Characterized by reddish skin, typically five to seven feet tall, most similar, biologically, to Earthlings.

Pringnette: Primoid race. Tall and gazelle-like. Nearly extinct thanks to the Rheans. Ugh. Rheans.

Rhean: A'Vilrial race. Characterized by purple skin in a variety of shades and hues and blue-ish blood. Likes to think they're as evolved as the A'Viltrians; they are not. Have colonized several star systems, destroyed a few cultures, you know, just fun humanoid things.

Titian: A'Vilrial race. Nearly extinct and distantly related to the Rheans. Titians have dark purple-red skin and an extra set of arms (usually underdeveloped and vestigial nowadays). Most remaining Titians have found refuge on Estrichi, a previously uninhabited and neutral planet.

Tuhntian: A'Vilrial race. Blue to green skin tones of any shade, pale white blood that dries green, close cousins to the Rheans, but diverged in their evolution many centuries ago by colonizing Tuhnt. Started the trend of ear-lobe stretching, where the plugs are typically made of expensive metals. The larger the plug, the richer the family.

Udonian: Panen race. Typically short, green, and mustachioed. Their lip hair grows so fast, no one has ever seen one clean shaven.

✳ ✳ ✳ ✳ ✳

Star Systems

Flotluex: Planets include Rhea I, Rhea II, Rhea IV, Tuhnt (scorched), Not-Tuhnt (aka Pontoosa or Rhea III).

Premerfherf System: Planets include Andolon (missing), A'Viltra (scorched), Estrichi, and Primox.

System 69F: Planets include Forn, Pan, and Udo.

THERE'S MORE WHERE THAT CAME FROM!

Visit CarmenLoup.com for updates and follow @Carmen_Loup42 on Instagram

The Audacity May's humdrum life is flung into hyperdrive when she's abducted and finds out that rocket racing is a quick, if life-threatening, way to make a living in space. Now, May has a career she loves and a friend to share her winnings with. Until a Chaos goddess decides to turn Earth into her personal sandbox and the Audacity is the only ship that can stop her.

The Audacity 2: Time Warp May and Xan are wildly successful rocket racers, but when a tea-sipping robot arrests Xan, and Chaos steals the Sphere of Time, May must team up with an adventure biologist and her undead girlfriend to save Xan, the Audacity, and Time Itself.

The Audacity 3: Be Kind, Rewind When Xan and Aimz succumb to the Carmnian Scourge, May must team up with old friends, enemies, and a haunted Big Mouth Billy Bass to find the cure before the goddess of Chaos enacts the final stage of her universe befuddling plan

The Audacity's Horrific Horrors: Sip In a haphazard grab at eternal life for the short-lived May, Xan gets reeled in by a killer pyramid scheme. Will either of them survive? No. The answer to that is no, they won't.

The Audacity's Horrific Horrors: Bite May, nostalgic for Earth carnivals, insists on visiting a shitty carnival on a distant asteroid, but when she and Xan get there, they find it abandoned. keen for an adventure, May breaks in to explore the empty park, which is exactly what the remains of the carnival staff want.

The Audacity's Horrific Horrors: Glug A vacation to the universe's most sinful city leaves May and Xan with an unholy mess.

Tarot in Space a 78-card Tarot deck set in the Audacity universe and based on the RWS Tarot.

Thank you for reading, starshine. You're the coffee in my fuel tank, the blueberry in my milkshake, and the good in my luck charm.